Perverse

By

Larry Rodness

ITOH PRESS

ITOH PRESS

Bowling Green, KY 42103

www.itohpress.com

Perverse by Larry Rodness

Cover Art by: Yegor Yatsik

Cover Image: Christina Perez

Edited by: Lisa Maine

Print ISBN: 978-1-939383-14-3

Digital ISBN: 978-1-939383-17-4

Copyright 2012 Larry Rodness

Printed in the United States of America Worldwide Electronic and Digital Rights 1st North America, Australian and UK Print Rights.

All rights reserved. No part of this book may be reproduced or distributed in any form, including digital and electronic or mechanical, including photocopying, recording, or by any information storage and retrieval system, without the prior written consent of the Publisher, except for brief use in reviews.

This book is a work of fiction. Characters, names, places, and incidents either are the product of the author's imagination or are used fictitiously, and any resemblance to any actual persons, living or dead, events, or locales is entirely coincidental.

Acknowledgements

To my colleagues: Reva, Anne, Herb, Diane, Marsha for their abundant criticism and unwavering support.

Additional thanks to Tara Fort.

To my family: Adam, Jonathan, Erin, and especially my loving wife, Jodi.

CHAPTER 1

"Perverse" was Emylene Stipe's signature response to just about everything. Others her age were more apt to say "cool" or "wicked" or "awesome," but you knew Emylene was in the house when you heard, "Loved that band last night—so perverse," or "She's hanging with *that* dude? Perverse!" Or, "I hate people who eat with their mouths open, they're so perverse."

This was not just an off-hand remark, but more an expression of Emylene's mantra, for she was the dark-haired eighteen-year-old willowy daughter of Goth parents which made her a rare second-generation Goth. Standing five foot four, she was the picture of teenage defiance: shoulder length hair dyed the color of India ink, ears decorated with numerous piercings and hoops, and two lip rings on either side of her lower lip. On anyone else the look would be tragic, but on Emylene it was beguiling. Like every teenager, Emylene was trying to figure out exactly where she stood in the world and how to rebel against it. But the trouble with growing up a "second-gen" was that Emylene's parents had already exposed many of the cracks and faults in society's thin veneer, leaving very few for her to question for herself. So, the conundrum for Emylene was how to rebel against a family of rebels.

What would a person in her position do? Become a civil servant or at the very least, an *uncivil* servant?

Emylene's journey began when she met her first true friend, Nancy, in her thirteenth year at a midnight summer solstice gathering in a large urban park. In a city of over two million it was easy to become lost, swallowed up or marginalized. To find oneself often meant joining a small group of like-minded people who shared a common yet distinctive vision. Various segments of society found a sense of legitimacy when their sect was recognized through cultural events. The Christians had their Christmas Day Parade. The Irish had St. Patty's Day. The blacks had Caribana. Even the gays had Gay Pride Day. Goths, however, were at a disadvantage because it was their nature to gather at night when the rest of the world was at rest. As well, their shyness, avoidance of the mainstream, and worship of all things dark was misinterpreted as being antisocial. This kind of ignorance by society at-large led to acts of intimidation, persecution and on occasion, violence against them. As a sect, they felt it was time to stand up for their rights. After all, what was good for the gays was good for the Goths. They were not necessarily lobbying for a parade down Main Street, but they did feel that establishing some sort of event would help confirm their legitimacy, and even protect them from further harassment.

The job fell to Theo and Vandy Stipe, Emylene's parents who owned a local Goth club, and were the acknowledged leaders of their community. Standing five foot seven, with raven black hair that settled around her shoulders, Vandy was a woman who prided herself in her appearance. Whether dressed in traditional floor-length black lace dresses or latex keyhole corsets, the truth was that—no matter what she wore—Vandy was a striking beauty. She was equally matched by her husband, Theo, who at six foot four, loved to show off his commanding build by wearing tight fitting black tee shirts depicting devils, dragons or enslaved angels, that were casually slung over cotton bondage pants. When this power couple put their minds to it, they could move mountains, and staging this event was the kind of challenge they were born to.

Vandy and Theo went to work immediately, researching countries all over the world that celebrated alternative festivals, the most highly profiled being held at Stonehenge. Summer Solstice Eve Festival, as it was known in England, celebrated a time for purification and renewed energy. People from all walks of life were invited to gather 'round a sacred fire and stay up all night to bring in the new dawn. After eight months of petitioning the local city council, June 21st was designated as the date to hold Toronto's own Summer Solstice Festival. For the inaugural event, a portion of High Park was set aside to celebrate the longest day of the year, it being the first day of summer, the wedding of Heaven and Earth.

Word was sent out to invite people from all faiths, including Christians, Muslims and Jews, but everyone knew this night was clearly owned by the Goths. Other like-minded sects, including Wiccans, Pagans and Druids applied for a demonstration license, which bought them a patch of ground inside the park for the event. The various clans brought food and drink and gathered to chant, light candles, re-commit themselves to their faiths, and make new friends. Over four thousand arrived in their fanciest, most outlandish attire—leather, latex, robes, top hats, and corseted undies. Halloween had *nothing* on this night! Much was riding on the shoulders of Theo and Vandy, so strict rules were imposed. If trouble found its way into the park that night, there would be no Summer Solstice Festival ever again. A perimeter was set up to mark the boundaries. No drunkenness, fighting, bawdy behavior, or sacrifices (human or otherwise) were permitted. Other than that, people were free to do as they pleased. Just to be sure, the police monitored the park and kept a tight rein on the activities.

It was on this night that Emylene met Nancy who, like her, was a "second-gen" Goth.

Nancy's family lived in the small town of Eganville, about 400 miles east of Toronto. Her father made his living by fashioning jewelry—grave stud earrings, barbed wire bracelets, stash tins and such, and most of his customers were online. After hearing about the festival through a number of Goth websites, he decided that attending might not only be a good way to expand his business but also give his wife and daughter a chance to make new friends. On the eve of the festival, the gates were flung open wide to the hordes of revelers who took over the park. It was Emylene's job to greet the participating dealers and check the validity of the permits. But as soon as she came upon the jewelry cart and the chubby tween with the flaming red hair, Emylene forgot about the permit altogether.

"Love your work," noted Emylene as she handled a necklace.

"Thanks. That's an ankh," offered Nancy, "Most people think it's a Christian-type cross, but it's really Egyptian."

She fingered the one around her own neck to emphasize that she knew what she was talking about. Emylene, however, would not be outdone.

"The symbol for eternal life," she commented. "When a person dies her heart is weighed against the 'feather of truth'. If the heart is heavier than the feather, it means the person has committed too many crimes…"

"…and can never cross over…"

"…and their soul is destined to wander forever. My name is Emylene Stipe. My parents are running this festival."

"I'm Nancy, Nancy Nostradamus. My folks had our last name changed legally."

"Cool," replied Emylene, "but it's way long. I think I'll call you, 'Nostra-dame'."

Their connection was instantaneous and magical. Conversation flowed between them like two long-lost sisters and they quickly became frustrated by all the passersby wanting to buy jewelry. Nancy pestered her mother, as only a teenager can, until the elder allowed her daughter to beg off, and the two girls stole away to talk. Finding privacy in a festival this size proved to be quite the challenge. They were constantly being pestered by children jumping out from behind trees to scare them, or lovers looking for a place to cop a feel behind some bushes. Matters of the heart for these two required solitude. And so they wandered through picnic areas, past the barriers and the heavy brush, until they came to a glade by a stream where they continued their discussions about the isolation from other kids at school, the judgment of their teachers, and all things Goth.

So deeply engrossed were they in conversation that they didn't hear the three teenage boys creeping up on them until one of the punks snickered.

"Well, well, what do we have here, a couple of Goth-tarts."

The girls instantly picked up on the intimidating vibe, but Emylene knew enough not to show fear.

"Lost, boys?" she asked innocently. "Party's way back there."

"So you guys're into death and everything, right?" remarked the second one.

The third boy didn't say anything. He just stood there like a zombie waiting to take his cue from his friends. Emylene offered a "whatever," hoping they would go away, but knowing they wouldn't.

"You suck blood, don'tcha." added the second. "What else do ya…"

"Don't even!" interrupted Nancy in a tone that suggested she'd heard the remark so often that it had become a cliché.

Emylene and Nancy were certainly not strangers to this kind of taunting, but knew there was no easy way out. If they said nothing, the boys would continue their insults, even if only to throw a scare into the girls. If the girls said the *wrong* thing, it might escalate tensions. When the leader pulled out a pocket knife the tweens knew that whatever they said or did next would determine the outcome.

"Boys with knives. Oh, goodie!" Emylene said perversely. "Will there be blood?"

"Not mine," smirked the leader.

The three boys began to circle the two young girls with slow, threatening steps. Neither group was sure what to do or say next until Emylene figured that - if she didn't take charge now - things would get a whole lot worse very quickly.

"Okay, so here's how we play. You cut me first and drink my blood. Then I'll cut you and drink yours. First one to puke loses."

"Drink your blood? Are you sick?" cried the third boy.

"What's wrong? Scared? No probs. We'll go first," added Nancy, matching the bravura of her new friend.

Nancy slid her sleeve up to her elbow and stuck out her forearm to receive the first slice.

"C'mon," Emylene urged the boys. "Nostra-dame and I do this all the time!"

Nancy turned to her friend with a look of conspiratorial anticipation.

"And then after we can play the pain game."

"Yeah, the pain game," mimicked Emylene. "Betcha we can take more than you."

The three boys hesitated, unsure of whether or not to call the girls' bluff. It was the sound of horse's hooves that made their decision for them.

"Friggin' Goths, man," said the first boy. "They prob'ly got 'hep' or AIDS or somethin.' I wouldn't go near 'em!"

The three boys slunk back into the bushes, after which Nancy turned to Emylene with a look of amazement, wonder and admiration.

"Were you for real?"

"I dunno. Were you?"

A moment later, two mounted police officers came trotting out of the bush on horseback.

"You two okay?"

"Yessir," answered Nancy.

"Those boys give you any trouble?"

"Nothing we couldn't handle," replied Emylene.

"What are your names?" asked the first officer.

"I'm Emylene Stipe and this is Nancy."

"Nostra-dame," Nancy corrected.

"We got a report that two little spooks've gone missing from Summer Solstice. Would that be you?"

The girls nodded, a guilty blush on their faces.

"Your parents are worried, and the whole camp is in an uproar thanks to you two. You better come with us."

Each of the officers offered a hand to pull the girls up behind them on their mounts. Before they did, Nancy took the Ankh pendant off her neck and gave it to Emylene as a gesture of friendship. Fifteen minutes later, the four of them cantered into the main staging area to the cheers of the crowd. Emylene and Nostra-dame couldn't be more pleased with themselves, especially upon seeing their respective parents so furious with them.

"You know all the hard work your father and I have put into this event and then you go and pull a stupid stunt like this?" barked Vandy. "The perimeter was set up for everyone's safety including yours. You of all people should know the…"

"Jeez, it's not like they caught us burning down the park or anything, Ma. We were just talking." This would remain a minor family infraction as long as there was no mention made by the police about the encounter with the three boys. So, to keep their focus on the reported aspect of the incident, Emylene pressed her point. "And 'perimeter'? 'Rules'? What, is Dad running for Mayor next?"

They were Goths after all, she continued, born to live outside the norm, beyond the ropes and rules of contemporary society. Vandy remained unmoved. So, as Emylene always did when she and her mother locked horns, the petulant teen turned to her father for support. Theo looked down at his daughter, gave her one of his mock scowls, and then took her up in his arms. Vandy fumed and stomped away.

Next day the front pages of all the city's major newspapers bore pictures of the two girls smiling down at their 'subjects' from on top of the two majestic horses. The story went on to say how the police found and returned the lost girls, putting a positive spin on the whole event. Best of all there was no mention of the altercation between the girls and the three older boys. Summer Solstice Festival was pronounced a critical success, and the Stipe family's stature rose even higher in the community; but the stars of the show were clearly Emylene and Nostra-dame, whom one reporter referred to as "Goth princesses". The moniker stuck, and the exhilarating experience not only served to bond the tweens, but set the standard for their relationship.

The end of June marked the holidays for most students. The event had such a positive effect that Nostra-dame's family decided to move to Toronto. Emylene was enrolled in an alternative school that ran through the summer. Her family's lifestyle had made her socially and politically aware at an early age, and she thrived on it. Let the norms go to camp or hang out at the park all day; Emylene had aspirations. Thus, it made sense that Nostra-dame enroll in classes with her new friend. The two soon became inseparable and it wasn't long before they began plotting to make their marks on society by becoming the first Goth dentists or the first Goth astronauts or the first Goth co-city mayors. One way or another, they would find a way to exploit their culture in order to change the landscape of their environment and then, of course, the world - and always with their traditions at the forefront. When most girls were planning trips to the mall, these two were on a quest to dip their toes into the dark Pool of Oblivion.

Life took its first turn, innocently enough one day, when a student in Emylene's class asked their teacher whether sneezing could actually stop the heart. Miss Hartman replied that it was probably an urban myth and continued with the lesson, aware that the question was more about trying to derail the instruction rather than to seek knowledge. But Miss Hartman's terse reply combined with the way in which the teacher nervously flipped the pages of her textbook confirmed to Emylene that her teacher was indeed aware of the insidious nature of the sneeze, and was trying to hide it from the more impressionable students. In truth, Miss Hartman had no idea but could only imagine the chaos the next time her students became bored in class—the clutching of hearts, the claims of cardiac arrest, and incessant trips to the nurse that a sneezing jag would cause. In any case, Emylene and Nostra-dame lost no time in setting out on their quest, and the two began experimenting with cayenne pepper in an effort to experience for themselves the sublime moment between life and death.

When another student mentioned *'La petite mort'* or 'the little death' (the French term for orgasm), the two girls began delving into the practice of bringing themselves to climax. But, in the end, they gave it up because it proved to be too enjoyable an experience and thus defeated the more serious goal of coming face-to-face with their elusive quarry. Further investigations led Emylene and Nostra-dame through the gamut of drugs, bulimia and the occasional cutting.
To outsiders they might have seemed like a couple of self-destructive teenagers, but the girls saw themselves as intrepid pioneers on a mission to discover the uncharted regions of higher consciousness.

It was the girls' next and ultimately final adventure that led to their undoing. That debacle was inspired quite unintentionally by Emylene's parents when the family happened upon an old movie on television one night.

It was not often that the Stipe family spent the evening at home together. Vandy and Theo ran a club named Pall Bearer's Paradise located in the basement of a factory downtown in the clothing district. Loud music, grungy surroundings and cheap liquor made it home to the local Goth community, but running the club required constant supervision. So, the nights all three found themselves at home were rare and special. Emylene's friends at school imagined the Stipe household being similar to that of the Addams Family—sacrificial alters in the kitchen, coffins instead of beds, hot and cold running blood baths. But Theo and Vandy knew the stigma that their daughter had to live with growing up Goth and were very careful to keep their lifestyle on the down-low so that Emylene wouldn't feel embarrassed if she ever brought a friend home. Thus, the decor upstairs in their small post-war bungalow consisted of simple rattan furniture, beige walls and Turkish rugs. The basement, however, was a different story.

As well, Emylene's schoolmates would be surprised and probably disappointed to find that, on family night, the Stipe family would cozy up on the sofa with a bag of popcorn to watch television. This particular evening they chanced upon an old flick entitled "The Graduate." This movie from the late 60s featured a character named Benjamin Braddock who returns home from university to face an uncertain future and is subsequently seduced by an older woman. Emylene's parents dismissed it as a smug, self-serving, bourgeois fairytale. To Emylene it meant if they disapproved, she just *had* to watch it.

After the first scene, she knew that she and Benjamin were kindred spirits. Even though they lived in polar-opposite worlds, they were both saddled with overbearing parents and faced their futures with trepidation. But it was one of the lines early on in the film that struck a nerve with Emylene, when Benjamin receives advice from a friend of his parents, which went something like:

"I just want to say one word to you, Benjamin: plastics. There is a great future in plastics."

In the movie, Benjamin totally ignored the advice, but Emylene took it to heart. The next day, she and Nostra-dame ramped up their experiments by wrapping each other's faces in plastic. At the point of blacking out, the one standing guard popped a hole over the mouth of the other who would then report on how close she came to experiencing Death… or Nirvana… or God… or Marilyn Manson. Despite their best efforts, most of the time this would only result in a headache. *Maybe Benjamin was smart to ignore the tip*, Emylene thought.

Their adventure came to an abrupt end one day when Nostra-dame's parents went searching for that very same roll of plastic wrap (which they used to indulge in a particular fetish) and walked in on the two teenagers who had wrapped themselves together like sex-charged sausages feverishly working their way to the summits of ecstasy.

The girls were forbidden to see each other again, which they interpreted as a triumph of sorts in that they had inadvertently stumbled on yet *another* way to rebel against their parents. Naturally, Emylene and Nostra-dame rebelled against their parents' decisions and continued to see each other, at which point the parents rebelled against their children's rebelliousness, and Nostra-dame's family moved back to Eganville.

Emylene was alone again. Generally, this was considered a state of grace for most Goths, except that, without Nostra-dame, Emylene had no one with whom to share her solitude. How perverse! Without her confidante by her side, Emylene's sense of purpose dwindled, and, as the days, months, and years bled into each other, she drifted aimlessly through time like a twig floating down the River Styx.

Ever since Emylene was a tiny tot, she had been told that she was special; yet up until now, her life had been cast in the most mundane shades of gray. Was it life that sucked… or did she suck at life? The only way to know for sure would be to get out and experience it on her own.

favorite character of hers, Edward Scissorhands…wasn't he the object of an older woman's affections also? Yes, she was in good company, but that didn't mean she'd be a pushover.

"Are you stalking me?" Emylene demanded as she approached his table.

Most men would have been put on the defensive, but her admirer only smiled.

"My name is Stelio. I have a business down the way, a men's clothing boutique. The truth is I've seen you on occasion when I passed by your shop and I was intrigued. But I felt that to get the attention of a woman with your obvious creative flair I would have to come up with an original approach. Was I wrong?"

Emylene thought, yes, he was wrong in that she was not as experienced as he may have suspected. Her position in the community as a Goth princess tended to intimidate most boys her age, and others she knew from school thought she was too freaky to bother with. In fact, strangers on the whole took one look at Emylene and walked the other way. But this man was also right in that his approach had definitely piqued her curiosity.

" 'Stelio', not a very common a name. I'm guessing your last name is not Jones or Schwartz?" she asked.

"It is difficult to pronounce. For now, just call me Stelio."

"Okay, Stelio, so what do *you* think about black?" she asked.

"I think black is the absence of color. In fact, I believe it's not even a color at all and the reason for that is because when there is no light, everything is black."

Full marks, she thought. But she wasn't sold yet.

"That's not really a black rose, you know," Emylene offered. "There's no such thing."

"I know. It's called a 'black Bacarra rose.' It's actually a deep red verging on black. The petals feel like velvet, don't you think?"

Emylene did not reach out to touch the rose petals. She was already familiar with their texture and was not about to give Stelio the upper hand. Then he added, "Bacarra is also the name of a singing group from Spain, a female duo. Ever heard of them?"

She had! This Stelio character, whoever he was, was well-dressed and well-traveled. His age didn't matter to her on one hand, and yet made all the difference in the world on the other, for it was his experience and sophistication that was beginning to sweep Emylene off her feet. Well, if not actually sweeping her off her feet, it was at least encouraging her to sit down.

In the coming evenings they would meet after work at Bob's, where she would talk about her Goth upbringing and he would fill her head with tales about his travels through the exotic cities of Europe during his misspent youth. Stelio could go on for hours about subjects like the rotting of modern day society and its efforts to keep the city alive at the cost of its own humanity, or the need for revitalization through the inspiration of the soul. Some might have slit their wrists out of boredom if they had to endure one more dinner conversation cum university lecture, but Emylene thrived on it. Stelio could be a bit taken with himself, but he opened up new worlds to her. More importantly, when she spoke, he listened and that made her feel as though whatever she said was equally important. To a nineteen-year-old introvert, his undivided attention was more intoxicating than the rice wine he ordered for her. Yet Emylene was not so naïve as to ignore that fact that Stelio might have an agenda of his own.

Each time they met she expected to hear the old song and dance about a wife who didn't understand, or a couple who had fallen out of love after inertia settled into their marriage. She also half-expected his hand to reach for her leg under the table or to feel a reassuring hug start at her shoulder and drift down to her rear, but it never happened. In fact, he rarely touched her, something that in time became an exquisite torture.

Still, the affair was ideal for both of them. For him, Emylene was an exotic, forbidden fruit that fed his over-sized ego. For her, Stelio's attention was totally intoxicating. And, knowing that he was married only fueled her obsession for the doomed relationship. On occasion, she would wander over to his store to surprise him, but he was never there. He had other businesses and was often away. This only further enhanced

Emylene's notion of the affair as a delicious mystery. And, it didn't help that as much as they would talk, Emylene felt that she hardly knew the man. On occasion though, she would get a glimpse into his character even if it was a sideways glance.

One night, after dining on bubble tea and egg rolls, they wandered down Queen Street West. Not many people took strolls on late December nights. This particular downtown district was a hub of activity during the day, and a Mecca for the suburban family who searched out funky holiday gifts they couldn't find in their own local mall. But at night, the winds whistled through the concrete corridors with an intensity that challenged only the bravest souls… lovers, mostly, who found the frigid weather a reason to huddle close together. On this night Emylene and Stelio found themselves treading several steps behind a young couple who, by the nature of their conversation, sounded like they were in the midst of just getting to know each other.

"So you would never hit a woman?" the girl asked demurely.

"Never," replied the young man. "I don't believe in physical violence. It never solves anything."

"What if I had a gun to your head, would you hit me then?"

"'Course not," answered the man.

"*I* would," answered Stelio.

Surprised, the young couple wheeled around to see who had intruded on their privacy. The young man frowned, but the girl smiled with intrigue over Stelio's forthright answer.

"Really?" she asked.

"Yes, and I would be doing you a favor."

"How do you think?"

"If you shot me, you would go to jail and serve a lengthy prison sentence, so by hitting you first and knocking the gun out of your hand I would actually be saving you from yourself, wouldn't I?"

"Yeah, well I think there's always a better way," interjected the young man who took his girl by the arm and tried to escort her away. But Stelio wasn't finished.

"Now I have a question for you," he said.

"Shoot," answered the girl, wryly.

Stelio leveled his eyes at the young man.

"If the young lady had a gun on you, wouldn't you want me to hit her to prevent her from killing you?"

"I dunno, I guess, but…"

"What if I had a gun to my *own* head? Wouldn't you strike me to stop me from killing myself?"

"This *is* a hypothetical, right?"

"Of course. But don't you agree that there are circumstances where you would strike a woman or a man?"

"What are you, some kind of freak?"

Stelio ignored the jibe and pressed on with his point.

"So it follows that the notions of right and wrong, hero and villain are not always an absolute, are they? Sometimes it's a matter of perspective."

Realizing he was clearly out of his league the young man took his girl by the hand and walked away.

"Whatever, dude."

"Have a nice night," Stelio added.

The boy gave a middle finger salute, but the girl turned back with a twinkle in her eye. Emylene giggled as she and Stelio continued their walk.

"That was cool."

"And sadly true," he added. "We are all capable of the greatest acts of kindness and the most horrific atrocities. It just depends on the circumstances."

"Cool and perverse."

Stelio suddenly came to a halt. Something caught his eye in the window of an antique store they had just passed. It was a withered old charcoal sketch that was propped up against the window, a somewhat amateurish depiction of a rural winter landscape that could probably be found in any third-rate art shop in any country in the world. Nevertheless, it was clear to Emylene that there was something in this picture that enthralled Stelio.

Sensing his fascination, she asked, "What is it about that sketch?"

"Nothing. Reminds me of home, that's all," he said wistfully.

When she asked him where home was, he answered cryptically, "A long time ago," and refused to elaborate. Emylene took Stelio's chilled hand in hers and they continued their walk until after ten more minutes, they reached her apartment.

"Would you like to come up? Warm those frosty hands?" she asked almost shyly.

"More than you know. But I cannot tonight," he answered.

"I'm a big girl, if that's what you're worried about."

"Of that I have no doubt. There will be a time, now is not it."

Stelio took her hand and kissed it. Then he turned back and walked the way he came. A gust of wind pilfered the scarf from under his collar and drew it up into the frigid night air, affecting a simple, esoteric wave goodbye. Disappointed, Emylene opened the door and trudged up the dark, dirt-encrusted stairs to her apartment. She turned the key to open her door, flicked on the light, and flopped down on her unmade futon. Feeling sorry for herself she gazed around at her sad-looking flat and remembered the ad that brought her here. 'One room bachelor, close to bus routes, separate entrance, comes with bed, table and chairs, dresser, three-piece bathroom, toaster oven, loneliness and despair.' *Who would want to get laid here?*

The next day during her lunch break, Emylene returned to the antique shop to find the sketch sitting there on the dusty floor, leaning against the grimy picture window. She looked at it more closely this time. The artist had framed the winter scene by drawing a weathered old wooden fence that zigzagged from the foreground all the way to a line of trees that met the horizon. In the center of the sketch stood the subject of the picture, a great cypress tree surrounded by a blanket of pristine snow. Aside from that there was nothing distinctive about the picture at all except that Stelio seemed captivated by it. And yet the more she looked, the more Emylene felt a strange emotional tug. The sketch was serene and unsettling at the same time, evocative but distant—just the right mix of perversity for the heartsick Goth.

Her mind firmly made up, Emylene pushed open the paint-peeled door that creaked as if it objected to the intrusion. The air inside hung heavy with the smell of melancholia. The items on display, not so much antiques as other people's castaways, were piled haphazardly onto shelves and tables in no particular order. This was not so much a store as a graveyard, a tomb for forgotten relics and memories. And if that wasn't bad enough, Emylene sensed an air of gloom emanating from the shopkeeper himself who was behind his counter, staring sour-faced at her. He was a tall, gaunt man in his late sixties with wispy grey hair who had lived in the district for over thirty years and suffered them all—

the druggies, the hookers, and the hustlers. He took one look at Emylene and made up his mind about her before she said a single word: *Goths. If they were so in love with death, why didn't they just slit their wrists and let the rest of us get on with our own miserable lives*? Nevertheless, Emylene greeted him with a cheery hello.

"Hey there. The picture in the window, the one with the tree? How much?" she asked.

"It's not for you," he replied with a trace of a European accent.

"Maybe it is."

"Why? Why would you want it?"

"I dunno exactly," replied Emylene. "It just kinda speaks to me."

"Really. And what does it say?"

"It says… 'I'm lonely, I need a friend, a nice place to live.' So, how much you want for it?"

The storeowner stared at Emylene at first with curiosity, and then with disdain. "A million dollars," he replied. "You got a million dollars? If not, don't waste my time."

Emylene offered her prettiest smile while she lifted the picture from the floor and eyeballed it like an appraiser from Sotheby's. There was nothing particularly artsy about it. The dust covering the frame and glass told her it had probably been lying around for months, if not years. Artistically, the scale was tipping more towards 'garbage' than 'antique.'

"I don't have that much, but I'll give you a hundred," she offered.

"You really want it? Tell you what. You come back here tomorrow…"

Emylene knew what was coming next.

"…dressed from head to toe in white. You wipe all that black polish off your nails and the paint off your face, and you come here dressed like…"

"…like a little lady?" asked Emylene.

"Yes, like that, and she's yours."

Emylene put the picture down where she found it.

"See you tomorrow then," she sang as she left the shop.

Although she had never met this man before Emylene knew him all too well. Her parents had taught her early on that whenever people were confronted with something odd or strange, they generally went into "fear mode." This man was afraid of something and desperate to keep control of his domain. To do that, he needed to demystify Emylene by degrading and shaming her into showing that beneath all the make-up and the gear, she was as dull and ordinary as he was. Emylene needed to show him that she was a grown-up, and no one was going to push her around. Both were in for a shock.

The next day Emylene returned to the store as requested, wearing the only white dress she owned and treasured—an exact replica of the bridal gown Miss Lucy was buried in, after Dracula turned her into a vampyre. When Emylene stepped across the threshold of the store, she looked more frightening than she did in anything she had worn in black, and the look on the store owner's face instantly faded to the same pallor of white as the dress. As Emylene approached him she slowly opened her hand.

The owner drew back, fully expecting to find a beating heart pumping away in her little palm. Instead there were five twenties. He hesitated a moment, wondering whether to deny her the purchase and shoo her out, but instead, he scooped up the bills. Emylene took the picture and exited the store. Not a word was said between the two. After she left, the owner crossed himself, and then oddly, tears began to roll down from his eyes.

When Emylene returned to her apartment, she hoped to find another note tied to a black Bacarra rose, which signified that Stelio was back in town. She was anxious to surprise him with the sketch, but there was nothing waiting for her.

The next morning she looked again. Still no rose or note. A week went by without any contact from Stelio, which frustrated Emylene to no end. Whenever she dropped by his shop, she was told he was away on business. Was he avoiding her? Had he grown tired of her? Never, she told herself, how could he? Perhaps his wife found out about them.

But she had to admit that that wasn't her biggest concern. Oddly enough it centered around her sexuality. All of her previous sexual experiences had been with Nostra-dame when, as tweeners, they had experimented by trying to reach a higher cosmic plane through orgasm. It was time to be honest with herself. Was it her rejection by Stelio that vexed her so much, or was it all an elaborate ruse to deny the fact that she was gay? Someone once said the best way to know whether you were straight or gay was to just close your eyes and fantasize. Whatever got your motor running gave you the answer. It sounded so simple that she decided, why not? Emylene consciously took a breath and let her mind float over a myriad of images until she settled on the one that got her heart beating. The object that triggered the desired effect was not soft and sweet, but strong and sinewy. It was of someone who would 'take' her in the most intimate and glorious sense of the word. Emylene opened her eyes, reveling in her confirmation, and made a plan. She would keep the framed picture until she saw Stelio next and use it to lure him up to her flat where she would seduce him and experience the delicious mystery life had waiting for her. And if his wife didn't like it, she could jump off a cliff!

In the meantime Emylene looked around for just the right place to hang the sketch. There really was only one place for it. A nail went into the plaster with two bangs of a hammer and the picture was hung upon the wall opposite the main door of the apartment so that it would be the first thing she'd see upon entering, and the last thing upon leaving.

That done, Emylene took a moment to appreciate her

new acquisition. Ignoring the slap-dash method with which the simple brush strokes were applied, she concentrated on the basic elements of the scene—a rickety wooden fence that zigzagged all the way back to a line of trees in the distant horizon. A few wavy strokes indicating a blanket of unblemished snow, and of course, the lone Cyprus that commanded center stage. So simpatico did she feel to the tree that, for a moment, Emylene fancied the artist must have had her in mind when he drew it—two lone entities against the world. That was all and yet, there seemed more although she couldn't put her finger on what, exactly. Perhaps it was in the hastily drawn strokes that she had all but ignored until now. What was the artist's intention? Was it just plain laziness or was there a sense of urgency? But then, because even Goths get hungry, Emylene stripped off Miss Lucy's bridal gown and bounced downstairs to grab a sub.

  It was 8:15 when she returned. When her world changed. When the glorious mystery of the picture began to reveal itself. When she gazed upon her new treasure and noticed for the first time *footprints* in the snow that were not there before.

CHAPTER 3

Emylene's first reaction was to grab the gold cross around her neck with her left hand and the Egyptian ankh with her right, as if she were bearing witness to a profound religious experience. Then she caught her image in a mirror and it reminded her of one of those crazies who claimed to see the Virgin Mary in a piece of burnt toast, except that this time the only one to mock was herself. She turned back to the sketch hoping to divine something more, but all that faced her were more questions. The footprints in the snow appeared to be sandals, a woman's, which was odd enough. But where did they come from? Who could have made them? Had they been there all the time and she had been too oblivious to have not noticed them until now? Could it have anything to do with Stelio, wherever he might be, or the antique shop owner for that matter? After a while Emylene gave up trying to explain away the conundrum and flopped onto her couch hoping things would sort themselves out in the morning.

Indeed, when Emylene woke up the next day, the footprints were gone and the winter scene was as pristine as when she first laid eyes on it. But far from pacifying her, it sent her into a deeper funk, for it only proved that she really didn't have a window on another universe as she'd secretly hoped, or a third eye, or that she was special in any way.

As the morning sun scraped over the hackled rooftops of the downtown core, Emylene stripped off the clothes she'd slept in the night before and padded into the shower feeling stupid, gullible and ordinary. She toweled off, put on a full body black leotard and black skirt, dabbed on some extra heavy black nail polish, and cursed the sketch as she left her apartment. "Traitor! Bitch!" she shouted.

That morning at work, Emylene dragged her Doc Martens from one end of the textile store to the other, growling at customers like a wounded werewolf. Lamereaux Textiles had been a fixture on Queen Street for over six decades. Back in the forties it was the Lamereaux Hardware Store owned and operated by Gus Lamereaux and his family. In the seventies, the retail hardware business was cannibalized by larger conglomerates that forced out the small independents with their now-infamous volume buying. Gus was facing bankruptcy, but he was a resourceful fellow. The energy crunch was on and people were looking for ways to cut expenses. The textile district was just a few blocks away, manufacturers who made suits and dresses for the large retailers in town. Queen Street had always been at the forefront of change in the city, and when Gus saw a few shops beginning to cater to the hand-made clothing industry he went to the manufacturers and begged them for their offcuts. Lamereaux Textiles, as it was now called, became the supplier 'direct to the public'. The shop wasn't fancy, but that's what gave it its strongest appeal. Gray concrete floors, open ceilings and the worst kind of fluorescent lighting, fairly shouted 'cut-rate'. Metal shelves stacked sky high with hundreds of bolts of cloth invited the curious and the thrifty from all over town. Gus and his family never looked back. The store was rarely quiet and the sales staff was in constant flux. After taking the apartment upstairs, Emylene became friendly with the owner's son and manager, Ronald. He was one of the few people who saw past her Goth trappings and realized that Emylene had potential in the retail business. Most of the time she was quite the personable little salesgirl and the regulars knew to overlook her occasional surly behavior. But today they were just thankful Emylene didn't sink her teeth into their throats before they got out of the store with their purchases. As the afternoon inched toward what Emylene expected to be another dreary evening, her mood grew from sour to vile. By the end of the day, Emylene was pricking her fingers with a staple gun and writing "Burn in Hell" on the backs of all the customer's receipts.

    When her shift was over at six o'clock, Emylene left the shop for some fresh air and headed over to a macrobiotic restaurant to 'detox' with a salad. Unfortunately, the salad did nothing to sooth her, and after a few bites she decided to march herself down the street to Stelio's shop to get some answers once and for all. When she entered, she was greeted by the same snooty employee as before.

"'Scuse me, I was wondering if you'd heard from Stelio yet?"

"As I told you the other day, miss, he's away on business."

Emylene lowered her voice to a whisper.

"Is it a family thing? His wife? You can tell me."

"Wife? Who told you he was…?"

The stunned look on Emylene's face gave the employee his answer. "We'll just forget this visit took place—for both our sakes," he said in a conspiratorial tone.

Emylene left the shop as her embarrassment quickly grew to rage. Not married? What else was he lying about? A few short minutes later that rage turned to bewilderment when she entered her apartment to find the footprints in the sketch had returned. She would have settled for bewilderment, but that was only the beginning of the evening's emotional rollercoaster ride. Emylene traced the footprints that led from the distant tree line and paralleled the zigzagging fence, to the center of the canvas where the large Cyprus stood. And there, peeking out from behind it, was the young peasant girl who had made them! She looked to be about the same age as Emylene, a cute blonde with short, pixie-like bangs that framed her broad forehead, strong cheekbones and expressive eyes. What was even odder was her choice of clothing for such frigid weather—a simple summer dress and a pair of red summer sandals. Emylene didn't know whether to praise the gods or wet her pants. This girl's appearance was so startling and incredulous that it didn't seem unnatural for Emylene to address her by saying, "Excuse me, I bought this random scrawl the other day in that dingy old shop and I don't remember your being a part of the bargain."

Incredibly, the apparition acknowledged her by mouthing a response, but stopped before actual words came out. Something else had caught the waif's attention. Back at the tree line a procession of flickering lights was snaking its way toward her. It soon became apparent that the lights were torches held aloft by a host of shadowy figures dressed in cowls trudging through the snow toward the girl. Emylene saw the instant fear in the girl's eyes and knew instinctively what to do—run to the closet for her tools. At the same time, the girl made her way to the bottom left corner of the sketch. When Emylene returned, she wedged a screwdriver between the seams of the frame. The girl in the picture pulled a small tube from her coat pocket and poured a few drops of a scarlet liquid onto the snow. The Cowled Men were pushing hard now toward the girl and in another five seconds they'd be on her. Emylene smashed the hammer down, separating the joints of the frame. The red treacle seeped from the snow through the crack and onto Emylene's apartment floor. In the same moment the first drop hit the wooden slats, the girl disappeared from the picture! The old men stared out at Emylene from under their cowls, their eyes filled with anger. Emylene was as astonished as they were outraged…and then she heard the voice.

"What took you so long?" the voice asked in a light Slavic accent.

The stiffening hairs on the back of Emylene's neck felt like pinpricks as she turned to find a figure standing in the corner of her room.

Emylene simply stuttered, "I'm sss..sorry?"

The peasant girl grinned and shouted with a most innocent and appealing voice, "I'm only joking! You saved my life!"

Both girls turned to the sketch to see The Cowled Men march back to the tree line in frustration.

"Who are *they*?" asked Emylene.

"Horrible creatures that have been after me forever! But not anymore! I am free now and I have you to thank for it!"

The girl grabbed Emylene by the hands and twirled her around, letting out a loud, joyful whoop. After which, the visitor jumped on the sofa bed, picked up a saucer, and played with the water faucet like a cartoon figure exploring the real world for the very first time. Then she turned to her host.

"Where are we? What is this place?"

"This place? Uh, North America, Toronto, Queen Street West."

"The year?"

"2011."

The girl thought for a moment as she digested the information.

"Sorry, it's been so long…"

"…since what, since you looked at a calendar?"

"What is your name?"

"My name is Emylene Stipe. What's yours?"

"Emylene. I like that," the girl answered.

"Thanks, it was a gift from my parents," snapped Emylene." "What's yours, if you don't mind?"

Emylene wasn't sure why she was acting so inhospitably to the stranger. The girl hadn't actually *done* anything to her. And she certainly didn't seem threatening.

The girl cast her eyes downward looking ashamed that she either didn't remember her name or didn't have one.

"I know… your parents named you, why don't you name me?" suggested the girl.

Emylene looked around the room while she thought out loud.

"Door…Dora…Cella-phone?"

But before the visitor could voice her opinion one way or the other she noticed something that filled her with dread. She ran to the window and placed her hands up against the glass.

"This is a trick! You have trapped me in another picture!"

It took a moment for Emylene to comprehend the girl's fear, and then she giggled.

"No, no. That's just the world out there, see?"

Emylene crossed over and opened the window to let a blast of cold winter air inside. The confirmation not only satisfied the girl but lit her up with joy.

"Can we go out? Please?" pleaded the girl. "Then you can introduce me to everyone and I can learn all their names."

"Well, I don't know everyone, but…"

Staring at this child of wonder Emylene felt something stir within her that she hadn't experienced since her relationship with Nostra-dame. Emylene opened her closet and grabbed two coats.

"Why not. Here, it's cold out."

The girl nodded her thanks and then Emylene asked, "Hey, you *are* for real, aren't you? I mean I'm not having a breakdown or anything?"

The girl pinched Emylene to prove she had substance.

"Ow!" shouted Emylene, "You're so cold!"

"You would be too if you were stuck in that frozen wasteland for as long as I have."

"So, I've got some boots…"

But the girl was already out the door. Emylene followed her downstairs into the night, both of them acting like a couple of giddy schoolgirls.

The forest glistened with a new snowfall. The Cowled Men sat hunched around a fire with deep concern etched in their ancient faces. How could she have escaped? This had never happened before, not since anyone could remember, and no one had any answers or suggestions as to how to get her back. The old men were accustomed to the cold, but the girl's new-found freedom chilled them even more.

CHAPTER 4

Emylene and her new friend headed down the windswept block past the Christmas lights and holiday wreaths that decorated the shop windows. It was brittling cold and only a few brave souls were out tonight, but the girl danced and sang as if this was her own private winter wonderland. Not even the icy snow that caked her sandals could dampen her spirits. Two blocks down, Emylene stopped at the Boar's Head Tavern.

"So, before we go inside, like, how old are you?" asked Emylene.

"I don't even know my own name and you're asking my age?"

"Good point. Okay, if anybody asks, you're nineteen—drinking age, okay?"

The girl shrugged in agreement. Emylene gestured for the girl to follow inside and leave the talking to her. Only the die-hards were at the Boar's Head tonight. Ellen tended bar as usual, dressed in a red Christmas cap and a low-slung cami that showed off her cleavage and encouraged tipping. Ross, the owner, chatted up a few of the regulars while he watered down the drinks. By the time Emylene appeared, the crowd was bored stiff and ripe for some new gossip.

"Hey, Emylene! Come on in, have a snog with us. Who's your friend?" they asked. Emylene smiled and dragged the girl back outside again.

"I'm not ready for this and neither are you," she said to her visitor as they returned to the street.

Emylene jogged on the spot to keep herself warm while she debated where they might go next without being harangued. After a minute she exclaimed, "What the hell. There's only one place to chill on a night like this." The girl followed Emylene for three more frostbitten blocks before they turned down a dark alley and came to a big black metal door. She fancied that the portals of Hades would look just like this.

"Don't be afraid, okay?" Emylene said.

"Of what?" replied the girl.

Emylene wondered for a moment if this girl might actually be a genuine *tabula raza*, someone new to the world who had no preconceived notions or expectations. If this girl was a true enigma, then Emylene had finally found her own uniqueness—if even only through association. Then again, the young female did have an aversion to those Cowled Men, which indicated that there must have been a history back there somewhere. Something to consider later. For now, *this* was where the adventure was leading. Emylene opened the door and led her friend down a short flight of concrete stairs along a dimly lit hall until they came to another large door, a bronze one. There were no locks on these doors because no one would dare to venture down here without knowing exactly where they were going—to Pall Bearer's Paradise. Emylene flung open the bronze door and escorted her protégé into another world, her world.

P.B.P., as it was often referred to, was a study in perversity—a gloomy Goth club punctuated by giggles in the dark, a disconsolate atmosphere that thrived on the joyous anarchy and utter despair of its inhabitants, a home for the lost boys and girls who both wallowed and reveled in the futility of life.

The atmosphere here could only be described as fiercely maudlin. The lighting was harsh one second and sexy-flattering the next. The music ran the gamut, from mournful sounds of a gypsy violin to a full-on guitar and drum sledgehammer assault, all of which was delivered by a $50,000 state-of-the-art sound system. Attending guests were dressed in everything from vintage Edwardian ruffled shirts tucked inside leather-tight pants to latex mini dresses and ripped leotards. The air was a pungent mix of sex, drugs and danger. Piercings, tattoos, and bondage gear made the scene look as frightening as one of Dante's infamous Rings of Hell, yet the girl seemed oddly at ease. When the denizens of the club genuflected and curtseyed to Emylene, her new friend clapped her hands with delight.

"Wow, what kind of special *are* you? She asked.

"She's a *princess* for one," shouted a nearby dancer wearing a scarlet bustier and spiked dog collar.

"Not to mention she pees black," shouted another.

"Huh?" exclaimed the girl.

"It's called Alkaptonuria," explained Emylene. "Makes your urine turn black. For some people, their ear wax, too. I get it from my Dad's side."

There were few second-gen Goths and even fewer with the rare genetic disorder more commonly known as 'black urine disease.' The condition was due to a defect in an enzyme that prevented the body from degrading a chemical named tyrosine. As a result, acid that accumulated in the blood was secreted in the urine. The condition is generally harmless except for one of its more serious effects being kidney stones which Emylene's father, Theo, suffered from. In any case, black urine was just another of the factors that elevated the Stipe family to Goth royalty. As the girls waded into the crowd Emylene whispered to her new friend, "We should've come here right off."

The best thing about a Goth club was that everyone there was too cool to ask questions, mostly because this was where they came to escape public scrutiny themselves.

P.B.P. was owned by Emylene's parents, but was managed by Thrall, their major domo who fashioned himself after David Bowie's vampyre character in "The Hunger."

Emylene depended on Thrall more and more these days to keep open the tenuous lines of communication between her and her parents. Secretly, she wondered if the tall, dark Goth had a crush on her, but didn't want to mix business with pleasure. When she left the family home, it was with the understanding that she needed her space. Soon after, her parents began to frequent the club less and less, which Emylene took as some sort of reprisal for her leaving. It left her confused and resentful, because not only were they abandoning their daughter, but the regulars who made P.B.P their second home. These people needed a Stipe figurehead. If Vandy and Theo were bowing out, that left Emylene. But having a nine-to-five job and making an appearance after eleven most nights… no one including a teenager had the energy to keep that up for very long. Moreover, the whole thing was just not fair. Emylene reasoned that it was a child's duty to move out and grow into her own, but how could parents justify withdrawing from their own progeny? Shouldn't parents be available to their offspring whenever they were needed? Wasn't that some kind of unwritten law? Furthermore, if Vandy and Theo wanted to punish their daughter for leaving the nest, so be it, but there was no need to abandon the entire clan. In truth, Emylene knew that if she wanted to contact her folks she could always phone them, but doing so too often would be a sign of weakness, and Emylene was not about to give them that satisfaction. In their absence, Emylene did her best to make regular appearances and relied on Thrall to run the day-to-day business of the club. He was also good for passing messages between the two camps without passing judgment. So, on this night when Thrall approached her, she expected that he was going to ask her opinion on the music or housekeeping or inform on her parents. Instead he whispered, "You have a guest." He nodded to a man sitting at the back of the room dressed in a well-tailored suit. Catching her eye, Stelio was already out of his seat and on his way over, pissing off partygoers as he swaggered past them. "What are you doing here?" asked Emylene, more as an accusation than a question.

"I'm sorry, I was away on business, I thought you knew," he replied, as if that was end-of-story.

"Oh, you can do better than that. Why don't you say you were lecturing at Oxford or confess that the wife you don't have found out about us? It wouldn't have sounded half as lame as the 'out of town on business' line your lackeys kept handing me. I don't get you. You romance me but you never touch me! You bring me roses but you don't want to sleep with me! And you're not even married! How perverse is that?"

Emylene's outburst had the immediate and unfortunate consequence of attracting the eyes and ears of everyone around her, and she cursed herself for having shown such lack of control.

Stelio, on the other hand, displayed great restraint by not even acknowledging the accusation.

"And who is this?" he asked, nodding to her friend in an off-handed manner.

Infuriated, Emylene wanted to stab him in the eye with her crucifix. But she reminded herself that she was a Goth princess, after all, and her tribe would be watching closely to see how she handled herself. Scanning the room for inspiration, Emylene's eyes came to rest on a small holiday shrub that someone had laid at the feet of the statue of Yama, the Hindu god of death.

"She's my cousin, Poinsettia. So… what are you doing here, Stelio? What do you want, exactly?"

"I've missed you deeply. I look at you now and I see the seed of something that could grow into a rare and magnificent flower…"

Emylene cocked her head, confused by what he was saying to her.

"…But, to realize this, you will need to take full control of your emotions, you will need to know what to do and when to do it without letting pride, remorse or misguided zeal get in your way."

Emylene had no clue what Stelio was trying to tell her because she was so keyed into the arrogance with which he said it.

"Whatever," was all she could manage.

Emylene's people, however, were not about to let him off so easily. Goths are generally a mild-mannered, even playful, people. But they had been intimidated, misjudged and reviled for so long that the last thing they were prepared to accept was the disrespect of their princess. As soon as Emylene voiced her displeasure the innocuous partiers transformed into a surly mob.

"Stelio, you better leave now, for your own good," said Emylene.

It wasn't the Greek's nature to let anyone dictate terms to him, but Emylene was right. Stelio came here to see who he wanted to see and say what he wanted to say, and now it was time to leave. As he strode to the door he made one parting comment.

"I'll be here when you need me." And with that he left.

"The arrogance of that man!" Emylene muttered.

"What did you call me? Poinsettia?" Distracted by her friend, Emylene nodded to the small bush with the brilliant red leaves sitting in the corner.

"I love it. And I love this music. Let's dance!"

Without waiting for a reply, Poinsettia dragged Emylene to the dance floor, threw back her head, and swung her hips with wild abandon to the thumping beat. Her mood was so infectious that Emylene was compelled to join her and grind out all her pent-up frustrations. Others joined in and the dancing grew wildly hedonistic. The lights began to strobe and soon the partygoers lost themselves in the music and the crush until one of the dancers actually dropped to the floor. Thrall was first to reach the girl who lay semi-conscious and bleeding.

"Another night in paradise," he mused.

"I love this place, Emylene!" screamed Poinsettia over the pounding music.

"Yeah, me too, but I gotta work tomorrow so..." Emylene took Poinsettia by the hand and elbowed her way through the throng back to the bronze doors.

"Goodnight everybody!" shouted Poinsettia. "I love you all! Can't wait to see you again!"

Emylene and Poinsettia made their way down the long, dank hall and out into the prickly night air.

"That man, Stelio? Is he your boyfriend?" asked Poinsettia.

"Was. It's over. He just doesn't know it yet."

"I love my new name, 'Poinsettia'!"

CHAPTER 5

It wasn't the evening chill or even Stelio's unwelcomed intrusion that bothered Emylene on her way back to the apartment, so much as a thousand stinging questions: Who was this girl, really? Where did she come from and how long would she be staying?

When they finally entered the flat and shook off the snow, Emylene felt the time was ripe for some serious Q&A.

"So, my new friend, what's the deal? Are you, like, staying, or going? Do you turn into a pumpkin at midnight and disappear back into that frame or what?"

"I hope to remain here a very long time."

"I'm glad. But I'm curious, what it's like being in a sketch? I know you said you had no name and you're not even sure how old you are but, like, how did you get yourself in there? Were you born inside the picture?"

"Born? I can't imagine being anything other than what I am now."

"Okay...so you were always you. What did *you* do from day to day? Do they even have days and nights in there? What about parents, a family, do you eat, do you pee?"

The questions seemed to draw a blank with Poinsettia. As simple and mundane as they sounded, the girl was simply unable to assign any meaning to them.

"Alright then! Tell me about those men. Why were they after you?"

At the mention of the The Cowled Men Poinsettia flew into a fury.

"Horrible creatures! They want to kill me! They can find me, you know, just by following my thoughts. If I even think about them or speak their names…!"

"Okay, okay! Don't freak out! I won't ask again, I promise. And don't worry, I won't let anyone hurt you."

Poinsettia calmed down a bit, but the fear in her eyes remained.

"And, you should know, if they come for me they could hurt you, too."

"Bring it on," replied Emylene. "I'm a Goth princess. I have warrior blood in me that goes back 1500 years, so if those butt-ugly farmers want a fight, I'll give it to 'em!"

It felt good just to say it even if she didn't fully believe it. A minute later Emylene took a more measured approach.

"Look, whatever happens we'll handle it together, okay? Anyway, I hope you stay. I could use a friend to hang out with."

"Stelio again?"

"Men are such bastards, aren't they? Look, the apartment's kinda small and I only have one bed, so as long as you don't mind sharing…."

"Are you crazy? After being stuck inside a two-foot sketch, your home feels like a palace. And I'll be good, you'll have no trouble from me," promised Poinsettia.

"I get that, and my intuition is generally pretty good," replied Emylene, trying to act cool.

"Thank you, really, Emylene, for saving my life…and thank you for letting me into yours."

A warm feeling came over Emylene, reminding her of her friendship with Nostra-dame. She handed the girl a pair of pajamas, a toothbrush, and a bar of soap unsure of whether or not a two-dimensional subject of a sketch had even considered personal hygiene before, but figured it couldn't hurt. Poinsettia accepted them quick enough and followed Emylene's lead like a little sister.

When the two finally crawled into the cozy double bed, Emylene was exhausted, but the questions wouldn't abate. She wondered if parallel worlds existed in every picture, or whether this one particular drawing was special? And what was the connection to Stelio? After all, he was the one who noticed it in the window in the first place. What was up with him anyway? What could have turned such a sweet man into such an ignominious asshole? Or was that the real Stelio she met last night, and the other a facade? Where *was* that bottle of Xanax?

The girl's escape could not be taken lightly. Deep in the forest a decision was made and a plan was hatched. The Cowled Men would take turns, four at a time, hiking out of the forest every night along the fence line to try to make contact. But not if the girl was present. That would be too dangerous.

The next morning Emylene opened her eyes to find Poinsettia cowering under the bed sheets trying to avoid the light that was streaming through the window blinds.

"That's exactly how I feel every morning," quipped Emylene as she got out of bed and went to the window to tighten the blinds.

After both girls showered and dressed, Poinsettia watched Emylene begin her morning make-up ritual. First the heavy application of white pancake, followed by a blood-red lipstick, blue eye shadow and a splash of black fingernail polish. When Emylene got up from her seat, Poinsettia sat down and began copying her look down to the very last detail.

"Such a poseur," Emylene giggled.

"What's a poseur?"

"Someone who dresses like a Goth 'cause they think it's cool. You see them all the time, kids desperate to be part of something they know nothing about, who have no idea what they're doing or who they…"

Emylene caught herself before she put her foot any further down her mouth. If any girl had reason to claim ignorance, it was this one. The fact that Poinsettia was copying her mentor's style was more flattery than anything else, so Emylene decided to take a softer, more philosophical tack.

"True Goths wear 'the black' as a reflection of how they feel inside, which is essentially that there is nothing after life except death. But, accepting that sets you free because it's only when you look death in the eye that you cease to fear it. Right? I guess what I'm saying is you shouldn't wear 'the black' if all it is to you is some kind of fashion statement."

Poinsettia thought for a moment before she spoke.

"I will wear it because it not only speaks to me, but it speaks *for* me."

"Brava! So are you ready?"

Poinsettia got up to follow Emylene out, but again shied away from the morning light. Sensing her discomfort, Emylene looked through her drawers and found a pair of large rimmed sunglasses for her.

"Glam Goth—a new sub-species! Cool! Come on, girl. We gotta catch you up!"

Poinsettia grabbed a coat and tam to cover her head, dabbed some more pancake on her hands, and let Emylene lead her downstairs. Now there were two of them to turn the world inside out.

CHAPTER 6

A generous new dusting inspired Poinsettia to kick her feet through the white fluff like a child enjoying a snow day. Emylene looked at the girl's red sandals, and could ignore the unseasonal footwear no longer.

"Come with me," she ordered as she led Poinsettia across the slushy street and down the block to Master John's Shoe Emporium. Master John was not a Goth himself, but a craftsman of fine footwear who was respected and admired by Goths, gays, transvestites and leather fetishists alike. Standing about six foot two and as solid as a grain silo, Master John wrapped his beefy arms around Emylene as soon as she entered.

"Princess Emylene, how nice of you to grace us with your presence this morning."

"Knock it off, John. Meet my friend."

Introductions were made and the search for Poinsettia's new shoes began. There were dozens of choices that included Mary Janes, black creepers and Demonia boots. In the end they found a pair of sturdy black lady-killers that said, 'I may be small but look at me sideways and I'll kick your ass into next Tuesday!' Poinsettia wore her new shoes outside, but insisted on keeping her old pair.

The girls ambled along the sidewalk while Emylene pointed out various businesses and buildings along the way. This particular strip of Queen Street was home to family-owned bakeries, fruit stands, vintage clothing boutiques, comic book stores, second hand furniture emporiums, and even a condom shop. It was an oasis in the heart of the big city where the small town mentality thrived, a twelve block stretch where it was still possible for the little guy to eke out a modest living. Emylene loved the people who worked here, and every brick and mortar edifice she passed. Until she came to his.

"What's wrong?" asked Poinsettia.

"You remember Stelio from last night? This is his store and I just don't need the hassle right now."

The girls crossed the street and walked back down the opposite side to finish up the neighborhood tour. Fifteen minutes later they had returned to Lamereaux Textiles.

"So, here's the thing: I work until six o'clock, and I don't know exactly what to do with you 'til then."

"Don't worry about me, I've got a whole world to explore," responded Poinsettia as she snapped off an icicle from an awning and jabbed it playfully into the palm of her hand.

"Okay, but this part of town can be kinda sketchy. So I'd stay away from the dopers, the pimps, the bums…jeez, I sound like such a parent, don't I? Know what, go have a good time and meet me back here at six. If you don't have a watch, just ask around. Here's ten bucks in case you get hungry. You *do* get hungry, right?"

"Oh, I have an appetite," replied Poinsettia who was so excited that she scooted off without taking the money.

The morning went unexpectedly well for Emylene whose elevated mood confounded the staff, as well as baffled her regular customers. While she flitted from one aisle to the next, they whispered to each other, "What's up with Little Morticia Addams? Why's she so…nice?"

Even her boss, Ronald, gave his employee an appreciative smile and a pat on the back. Emylene couldn't wait to call her mother when noon rolled around. She hadn't been home in months, and Poinsettia's arrival would be as good an excuse as any to get in touch. True, she would see her parents whenever they'd drop by the store for a quick hello or at P.B.P., although those occasions had become less frequent of late. It was apparent to Emylene that they needed their space as much as she needed hers. The truth was that the title of Goth Princess had become as much a curse to Emylene as a blessing. Chiefly, because it spoiled the girl to a degree, making her a little lazy and entitled. Both Emylene and her parents knew she needed to grow up and meet life on its own terms. No one was sure whose idea it was for her to move out first. Each side claimed it was theirs, but in the end it had been best for them all. Today, however, Emylene needed her parents' approval and support more than ever.

So she practiced out loud the story of how Poinsettia came into her life. Hopefully, when she recited it back, they'd tell her how especially blessed, or especially worthy, or especially special she was. However, all that would have to wait because there was no answer on the other end of the phone. Damn!

The rest of the day jogged along uneventfully until a passing ambulance broke the calm of the afternoon. For a second, Emylene wondered if something happened to Poinsettia. The gremlins in her mind continued to torment her until Emylene worried whether she might ever see her new friend again. Then she scolded herself for growing attached to someone so quickly. This only put her into a deeper funk. The closer her shift came to quitting time the more morose Emylene grew. So when old Mrs. Cotter asked her to fetch a bolt of worsted wool, Emylene completely lost it.

"You mean fetch, like a dog? Why sure, Mrs. Cotter."

Emylene barked all the way over to aisle one, grabbed the step-stool, and barked all the way back. Worried that a stray dog might be loose in his store, Ronald raced around the aisles to find that the only bitch in the shop was...

"Emylene!" commanded Ronald.

"Sorry. I'm sorry, I'm just worried about my friend," she replied, which immediately drew both Ronald's and Mrs. Cotter's sympathy.

"She's visiting from the forest and I'm worried that Queen Street might be a little too much for her, ya know?"

"She lives in a forest, your friend?" asked Mrs. Cotter. "What kind of person lives in a forest?"

Ronald shook his head as he climbed the step-stool to get the bolt of wool for Mrs. Cotter, and then directed her to the cash register. After the elderly woman left, Ronald turned back to his employee.

"Emylene Stipe, are you stoned?" Ronald peered suspiciously into her eyes to find she was not, which only troubled him more.

"I like you, Emylene, because you're not afraid to be you, and I think that's kind of brave, if you want to know the truth. For me it's different; this store was an inheritance of sorts and because of that and I've got responsibilities. In a way, I am the store and the store is me. Though, figuring out who the hell I am these days...anyways, I think I've been cool about how you dress and I've given you a lot of slack about your whole Goth deal because, as strange as you make yourself out to be, you know your stuff. But part of our job here is 'client relations' and if we walk around yapping at the customers like rabid dogs all day long, we're not going to be selling any of these magic bolts of cloth that keep us in business, are we? And if I lose this store, I would, in essence, be letting down my whole family and I've got enough to feel guilty about without...anyways, capisce?"

Emylene didn't 'capisce' because her eyes were trained on the end of the aisle where Poinsettia was listening in on the whole diatribe. Emylene's mood suddenly brightened and she smiled at her boss contritely.

"I totally get it, Ronald, and I'll be cool as an arctic cucumber, promise. A thousand apologies."

"Great, so be a good little Goth and say your sorries to Mrs. Cotter."

Ronald hurried off to his office while Emylene skipped down the aisle to Poinsettia.

"Gimme a minute and then we're outa here, okay?" she whispered.

Poinsettia nodded as Emylene raced to the cash register, shouting, "Mrs. Cotter, lemme help you. Sorry about that before. Time of the month, ya know?"

After Emylene checked Mrs. Cotter out, she and her new-found friend traipsed upstairs to their apartment while Poinsettia showed off her new hat, an aging fedora with a wide brim.

"Where'd you get that? You didn't buy it. I know 'cause you forgot to take the money," Emylene said as she poured some mac and cheese into a boiling pot of water.

"It was a gift. Oh, I had the best time today, Emylene. I met some musicians who asked me to join their group, then I saw some beggars begging for money but they didn't want me to join their group, but they told me I could have this hat if I moved on. I like hats. Then I saw some people who wore the black, and I asked them if they thought life was empty of pleasure and full of pain like you, and they smiled and nodded like they knew. But they weren't Goths, they were Hassidic Jews."

Poinsettia prattled on about her adventures for the next few minutes, which brightened up the apartment like a new coat of paint. Emylene managed to squeeze in the occasional "really," "wicked," and "perverse" and waited patiently until it was her turn.

"Well, things were pretty much normal except for some random ambulance this afternoon. I mean… downtown you hear them all the time, but this one stopped maybe a block or two away so I got worried for a minute that it might have come for you. Stupid, huh?"

"Yeah, it didn't come for me. It came for your friend, Stelio," replied Poinsettia matter of factly.

"Stelio? What happened?"

"Not sure exactly, except they wheeled him out on one of those stretchers and put him in the ambulance. Somebody said something about a heart attack."

Emylene felt as though she'd been hit by a bus.

"Heart attack?"

"Anyway, he won't be bothering you anymore," continued Poinsettia.

"Why? What do you mean?"

"I mean he's dead, silly," she replied as easily as snapping shut the cover of a book.

"And if anyone knows what 'dead' is, that would be my new best friend, Emylene Stipe. So tomorrow, do you have to go to work or can we go out exploring together? Emylene?" she whined.

Stelio was dead…from a heart attack…in the store where he could rarely be found! Emylene was speechless. And if that wasn't enough to deal with, Poinsettia didn't seem to have a clue as to what that even meant. Was this girl as naive as she sounded or just a callous, cold bitch, or did she hold death in such disregard? As the gravity of Stelio's death filtered through her brain, Emylene recalled some of her own lame jokes about death as the great Vaudevillian slip on the banana peel of life, or a one-way bungee-jump into the great beyond, or 'taking the last train to Clarksville', things that tripped so easily off her tongue. Until now. Now, someone close to her had died and for the first time in her life, Emylene felt death's awful weight.

"I can't take off work. You know that," Emylene muttered flatly.

With that she picked up the dishes from the table and dumped them in the sink. Then she put soap to sponge and scoured the countertop, table, and even the chairs in an attempt to ground herself to something familiar, to connect in some way with life. Poinsettia must have gotten the message because she held her tongue for three whole minutes before chiming in again.

"You know what we should do? We should go back to that club of yours. That will make you feel better."

"That would make *you* feel better. I'm a little out of it," was all Emylene could manage to say.

As if to validate her condition she peeled off her clothes and slunk under the covers. Poinsettia joined her a few minutes later and together the pair lay in silence. But sleep would not come easily to Emylene whose mind spun like a pinwheel as she re-evaluated her relationship with her old friend, Death. Growing up she'd always held this fanciful image of Death as an elegantly dressed gentleman in a Mardi Gras mask that, when the time came, would step up and ask her for one last dance. Now that image had morphed into a stubble-faced thief slinking into the night with a bag full of souls slung over his shoulder. That skulking specter toyed with her until sleep mercifully overcame the little Goth. But blessed rest was short-lived.

Later that night an odd feeling awakened Emylene. Instinctively she turned to check on Poinsettia who was also awake, sitting bolt upright in fact, staring at the sketch on the wall. Emylene followed her gaze, and, for the second time in twenty-four hours, was agasp. There they were—unmistakable and undeniable footprints in the snow. This time, *four sets* of them! The Cowled Men? Could they be the ones responsible for Stelio's death? And if so, what about Poinsettia? Was she in danger now too?

"We should rip it to pieces," whispered Emylene.

"No. Don't touch it, don't go near it. They can't get me as long as you don't make contact."

"Or if you don't think about them, right?" Emylene added.

"What?"

"You said last night, they can find you if you even think about them."

"Right, just trust me. Leave it alone," was all Poinsettia said.

Emylene nodded her head and was determined to stand guard for the rest of the night just in case. The next morning she shuddered awake with the sinking feeling that she had failed her friend. Thankfully, Poinsettia was safe and asleep beside her. When Emylene looked at the picture again, she found that the four sets of footprints had disappeared, and the snow around the Cyprus tree was as pristine and untouched as ever. Had she dreamed them? Had Stelio's death inspired the ominous hallucination the night before? There could be a thousand reasons or there could be one. She debated with herself whether or not to mention anything more to Poinsettia. No, she vowed, today would be a normal day…or as normal as times like these could be.

CHAPTER 7

"Are you getting up or what?" asked Emylene as she tugged at Poinsettia beneath the bed sheets.

"Not much of a day person. Think I'll stay right here," Poinsettia muttered.

"Cool. Hey, you know what? I've been thinking, why don't we have lunch later?"

"Where, at Old McDonald's? They give you toys with your food, you know. And they have the most delicious children there, too!"

"Jokes. I'm thinking my parents' place."

"Really? I would love to meet them!" replied Poinsettia with even more enthusiasm.

Emylene wanted to believe that this hairpin turn in her life was something she could handle on her own, but the combination of Poinsettia's unexpected arrival and Stelio's sudden death were too much for one little Goth to take all at once. Her nerves were frayed and she needed the comfort and support of her family. The question was, would she get what she needed? Unfortunately, Emylene's cutting of the umbilical cord in the name of teenage rebellion had left an ugly scab, though if there ever was a girl who enjoyed picking at a scab, it was Emylene. Resigned to making the trip to her parents, she finished dressing and ate breakfast, while debating whether to call ahead or just show up. As she left the apartment she glanced once more at the sketch to make sure no fresh footprints had appeared. Nothing. Before heading out the door, she reminded Poinsettia of their date at noon and then hurried downstairs to work.

When she entered the shop, Emylene told Ronald she would need to take an extra long lunch hour because of a dentist appointment. News traveled fast on Queen Street and Stelio's death was common knowledge by the time the shop doors opened that morning. Wise to her affair with the pretentious businessman, Ronald nodded his okay and even asked the rest of the sales staff to respect Emylene's feelings by keeping gossip to a minimum. Of course, that only encouraged them to speculate more. Some whispered that Stelio died while he was arguing with a particularly prickly customer, others said the heart attack occurred when he was having a quickie with one of his salesgirls in a change room, for he had a reputation as a womanizer. In the end all agreed that, although he was too young to die, if anyone deserved to go sooner than later, it was the snotty Greek haberdasher.

Fetching bolts of cloth for customers all morning long proved to be good therapy for Emylene who tended to live too much in her head anyway. She reminded herself that relentless self-introspection was the number one cause of mental breakdowns and the number three moneymaker for pharmaceutical companies. She envied some of the staff that went through life like they didn't have a care in the world. Maybe that was the better way, she thought, living the unexamined life. But, personal wisdom told her everybody, smart or dull, had their demons whether they admitted it or not. So Emylene made the healthier choice and spent the morning dwelling on everybody else's shortcomings instead of her own, until before she knew it, noon hour had arrived, and it was time for her 'dentist appointment.'

Well, one decision was made at least—she wouldn't be calling ahead to prepare her folks for her visit. Maybe that would give her the upper hand.

Emylene found Poinsettia waiting outside on the sidewalk wrapped in a jacket, toque, scarf and large sunglasses, covered under so much clothing that Emylene could barely make her out. For a girl who had lived in a cold climate for God knows how long, you would have thought adjusting to the local weather would have been a snap. Maybe there was a dry chill/wet chill differential between picture life and street life, something akin to the visual differences between 2-D and 3-D movies. Cold withstanding, the girls climbed onto a westbound streetcar, traveled a dozen blocks, and walked south on Manning Avenue to the Stipe house.

Emylene was uncharacteristically quiet as she tried to sort the details of the story in her head and prepare herself for her parents' reactions. Then it struck her that it might be a good idea to prepare Poinsettia for the meeting, as well.

"Listen, my folks are like me, except first generation, so the duds and the piercings, be cool, okay? And, like, they have a side business selling 'Goth cloth' and accessories over the Internet, so if you see some weird shit lying around, it's no big deal."

"Whatever you say," replied Poinsettia, unfazed.

"And most of all, don't let 'em hook you. I mean… they'll be courteous and all, but they can be devils, especially Mom."

Emylene stopped when they reached the walkway where, as a child of four-years-old she broke her leg. Her mother was pushing her on a tricycle from behind that day and didn't notice that her daughter's foot had become trapped in the front spokes of the big front wheel. Vandy was so gleefully carried away with the moment that she didn't realize her daughter's predicament until she heard the awful snap like that of a twig breaking. By the time Vandy pulled the trike to a halt Emylene's leg had become enmeshed in the spokes and the child was screaming in pain. The doctors set the leg and it healed in less than six weeks, but Emylene would tease her mother for years after that. Stepping up to the front door now she wondered whether today would end with a healing or another bad break.

"Hey!" shouted Emylene into the house.

"Hey back. Is that you, Emylene? Downstairs," came her mother's reply. "And if there's a package, can you bring it?"

Sure enough, there was a small brown box sitting on the porch to the left of the door. Emylene brought it with her as the two girls unlaced their boots and left them on the inside mat. They walked across the wood floor, past the bland-looking rattan furniture, and into the next hallway where the even blander Robert Bateman prints hung. Somewhat embarrassed, Emylene explained, "Most people, when they come over, expect to find a cauldron in the kitchen or an alter for devil worship next to the fireplace. My parents didn't want to turn off any of my friends when I was a kid so they kept their lifestyle out of view. So what you're about to see, don't freak, okay?"

"No freaking, I promise," smiled her friend.

As Emylene led Poinsettia downstairs to the basement, she sensed something very, very wrong. The ink blue carpeted stair-runners had been replaced by a sickly oatmeal color, and the heavy crimson drapes she'd grown up with were gone. From there it got worse. The basement housed a treasure-trove of early European artifacts including a maple libraria bookcase, a cypress wood armoire, and an authentic 16th century hard wood table and chair set bearing the crest of 'Vlad Tepis' (Vlad the Impaler), a gift from a distant relative. They were gone too. It was as though the upstairs had somehow crept downstairs one night and overtaken it like a cancer. In place of all the old world furniture, was a pair of gun metal desks and business filing cabinets that stood out like ulcers in a God-awful sea of beige.

"Perverse!" gasped Emylene.

But, the most hideous metamorphosis of all lay in the people Emylene knew as her parents. Her mother, Vandy, who once bore a glorious, jet-black mane of hair now sported a short, cropped head of natural gray. Gone were the black lace corset and the steam punk heels that accentuated her mother's voluptuous body. In their place was a Corvette yellow Lululemon sports top and leggings that hugged a much slimmer version of the woman. Working away at a computer, she looked like some kind of Stepford soccer mom. Her mother had obviously flipped out, but what about her father?

"Ohhhhhhh," came a long moan emanating from the adjoining bathroom.

"You okay in there, Theo?" yelled Vandy in the direction of the moan. "She brought a friend, so easy on the dramatics and don't forget to flush."

Then she whispered the words 'stones' to Emylene who in turn discreetly informed Poinsettia that her father must be having a kidney stone attack. On cue a toilet flushed, the bathroom door opened, and out walked Theo Stipe, stuffed into a hideous royal blue jogging suit and white Adidas runners.

"There she is. How's my girl!" smiled Theo.

"Mom, Dad, what the Hell?" said Emylene, looking shell-shocked.

Theo wiped the sweat from his brow with one hand and grabbed his crotch with the other as he grimaced from an involuntary whoop of painful laughter.

"I told ya, didn't I, Vandy?"

Turning to his daughter he explained, "It was time, sweetheart, that's all. Times change and people change with 'em. A half hour ago I was at my desk taking an order. Next thing I know I'm on my knees in the bathroom, praying for a quick death. A few ticks later, I've got the bastard that was trying to kill me right here in this Kleenex—its life in *my* hands. Wanna see?"

"Ugh, no!" she replied.

Theo shrugged and stuck the Kleenex in his pocket.

"And that's just in the past thirty minutes, so you can imagine all that's happened since you moved out. Pass the package, dear?"

Emylene shook her head and handed the small cardboard box to her father who used the gold razor he kept hung around his neck to slice open the package, and pulled out a foot-long purple vibrator. He jiggled the 'on/off' switch a few times and pronounced, "Lousy connection. We're dropping this supplier, pronto, Vandy."

"I repeat, what the *Hell*?" Emylene shouted with exasperation.

Reading the bewilderment in her daughter's eyes Vandy sighed and reluctantly offered her a terse explanation.

"I know, I know, Goth is good, but sex pays the bills. We would have said something, but we hadn't heard from you in almost two months and we know how you like your space."

Emylene paused for a long moment and then suddenly brightened.

"You know, I'm kinda glad, because if you think track suits and kidney stones and plastic dildos are life-changing, then man, am I going to blow your mind! Meet my new friend, Poinsettia."

Over the next half hour, Emylene carefully related the story of how Poinsettia came into her life, and how Stelio had so suddenly exited it. Her parents listened patiently until Emylene got to the part about discovering the new sets of footprints in the sketch the previous night. At that point her mother could hold back no longer.

"Somebody from Pall Bearer's Paradise tipped you off about us and this is your revenge, isn't it? This little 'Nightmare On Stipe Street.'

Emylene stiffened immediately.

"Mom, I swear this is the first I've heard about your metamorphosis or whatever you wanna call it, and to tell you the truth, I guess I was a little freaked out, but I'm cool with it now. It's your life and you can do what you want. But coming here today was not about you, it's about me."

"Daughter dearest, this fantasy of yours is *all* about me, about us. You're obviously upset and this is your way of showing it. Really, when we suggested you move out we hoped you would have outgrown this adolescent need to define yourself by rebelling against us, but I can see…"

"…moving out was my idea, lady, all mine!"

Theo, the mediator between the two headstrong women, felt it was time to wade in. "We are not Wiccans, Emylene, we don't subscribe to magic. So assuming everything you've told us is true, what would you like us to do?"

"For one, you can start by not being so damn condescending," she snapped back.

"Fine, have it your way," replied Vandy who began tapping away at her computer keyboard.

"What are you doing?" asked Emylene.

"Come on, Emylene, you actually expect us to believe that this little poseur of yours climbed out of some picture on your wall and a bunch of ancient forest dwellers followed her, killed your boyfriend, and now they're after you? I'm looking up your friend on Facebook, and all the local Goth sites. And when I find her, you'll be lucky if I don't shave your head for lying."

Plainly, Emylene was not getting the healing she'd hoped for.

"Lying? You'd be doing me more of a kindness if you called me crazy."

"Chill, Emylene, nobody's calling you a liar, exactly," interjected Theo. "We just know how creative you can be with the truth sometimes. I often thought you should write for a living."

Vandy grunted over her husband's passive-aggressive stance.

"Theo, quit mollycoddling her. You're not doing her any favors. You want a story, hon? I've got a story for you. How about you were screwing that old dude and he died in the sack, and now you're so guilt-ridden about it that you're talking yourself into a nervous breakdown."

"Great! Feeling much better now, Mom!"

"Vandy! You're not helping!" shouted Theo.

"Well, she can't have it both ways. Either she's lying to us, or she's asking us to support her in this sick fantasy."

Emylene wasn't about to let her mother get away with a single point.

"Your meltdown scenario might make sense, mother, if Poinsettia appeared *after* Stelio kicked, but she appeared *before,* so how do you explain that? And if you think I'm trying to bullshit you, what about all the bullshit you shoved down my throat for these past nineteen years? And now you turn around and pull this?"

Locked and loaded, Vandy fired back.

"Truth is you never dealt with those latent daddy issues, so you had to act out by taking up with a man old enough to be your…"

"…you're just jealous because my father loves me more than he ever loved you!"

"Oh, God," interjected Theo. "I love you both equally!"

Vandy threw her husband such a disparaging look that Theo knew that whatever he said next would only make things worse. So he just shook his head, took a seat and shut up. As for Poinsettia, she was as amused as a kid at a Punch and Judy show.

"Now you're just being cruel," replied Vandy to her daughter. "And for your information it wasn't bullshit, being Goth. It was a lifestyle which suited us at the time and made you the person you are today."

"So what does that make you? Phonies, poseurs! *You're* the ones who turned your backs on everything you taught me!"

"We didn't turn our backs. We *evolved*," exclaimed her mother.

"Evolved? More like, deserted!" screamed Emylene. And to press her point she deserted her parents by storming upstairs.

Poinsettia let the silence hang in the air a moment before she smiled politely and said, "Very nice to meet you," and then followed after her friend.

Emylene fled her parents' icy rejection for the cold comfort of a winter's day, which felt 100 degrees warmer by comparison. It wasn't until she was about a hundred yards down the street when she stopped and lifted her voice to the heavens to exclaim, "I am alone!"

A hand reached out holding the pair of boots that she had forgotten in her parents' house. Poinsettia hugged her friend to shield her from the inhospitable elements, both natural and familial.

"All my life they told me I was special, but now all I feel is stupid."

"You are special, Emylene, more than they know or even you do. And you're not alone. I'm here with you," she said.

After the tears subsided, it was Poinsettia who comforted Emylene and promised her that everything would be all right as they made their way back to her store. They agreed to meet that evening and do something special, but in her heart Emylene knew that things were way past the point of being 'alright.' Her parents' lives might be evolving, but Emylene's was turning upside down and inside out.

CHAPTER 8

The rest of the afternoon at work was torture for Emylene, and not in a good way. When she finally traipsed upstairs that evening, she found the apartment empty. Looking forward to some downtime, she turned on the kettle and made herself a cup of oolong tea to sooth her jangled nerves. Emylene generally loved her solitude, but tonight the quiet was so unsettling that she put on a CD in the hopes that some classic Evanescence might bring her some comfort. Curling up in a chair she sipped her tea and sang along:

"Wake me up inside
Wake me up inside
Call my name and save me from the dark
Bid my blood to run
Before I come undone
Save me from the nothing I've become"

But nothing could save her from the feeling that her little world was about to crumble like a condemned building facing the wrecking ball. Was she still upset over the confrontation with her parents earlier? Or was it Stelio's death? Or was it a combination of both? And where was Poinsettia?

Omigod, how pathetic! Had she come to rely on Poinsettia's company so much that she couldn't even bear to be alone with herself anymore? Then she realized that, no, what she was experiencing was much more than that. It was a feeling of anxiety, a tsunami of fear cascading over her, waves of a thousand stinging needles. But from where was this coming and, why? That's when it hit her. Turning her head toward the sketch, Emylene's worst fears were realized. They were back! The footprints in the snow, and along with them, four Cowled Men standing by the rickety fence staring directly at her. Emylene's gut told her to go for the nearest pair of scissors and slash the canvas into bits once and for all. But something stayed her hand. That 'something' lay in the expressions she saw in the faces of the old men, which were not menace, but worry and concern.

"Who are you? What do you want? You can't have her back! I won't let you take her from me, you hear?" yelled Emylene in a voice rivaling the head-banging music.

One of them moved his lips in an effort to speak, but footsteps coming up the stairs prevented him from uttering a sound. Instead, all four of them turned, and with heavy leaden footsteps, trudged back to the cover of the forest. A moment later Poinsettia burst into the apartment, as giddy as a child who had spent a day at the circus. Emylene was desperate to tell her about the manifestation, but didn't want to upset her friend's spirits, so all she could manage was, "Want some tea?"

Poinsettia related all the new wonders she witnessed that day as they drank their oolong and shared a dinner of canned soup and peanut butter sandwiches. Then she asked Emylene if they could *please* go out tonight. The holiday known as Christmas was upon them and Poinsettia was anxious to see what all the fuss was about. At the mention of the event Emylene smacked herself on the head.

"I almost forgot. We have to go to P.B.P. It's tradition."

"Wheeee!" shouted Poinsettia.

"Jesus, girl, did someone shoot you up or something?" asked Emylene. "Where do you get all the energy?"

CHAPTER 9

When they arrived at Pall Bearer's Paradise that night, Goth Christmas was in full swing. The disinterred bones of Old Saint Nick were propped up at the entrance for everyone's acknowledgement and edification. As per the custom, Emylene instructed Poinsettia to kiss the mistletoe that hung around his neck before they proceeded. "Most people kiss each other *under* the mistletoe," she explained to the girl. "But the plant was actually worshipped by the ancient Celts and Druids as having magical powers. Protected them against poison, warded off evil spirits, and even used as an aphrodisiac. A kind of all-purpose cure-all. So we kiss the actual plant."

The girl nodded and did as she was told, whereupon the fabulous Damiani Sisters who were decked out in their traditional red Lolita unitards ushered both inside. Emylene and Poinsettia made their way toward the hub of the festivities where the large blackened Christmas tree stood, and from which little voodoo dolls hung, and the many wrapped gifts that lay beneath.

"We didn't bring a gift," whispered Poinsettia.

"No worries. As Princess, it's my job to give out the gifts."

Emylene had mixed emotions when it came to her position in the Goth community. She loved the idea of being part of the 'royal family' who presided over their clan. That it was her parents on whose advice the tribe relied on to settle their internal squabbles and issues of decorum, gave Emylene a great sense of pride. The flip side of this was that whenever disagreements with her parents' judgments were voiced, Emylene generally bore the brunt of it. "Do you know what your father said about that thing the other night? How random!" The ugly truth was that Emylene knew her parents were as fallible as anyone else and, whenever their bad decisions ricocheted back on her, she made it hell for them at home. Yet, at times like this, being a 'princess' did have its upside, even if handing out holiday gifts was about the extent of her authority. Aside from that, nothing she ever did felt particularly inspiring.

Friends, wannabes, and lackeys came over to greet Emylene, but it was Poinsettia who quickly became the focus of attention. Somehow word had spread as to who she was and how she came to be. Emylene wondered if her parents had something to do with the rumors, even though they were rarely in touch with the club-goers these days.

"How did you get here, Poinsettia?" people asked. "What's your world like?" "Are there Goths where you come from, too?" "Are the dead over on your side? Can we speak to them?"

Emylene thought it odd that whenever she raised these kinds of questions with Poinsettia, the girl shrank from answering them. But tonight she was quite talkative. In fact, not just talkative, but downright bubbly and effusive. After a while it looked to Emylene like her friend was getting more attention than she. And so what if she was? Why did this irk Emylene so much? A few minutes later, a gong rang out and everyone gathered around the tree. According to their holiday tradition, Emylene picked names from a bowl and passed out a gift to each person until everyone had received something, be it a bottle of nail polish, an amulet, a dog collar or just a small piece of candy. Only Poinsettia was left empty-handed, leaving a few people to boo with disappointment.

"Oh, I've already received my gift," she announced. "If not for Emylene, I would be celebrating Christmas in some horrible dark forest instead being here with all of you."

Thrall handed Poinsettia a small glass filled with green liquor.

"At least accept this on our behalf, absinthe—the green fairy," he said in a seductive tone.

Emylene wondered if Thrall was coming onto her friend. Poinsettia downed the potent liquid in one gulp and challenged Emylene to match her shot for shot. With everybody's blessing the bacchanalia of dance and drink began. As it turned out Poinsettia was one little lass who could hold her liquor. But, instead of easing tensions between the girls, the alcohol was accessing Emylene's primal feelings and playing havoc with them. The last time they were at the Club she'd had a fight with Stelio. This afternoon she argued with her parents, and now she was jealous of her new best friend. Emylene had an ominous feeling that her life was quickly spinning out of control, and there was nothing she could do about it.

By the time the party peaked Emylene was so envious of the attention given to her friend that it was all she could do to stop from tying the mistletoe around Poinsettia's delicate little throat and asphyxiating the wench. The party continued to devolve through the night until a few of the party-goers collapsed, not an common occurrence at P.B.P. Ultimately, the festivities wore themselves out and Thrall ushered the last of the degenerates through the brass doors before he closed up, Emylene and Poinsettia included.

Stumbling through the alley on the way home, Poinsettia gushed.

"Oh, Em', I had the best time tonight! Thank you for introducing me to your friends, I love them all."

"You must have felt pretty damn comfortable yourself to be gabbing so much about your life in the forest or wherever it is you come from. Did I hear you tell somebody The Cowled Men were after you for stealing a rabbit? You never told me that."

"Oh sure, I did. You saw the blood, don't you remember? When you helped me escape?"

"That was rabbit blood you dripped onto my floor?"

"It was my only way out. Don't be angry. The Cowled Men were much more cruel than that, believe me. I could tell you some things, but you look tired, we need to get you home."

Emylene was not sure whether she had heard the story correctly or not, but for the second time in twenty-four hours she felt betrayed, and this kicked her anger level up a few notches.

"I am not tired and I'm not drunk! For your information, I didn't wanna say anything—you were having such a good time. But you should know I saw more footprints in your little charcoal sketch earlier before we left for P.B.P."

Poinsettia stopped dead in her tracks.

"You saw and you didn't tell me? I thought you were my friend. You promised you'd protect me. Did you see anything else, those evil hooded devils?"

Maybe the absinthe had gotten to Emylene more than she was prepared to admit. Poinsettia's heart-rendering plea made Emylene feel more ashamed than she had in years.

"No," she lied. "And of course I want to protect you. I'm sorry."

Nothing more was said between the girls as they made their way back to the apartment. However, that didn't prevent Emylene's mind from buzzing with more unanswered questions. What did these Cowled Men want from Poinsettia?

What could she have done to make them pursue her like this? And could they actually escape from that painting and come after her? Mostly she wondered what they were trying to say to her before Poinsettia's arrival scared them off. The best Emylene could do for now, she figured, was to get some sleep. Perhaps the morning would bring a few sobering answers. As it turned out she wouldn't have to wait that long. It was 5:15 A.M. when her next life-changing event struck.

CHAPTER 10

"Emylene, get up! Get up!"

Emylene awoke to the sounds of Poinsettia's urgent pleas and her own choking cough as she realized that her apartment was filling up with smoke. Through the acrid tears filling her eyes, she could make out Poinsettia by the bed, shaking her.

"We need to get out of here now!" Poinsettia commanded.

Emylene fought the hangover that gripped her head like a vise while she searched for her sweatpants and boots. Then, instinctively, she ran for the front door to make her escape, but Poinsettia pulled her back just in time. The fire on the stairwell outside had already super-heated the door and was eating its way through the cheap particleboard. She would have suffered severe burns if she even touched the doorknob.

"The window!" Poinsettia cried.

Poinsettia led her friend to the window at the back of the apartment that opened onto a fire escape. Emylene wheezed and hacked as the two climbed awkwardly down the stairs. By the time they reached the soot-covered ground, the entire building was engulfed in flames.

"We can't stay here. The whole thing could come crashing down any second. Come on!" shouted Poinsettia.

"Where?"

"The club. We'll go back to the club, we'll be safe there," she answered.

Emylene stared stupidly at her friend as she tried to clear her head from the drunken fog.

"You're already dressed?" Emylene asked.

"I heard something downstairs earlier, so I got up to check. That's when I smelled the smoke, and came back to get you."

"Ya think someone set the fire?"

"I don't know for sure, but we need to go now. It'll be light soon."

As they stumbled away, Emylene noticed footprints in the snow—fresh footprints heading toward her building. The arsonist's footprints? As the girls hurried down the block, all Emylene could think of to say was, "Poor Ronald, what's going to happen to his store?"

"Who cares? But, I guess you'll finally be getting that day off, won't you?" mused Poinsettia.

Emylene had more questions, but her friend wasn't answering. She was focused on reaching their destination and getting them to safety. Poinsettia was proving to be not just a friend but a true godsend. A moment later they arrived at the alleyway. It was almost dawn when the girls trotted down the stairs and jogged along the dank hallway.

"We can stay here as long as we want," said Poinsettia.

"The door, it's open. Thrall never leaves it open when he's not here, and he never lets anyone stay after he's gone."

"He did for me—after I gave him his gift."

"What gift?"

"Remember how everybody brought a gift last night except you?"

"I told you, I'm the Princess, I don't have to…"

"Yeah, well, Princess, it turns out that that was getting kind of old. But don't worry, I fixed it."

"What do you mean, you fixed it? What did you do?"

Had Poinsettia rendezvoused with Thrall at some point in the night and had sex with him? That would have been the last straw. Poinsettia yanked open the bronze door and steered Emylene into the club. That's when she saw it—the framed sketch that sat on the floor, by the bar. What the hell was that doing here?

"I knew how it bothered you, so I brought it here yesterday. Thrall loves it and thinks it belongs here. So do I."

The more Emylene tried to make sense of it all, the more her head pounded. How could Poinsettia have brought the painting over the other day when she saw it hanging on her apartment wall last night? Emylene gazed stupidly at the floor, for an answer—and then she noticed it—the wet footprints on the cement floor next to her! In that moment, all her perplexing questions, fears and answers crystallized in her mind: This had nothing to do with Thrall, but it did have something to do with someone else she once cared deeply for. Stelio had bothered her, and now he was dead… Emylene, who couldn't get a day off work, now had all the time in the world….The Cowled Men in the painting didn't look menacing, they looked worried…and the footprints in the snow behind the apartment leading *to* the building were the same as the ones leading *away*—the very same wet footprints she was staring at now—made from Poinsettia's new boots, the ones that Emylene bought for her.

"All these things, Emylene, I did for you," said Poinsettia, in reply to her unspoken question.

"You tell me that life has no meaning, but look how you suffered when Stelio died. You argue with your parents like their opinions actually mean something. A stupid building goes up in flames and all you can think of is your boss. If life is so meaningless, why should all these things matter so much?"

Emylene stood there, astonished as the pieces of this cosmic puzzle came together, a Rubik's Cube of random thoughts being aligned by invisible hands.

"You killed Stelio! You set the fire!" Emylene accused.

As she spoke the words, she knew they were true. But why? Neither Stelio nor Ronald had harmed Poinsettia in any way or had anything to do with her. The only connection between them all was Emylene, but why would Poinsettia want to harm the one person who saved her from those cursed Cowled Men…the same men who came to *warn* Emylene?

"It's a cruel world, Emylene, you're much too fragile to live in it. Believe me, I'm only trying to protect you."

Poinsettia pulled a kitchen knife from her pocket and Emylene steeled herself for the attack. But instead, Poinsettia placed the blade into the corner of the picture frame and gingerly pried the wood apart. Now it was clear to Emylene what was about to happen.

"It's better for you in there, Em', trust me."

Emylene turned reluctantly toward the sketch to see The Cowled Men marching out of the woods. They made their way along the fence line, past the cypress, and waited at the forefront of the picture. While Emylene was distracted, Poinsettia nicked the little Goth's arm with the knife and drew blood. The faces on The Cowled Men that once looked menacing, and then worrisome, were now filled with sad resignation, helpless to stop Poinsettia from accomplishing her mission.

"Please, I don't want to go," pleaded Emylene.

Emylene tried to retreat to the door, but Poinsettia threatened her with the serrated blade.

"There's nothing for you here, Em', believe me," she said. "You have no home, no work, and no lover."

"My parents…."

"They deserted you a long time ago. We both know that."

"I'll change, they'll take me back!"

"Back to what? You had it all wrong. You Goths, you all dress the part and look the part, but *you* are the fakes, the frauds, the poseurs. You have no idea what the true nature of black is or the world that lies within it. Your parents were pathetic enough, but you, Princess, are so much worse. You only embraced their lifestyle to please them. You would have been just as comfortable wearing a white confirmation dress and going to church every Sunday if that's what they did. As much as you claim to be a rebel, you're afraid to draw a breath without their approval. The pity is that even after you left home, you never learned to think for yourself. Well, this is your chance. You'll see. Trading places will be best thing for you, for both of us."

Poinsettia grabbed Emylene's arm and held it over the crack in the frame, watching her blood trickle onto the wood and into the wet snow of the charcoal drawing. Then she brought a drop of Emylene's blood to her lips and said. "You never knew, never even suspected, did you?"

"What?"

"What I am, silly."

That's when Emylene saw it! The gleam of an enlarged bicuspid peeking out of Poinsettia's upper lip. She bared her teeth in full now, proudly displaying her true nature for the first time.

"What are you?"

"I am the real thing."

Emylene couldn't believe it! Those were not teeth, they were fangs! As soon as she saw them, the more quirky aspects of Poinsettia's personality began to make sense—her aversion to the morning sun, her way of overdressing whenever she went outside, the party-goers at P.B.P. who dropped unconscious and bleeding onto the floor during the orgies of dance.

Emylene stared transfixed at the entity, its true nature revealed for the first time. She had fantasized about this supernatural being ever since she could remember. A romantic, childish notion of vampyres, a mythical race scorned and misunderstood for centuries. But now, actually looking into the eyes of one terrified her. Those eyes. If ever there was a Pool of Oblivion, it was in those two soulless orbs. But what was equally disturbing was that beyond the fiend's obvious bloodlust, was the method in which she had so cunningly cut off Emylene from her friends and family. The vampyres she read about were only concerned with quenching their thirst, with satisfying their bloodlust. This one sought to banish Emylene from the world entirely. Why? As her head grew light and her mind grew dim she realized this question might never be answered. The last sad thought in Emylene's head was that Poinsettia was right; Emylene had been the poseur all along. How perverse!

The fire was a three-alarmer that took hours to douse and, in the end, sent two firefighters to the hospital. Ronald stood outside his store weeping for the loss of his business and his legacy, and for Emylene, whom he believed had perished inside.

The next night, Thrall threw a great party at Pall Bearer's Paradise in celebration of Emylene's death. Every Goth in the district arrived to pay their respects to Theo and Vandy Stipe, and all were held spellbound by Poinsettia who regaled them with stories of her brief, but intense, relationship with Emylene. Toasts were made and prayers were offered to a dozen gods and goddesses to honor the spirit of the young Princess who would never pass this way again. Little did they know that the spirit was just few feet away, watching over them from a black and white charcoal sketch that had been placed over the bar.

The Cowled Men had failed. They had been entrusted to keep the succubus in their netherworld over forty years ago until such a time as a cure for her affliction or a final solution might be found. But the wicked never rest, and neither had this one until she found a way out. She had not pilfered a rabbit, but killed a child and used its blood to escape, then tricked Emylene into taking her place. Now horrible things that had laid dormant for over four decades were once again set in motion, and all any of them could do was to stand by helplessly while evil went on its merry way.

CHAPTER 11

(16 MONTHS LATER)

Mid-summer. The stench from these deserted streets was as foul as the sour cough from a dying man's breath. No man, woman, child, bird or stray dog dared to traverse the roadways. The stretch of Queen Street used to be home to a hearty little blue-collar district filled with funky boutiques, tasty bistros and watering holes. But those stores had long been abandoned and, in fact, most signs of life had abandoned this part of town months ago. If a car or cab found its way onto these avenues during daylight hours, it was strictly by accident, and both the wise man and the fool knew their survival depended on putting pedal to the metal until they were safely out of the neighborhood. No threat of a speeding ticket here. Not even the police patrolled this quadrant, a patch of land that roughly covered twelve city blocks. They called it 'Other-Town' and it came into being just after the Lamereaux Textiles fire, maybe because of it. Along with the soot and smoke that settled over the area came a kind of malaise or torpor that slowly but surely discouraged people from patronizing the once bustling neighborhood. Choked out of business, shopkeepers simply closed their doors and quit the sector until it became nothing more than a ghost town. Their absence left it wide open to street thugs to loot at will and use as a drag racing circuit. But, even that was short-lived. Looters who broke into stores didn't always emerge again. Car jockeys would begin a race at one end of town, but not necessarily arrive at the other. Eventually even the criminals deserted it. Not to say there was no life there. Even though the streets appeared empty by day there was life of sorts. For Other-Town had become a living organism unto itself which needed to feed and grow. And like every organism it needed something to feed on.

Generally speaking, no time of day or night was safe to wander about in Other-Town, although mid afternoon would offer the best odds for survival. Only a handful of people knew that, people who had gained the knowledge in faraway lands or through tragic experience.

He had both. At the stroke of two, when the sun was highest, he left his dwelling at the edge of the demarcation line and moved westward into the zone. Even though it was sweltering outside, he wore an old fashioned greatcoat that holstered the weapons he would need, weapons he hoped he wouldn't have to use. He was not a young man anymore, somewhere in his late 60s, but his mission imbued him with a vigorous and determined spirit. He had worked on these plans for over two months, and knew exactly where was he was going and what he had to do. If he made one wrong move or miscalculation, well, death was a great motivator for getting a man's homework done right.

He strode down the sidewalks of the main street, careful to avoid being exposed out in the open or getting caught too close to a window or a doorway. They could be lurking anywhere. As he turned onto a side avenue he took a breath and began his gallop. Quick-footedness would be his best ally now. A left turn into an adjacent alley brought him to his destination, the stairway leading down to the old Goth club known as Pall Bearer's Paradise. He hadn't even let himself imagine he'd get this far without a fight, but the next hundred feet would prove to be the real test. He checked his wrists, ankles and throat to make sure the talismans were all in place, and prayed to God that the myths he learned back in the old country as a young man would serve him well today. If not, what the hell? No one lived forever. Well, that wasn't necessarily true either.

The stairs leading down to the long hallway were greasy and slick under his boots. Remnants of past victims, he wondered? His stomach churned at the thought of their wretched fate, and he used that to push himself onward, knowing that the putrid stains were confirmation of the horror that had set him on his mission in the first place, the horror he was determined to stop.

Treading along the dank hallway he thought it strange that they hadn't ambushed him yet. Either the talismans were working like a charm—he smiled at the pun—or he was being set up for the kill. There in front of him stood the great brass door. Beyond that was where the prize of his macabre quest lay. He pulled a crowbar from his greatcoat to jam it between the door and its sturdy metal frame. The sound of this behemoth being opened would certainly alert those inside. But the element of surprise was never part of the equation. He cracked the door away from the jamb and listened for any threatening sounds. Nothing. He reached into his greatcoat again for a flashlight and a Bible, and squeezed through the opening into the maw of the great room, singing an old song in his soft, scratchy, European accent:

> "She's Venus in blue jeans,
> Mona Lisa with a ponytail.
> She's a-walkin' talkin' work of art.
> She's the girl who stole my heart…"

They were there all right, ruby-red bloodshot eyes staring menacingly at him from the shadows. They did not attack however, only watched. Perhaps they were amused; perhaps his visit broke up the monotony of the day. He knew it wasn't the old Jimmy Clanton song that prevented them from swarming him. The tune was a sentimental favorite, and he sang it more to steady his nerves than to repel revenants. Cautiously he moved toward the bar where the sketch hung, making no effort to conceal what he was after. The only question was how far they would let him get before…

"Stop!" shouted a host of rancorous voices.

"Venus in blue jeans," he replied.

"We have let you come farther than any other."

They sounded like a chorus from a Greek tragedy, or some kind of gruesome tragedy about to occur.

"…*is the Cinderella I adore*," he continued, bound to sing the bridge and chorus of the song before the chorus of malevolent voices descended upon him.

"They say there's seven wonders in the world,

But what they say is out of date.

There's more than seven wonders in the world,"

"Leave now if you hope to draw another breath!" they howled.

But he had come too far to turn back. So on he sang,

"I just met number eight."

"You think those ludicrous charms keep you alive?"

Well, something did. It definitely wasn't his vocal talents. He stepped carefully, but determinedly, around the back of the bar, continuing to hum the tune. Meanwhile, the timber of their pernicious voices intensified.

"We will snap your wrists, peel your flesh and suck the marrow from your bones!"

Ignore them. It was the only card he could play. Without flinching he reached for the sketch that hung above the bar and lifted it off the rusty nail.

"Stop him!"

"Rip him!"

"Annihilate him!"

But they did not. Emboldened, he turned around and made his way out from behind the bar toward the brass door, humming the ridiculous tune. This was too easy, he thought. And at that precise moment the atmosphere in the room suddenly dwindled, as if the oxygen in the chamber was being sucked out by a giant vacuum. Not a finger was laid on him, yet their suffocating presence became as crushing as though they had all climbed onto his chest and, with their combined weight, pressed every molecule of air out of his lungs. In spite of the excruciating pain, he willed his legs to move one past the other, while these creatures bore down upon him with their cruel eyes and fetid breath. Finally, he reached the great door and lurched though the opening to freedom, gasping for air while their tumultuous voices screeched like vengeful banshees.

"There is no escape!"

"You have been marked!"

"Nice to meet you, too! I left you some reading material!" he shouted back as he wedged his Bible in the doorway. He wasn't certain whether or not it would prevent them from following him, but it couldn't hurt. On he stumbled along the dimly lit tunnel, gulping air into his burning lungs until he made his way back to the daylight:

"My Venus in blue jeans
Is ev'rything I hoped she'd be
A teenage goddess from above
And she belongs to me."

CHAPTER 12

He pounded the flinty nail into the water-stained, pockmarked wall of his house with the hammer he found in the basement. It wasn't *his* house per se, but the one he commandeered after fleeing his own home, before Other-Town over-ran the district and forced him out of it. Its owners had abandoned this one months ago, a hovel that looked like it belonged more at home in the infamous war zones of Bosnia, Syria or the Sudan. A fixer-upper, he joked to himself, not that anyone would set foot in it these days except him. He hung the charcoal sketch on the nail, placed the hammer on a nearby chair, and stepped back. He hadn't laid eyes on the picture for almost two years. Even when it resided in his shop, he could barely bring himself to look at it, which was one of the reasons why he turned it face-out. The other reason he did that was in the hopes that someone from his country might recognize the picture and help him solve his dilemma. Ironically, someone did just that, and created more problems than he could have imagined.

He took his time to look at the sketch more closely now, this hastily drawn winter scene of a field just outside Dubrovnik, on the farm owned by his family. The zigzagging wooden fence that stretched from the forest all the way to the great cypress tree…it was as haunting now as the night his uncle drew it forty years ago. Looking back, this was not how he imagined the original plan would unfold, but it was the best he could hope for. All that was left to do now was wait for the footprints to appear in the snow. It had to happen soon. After sunset their power peaked, and even though he lived to the east of the demarcation line, there were no assurances they couldn't cross over and ferret him out, especially now that he had entered their Sanctum Sanctorum and they had his scent. "You have been marked!" he recalled. And, if that was true, then no charm, talisman or "Top 40" hit in the world would save him. He stood staring at the frame for a full fifteen minutes, revisiting the days that led up to the creation of this cursed picture. Then, he reminded himself of that old adage 'a watched pot never boils' and went to the kitchen to boil a *real* pot of water to take his mind off the metaphor hanging in the main room. He turned on his old Coleman stove and took two teacups from the cupboard, his only cups. Who had need for more when there was never any company? As the water came to a boil he checked the slats over the windows to make sure no one could see inside. It was vital that anyone living or otherwise believe this place had been abandoned along with all the others in the neighborhood. In any case, if all went as he hoped, he would be gone soon, too.

    He glanced up at the sky and noted the position of the sun, estimating the hour of day to be somewhere close to five o'clock in the afternoon. He smiled remembering how he learned the art of telling time by the sun when he was a young man. It brought him back to happier days when he worked on the steamer, where the warmest moments of his life burned the brightest. Was this more trouble than it was worth, he wondered? This plan of his was so far-fetched and riddled with so many holes that any one of a hundred mistakes could easily spell his doom. And yet it was the best he could come up with in over a year and a half, after he discovered what really became of the little Goth horror who entered his shop that day.

The whistle on the kettle blew, jogging him out of his reverie. He yanked the pot off the coil to stifle any sounds that might attract the attention of passersby. Then he felt around in the cupboard for the tin where he kept his teabags, and poured the hot water into one of the cups, pressing a spoon against the bag to squeeze out the last drop of flavor. No sugar, no milk. He had made do without the extras for a long time now and was stronger for it. It wasn't for lack of money, as he had more than he needed. When shops began closing around Other-Town, people left in a hurry. The area was a treasure-trove if you had the cahones to go after it. Of course you took your cahones into your own hands if you did.

He craned his head to peek at the sketch again. Nothing. To pass the stubborn ticking minutes he shuffled down to the basement to check on the room one more time, the room that took him six months to build. It was strong, secure and well-stocked. If everything went as planned, he'd be spending a good amount of time down here. The evidence better show itself soon, he thought, or else he'd have to bug out—all that risk and effort for nothing. He climbed back upstairs to the kitchen and made his way to the living room, allowing himself the tiniest grain of hope, for which he was rewarded. There they were, footprints in the snow! With as much authority as his raspy voice could muster, he spoke to the sketch like a modern-day Aladdin coaxing a genie out of the lamp.

"Come out now, don't be shy."

There was no movement or sign of life in the frigid two-dimensional landscape.

"Please, I have risked everything for you. We have one chance only. The sun sets in less than an hour. If they catch us, we will be finished, you and me both."

Still nothing. His anger and frustration began to mount.

"It's been almost two years. Are you so happy where you are? Never to see your parents again? Never to punish the bitch that banished you?"

From behind the great cypress, a head peered out; it was Emylene. The old man was not exactly sure if she saw him standing in front of her, or if she was responding to his voice, but it didn't matter, contact had been made!

"Yes, that's right! Come, *babika*, if you want your freedom," he coaxed.

He pointed to the bottom left hand corner of the frame. He continued, "You know what to do."

Another figure peeked out from the behind the great tree—one of The Cowled Men. The Ancient reached into his pocket and pulled out a knife. Then he took Emylene's finger and cut the tip. There was no hesitation or fear in either of their eyes, only determination. Emylene let the droplets of blood fall onto the snow where it pooled in the corner of the frame.

"Good."

Magically, the blood dripped through the frame and onto the dirt encrusted floor of the squat. Then it happened as it did nearly two years ago. Emylene disappeared from the sketch and re-appeared in the room, face to face with the old man. Both stared at one another until the old man finally said, "Welcome back."

They turned to see the Cowled Man give a gentle wave and trudge back along the fence line into the distant forest. Emylene opened her mouth to speak, but the sound that came out was more like that of somebody trying to open a rusty can with the edge of a spoon.

"Back off," she croaked, " 'less you want me to stick this blade in your gnarly old eye."

He looked down at the knife that the Cowled Man slipped into her hand.

"Or we could have tea," he replied with a smile. "Would you like some tea? It will help your voice, though I see you haven't lost your command of the language."

"Who are you?"

"My name is Laszlo Birij. I…"

"I know you! Antique shop… tricked me into buying that picture…set that witch free… trapped me in a frozen wasteland!"

Emylene pointed the blade at the old man and took a threatening step toward him. In response, Laszlo politely offered her the cup of tea. Emylene waited one deadly serious moment, and then accepted the cup. It was the first thing she'd tasted for a long time, and the sensation was like swallowing hard whiskey for the first time.

"Good, Emylene?" he asked.

"You know my name."

"Now, if you've finished, we should go."

"You just gave it to me, Doctor Demento, and I'm not going anywhere with you!"

Looking around the dilapidated house, Emylene noticed the slats haphazardly nailed to the windows. Curious, she peered between them to look outside. The cityscape that was so familiar to her seemed barely recognizable now, devoid of cars, people, birds and most signs of life.

"That is Queen Street, isn't it? Looks like a ghost town out there."

"'Ghost town' is more correct than you know. Please, soon it will be sunset, everything will change, and not for the better. We must go now."

"Why? What the hell is going on?"

"I will tell you after we leave."

"And I'm not leaving until you tell me what's going on."

"As you wish."

Laszlo grabbed the knapsack sitting on a nearby chair and began stuffing various food staples into the half filled sack: a jar of peanut butter, a bag of crackers, and a few chocolate bars. He would leave without her if he had to. Emylene sensed that if she wanted to get any more answers out of him, she'd have to play along. She handed him a bunch of bananas from the counter. It was a small gesture, but it gave them both an excuse to continue the conversation.

"What's the last thing you remember before you disappeared?" He asked.

Emylene handed him a pack of licorice drops as she thought back.

"Mmm… footprints in the snow, on the floor… the sketch… Poinsettia…"

"Her name is not Poinsettia. It is Mira."

"Mira? How do you know that?"

"Because she is my wife."

Emylene stared at the withered old man in front of her. With his scraggly white hair and beard, he looked more like a cross between Jesus of Nazareth and Charles Manson than the husband of some twenty year-old.

"In your dreams, grand-dad! Poinsettia is my age. You gotta be pushing 60!"

"Actually, sixty-eight, the golden age. Half price movie tickets, cheap public transit, early-bird dinners, the good life," he said wryly.

Laszlo peered through the slats to see the sun begin to slide behind the buildings.

"We need to go. I have been marked," he repeated.

"Marked? What does that even mean?"

Emylene watched as Laszlo tied off the clips to his knapsack and shrugged it onto his back while making for the door.

"Who's after you?" she demanded.

"I managed to stay one step ahead of them until now, until I broke into that godforsaken club of yours."

"Pall Bearer's Paradise?"

"But now they have my scent. They'll track us and that will be the end unless we get far enough away."

The old man opened the door carefully to make sure the streets were still deserted.

"Wait a second. Why should I even trust you?" she asked.

Laszlo took a calming breath and tried a different tact.

"The men in the forest, they were not monsters. They were your protectors, am I right?"

He was right! For all the time she'd spent in the cypress forest she knew in her heart The Cowled Men were good souls.

"How did you know that?"

"They are my ancestors, elders from my village, and you ask too many questions! Now, I can either fill you in after we make it to safety, or you can wait here for Mira and her revenants to drain you dry. Your choice."

CHAPTER 13

No sooner had Emylene stepped into the dead heat of the fading afternoon than the seductive pull of the west was upon her.

"You feel it, don't you? Ignore it!" Laszlo ordered as he escorted her eastward.

"No, but my parents, they live that way."

"If you ever want to see them again, we go this way."

The pull of Other-Town was always strongest just before sunset, and Emylene was experiencing the phenomenon for the first time. It was like a deep sensual yearning, a combination of thirst and desire too complex to rationalize and too difficult to ignore. Emylene took two steps and then dug in her heels, trying to shake Laszlo off. She whined and wriggled, but he clutched her even harder and dragged her relentlessly eastward while she acted like a crack addict jonesing for her next fix.

They continued in awkward starts and stops until Emylene eventually began to relent. Nobody paid them much attention, for everyone in the vicinity was falling under the influence of Other-Town. As they made their way along the sidewalk, Laszlo monitored Emylene's eyes, trying to gauge Other-Town's diminishing sway over her. Slowly, but surely, the combination of the ever-widening gap plus the familiar sounds and sights of a normal neighborhood helped to bring her back: the cars and pedestrians fighting for the right-of-way over the streets, kids hanging out on the sidewalk, a driver arguing with a parking cop over a ticket. Soon enough she became tired and docile.

"Feels like there's a hole in your belly, I'll bet. You're hungry, aren't you?" he asked.

When she nodded yes, he knew he'd won the first small battle. Hunger, one of the basic human needs, could be a most effective tool when used judiciously. Laszlo ushered Emylene into the first greasy spoon they came to, and sat her down at a booth. The matronly waitress spotted the odd couple in the half empty diner and meandered over with two mugs of coffee in hand. *What was the deal with these two,* she wondered. She placed the mugs in front of the sorry-looking souls and sensed that no matter how good her service might be, a tip would be minimal, if any.

"You got money to pay, right?" she asked while scratching an irritating sore on her neck.

Laszlo laid several bills on the table after which the waitress poured the java into the mugs.

"So, Miss, what can I get ya?" She asked.

Emylene ignored the question. She was still trying to acclimatize herself to her surroundings. "Orange juice and menus for now, thank you," said Laszlo smiling at the waitress who, in turn, frowned at Emylene.

"She alright?"

"Are you?" Laszlo asked, noticing the waitress's constant scratching at her neck.

Insulted, the waitress grabbed two menus from the next table and dropped them in front of her customers before walking away in a huff.

Laszlo handed a menu to Emylene.

"I'll bet you can't even remember what food tastes like, can you? What was it like in the forest? What do you remember?"

"All I remember is…being gone. How long?" she asked.

This was going to be tricky. Laszlo couldn't afford to alienate Emylene before getting her onboard with his plan. Yet he knew she needed to understand what had happened while she was away. When he made his decision to bring her back, Laszlo hoped he might get Emylene to cooperate on a 'need-to-know' basis. But she had already proven feisty. Recalling the first time she entered his shop, he remembered her as stubborn, yet smart. So far she fought him at every turn, proving she still had 'stubborn' going for her. He wondered how smart she really was.

Laszlo sipped his coffee and considered how best to play this. Like a shrink to his patient? Like a teacher to a slow student? He decided on 'favorite uncle to a niece.'

"A while. You look good, though. Tough, stronger even."

The waitress brought over two glasses of O.J. and placed them in front of Emylene before she skittered away again.

"Drink up, *babika*, you need your nourishment."

"How long?" she repeated.

A silent tug of war was being played between the two. Both were stubborn, but only one could win. Finally, Emylene brought the glass to her lips and drank. At which point Laszlo smiled, and answered her question.

"A few months. Sixteen months."

Emylene stared back at him with the look of a prizefighter taking a sucker punch.

"That bitch cheated me out of almost two years of my life? I will hunt her down and kick her ass back all the way back to that frozen, freaking north!"

Laszlo didn't respond right away. He had jeopardized much to resurrect Emylene and knew better than to risk losing her so early in the game. Throwing roadblocks in her way or lying to her would only alienate her further, and he could not afford to do that. Though he would never admit it, he needed Emylene more than she needed him, and decided to continue with the same kid glove approach.

"I'd feel the same if I were you. Believe me, justice will be done, but before you go anywhere or do anything, you need to know what you're dealing with.

"I know what she is."

"And how she came to be that? And where you've been for that matter?"

"I know where I've been—stuck in some snow-bound, frost-bitten forest with a bunch of foreign-speaking dudes…"

"…a frost-bitten forest in Croatia. The field with the big cypress tree standing by the old wooden fence is on the farm that belonged to my aunt and uncle."

"You mean *the* Croatia, like in Europe?"

"The same. How do you like your eggs?"

"What do eggs have to do with this?"

"Nothing, except you need to eat and this will take a while."

"I don't have a while!"

Emylene stood up to leave, but Laszlo's hand shot out to stay her. For an old guy he had surprisingly quick reflexes.

"You can walk out that door right now to seek revenge. But if you go unprepared, you won't live through the night. I promise you."

"Ya know I've been listening to your bullshit for the past hour, and I haven't seen one piece of evidence to back up your lame-ass story."

"I knew where to find you and how to bring you back, didn't I? Surely that accounts for something."

Reluctantly, Emylene took her seat again. Then he gestured at the waitress who shuffled over like a tired old mare.

"I know things that could help you. And you have been places where I could not go. Together….two orders of fried eggs and toast…" The waitress scratched her neck and jotted down Laszlo's order. Then she turned to Emylene, giving her a cold, hard look.

"She's been to Other-Town, hasn't she? We got a policy…"

Suddenly, the waitress started twitching like a victim of a stroke, and fell unconscious onto the floor. Laszlo kneeled by her side and stuffed some newspapers under her head. Then he pointed to the two puncture marks on her neck.

"What are those?" asked Emylene.

"Part of the evidence you seek," he replied.

The restaurant manager rushed over with a glass of grapefruit juice while Laszlo patted the waitress's face to bring her around. A moment later the old mare's eyes fluttered open.

"Easy," he advised the woman, "Sit up slowly, and put your head between your knees. Allow the blood come back to your head, what little of it there is left. Juice?"

The manager handed Laszlo the glass of juice, and watched him administer it to the waitress.

"Second time this week, Doris," clucked the manager. "You gotta take it easy. Women your age need more iron in their blood."

"What she needs is more blood," replied Laszlo. "Maybe we can get that plate of eggs now?"

The manager nodded as he got Doris to her feet and walked her to the back of the restaurant.

"What the hell is going on?" demanded Emylene.

"I think you know, but first things first. And the first thing is, I will tell you a story. You may choose to believe it or not, I don't care, it won't change the truth. If you take my words seriously, it will help you decide what to do after we leave here. If not, I'm afraid you will end up like that waitress… or worse."

The manager came over with two plates of eggs and a fresh pot of coffee, then went back to tend to Doris. Emylene took a bite of the eggs and leaned in.

"Okay, I'm listening," she said.

CHAPTER 14

Laszlo begins. "I am an old man now, but I was young once like you. In the year 1962 I was eighteen, and a man in love. Mira was my *babika*, my little doll with blonde hair and proud Slavic cheekbones. We were born in neighboring villages not far from Dubrovnik, a major port on the Adriatic Sea. The big luxury ocean liners would arrive every week or so with their rich passengers and, because the staff was so unreliable, they would always be in need of new help. This was how Mira and I met, on The Adriatic Star. I signed on as a kitchen attendant and Mira, a chambermaid. Our ship took us to all the great countries that bordered the Mediterranean Sea—Italy, Greece, and Turkey. We saw them all. For two young people like us, working on one of these magnificent steamers was a dream come true.

"In the beginning I would see Mira daily in the hallways as the ship made its way from one port to the next. Part of my job was to pick up the trays of food left outside the cabins in the mornings, and her job was to make up the staterooms. Often our paths would cross. Talk came easily to us, having been born not a hundred miles away from each other. I soon learned that if I worked fast, I could spend a few extra minutes with her while she made up one of the staterooms and then we would share some of the leftovers we found. We were both young, away from home on our first adventure, seeing all the wonders of the world. How could we not fall in love? Things might have continued just so—two little mice having our own private shipboard romance—but love was not to be denied. Soon, it became difficult keeping our relationship a secret, and we worried that if the other crew members found out, it might endanger our jobs. Also, we were both God-fearing people and wanted to do the right thing, which, to us, meant marriage. I decided the right thing would be for the captain to hear about our secret from us rather than the crew. Then he could do whatever he thought best. As it turned out I shouldn't have worried. Not only did he approve, he even offered to marry us! Maybe he reasoned that with his blessing, we'd not only be married to each other, but also to the ship. Cruise lines were notorious for being short-staffed because the help would jump ship in an instant for a better wage. Not only did he say he would he marry us, but as a wedding present he would drop us off for a three-day honeymoon at our next port of call, one of the most romantic of the Greek islands, Santorini. We had jobs, we had love, and we had a future. Life could not get any better.

"Santorini is a small island off the coast of Greece that grew out of the Aegean Sea from volcanic eruptions over thousands of years. The main town, Fira, actually sits at the top of the mountain not far from the volcano's caldera, overlooking the steep cliffs and azure waters below. Santorini is famous for its romantic sunsets, idyllic weather, and its black sandy beaches. It is also famous for something much more sinister, but I would not learn that until the night of my honeymoon.

"Just as the captain promised, our ship weighed anchor in the harbor early the next morning. The weather that December was mild enough for us to say our vows outside on the deck. Friends, shipmates and even some of the passengers attended as the captain performed the marriage ceremony for us. Upon pronouncing us man and wife, our shipmates surprised us by striking up our favorite song, the most popular one on the American Hit Parade at the time:

> "She's Venus in Blue Jeans.
> Mona Lisa with a ponytail
> She's a-walkin' talkin' work of art
> She's the girl who stole my heart."

Emylene cracked a smile at the off-key rendition and waited for Laszlo to continue.

"Afterward, we boarded a skiff that was filled with boxes of supplies for the island. We laughed about being dressed in our wedding clothes and sitting on crates, but we were young and all we really wanted was each other. Once we landed, we were told that the only way to reach Fira from our side of the island was by donkey. There we were, bride and groom dressed in our finery, sitting astride two pack mules, zigzagging a full 600 steps up the mountain! We looked so ridiculous that we didn't stop laughing until we reached the summit. After arriving in Fira twenty minutes later, it felt like we were standing on top of Mount Olympus because the view of the harbor down below the cliffs made us feel like gods. We walked along the cobblestone paths with our suitcases in hand to the small villa that the captain arranged for us. I wanted to take my bride to bed then and there. We had touched each other over our clothes when we could steal a few minutes alone, but we had never laid down together skin to skin, never consummated our love, and I was a very eager groom. Mira wanted to wait until the evening to make everything just perfect. What was a few more hours? I agreed and we changed into more comfortable clothing. One of the rich passengers on board took a liking to Mira, and let her borrow a pale pink dress and red sandals. What a vision she was as I escorted her out to explore the town.

"This being the off-season for tourists, we had Fira all to ourselves and wandered giddily past the churches, shops and inns thinking that the whole town must be here for our pleasure only. The locals appeared shy at first, but after we introduced ourselves and entertained them with our wedding story, they became friendly. By the end of the afternoon, people seemed to know who we were even before we met them. We were told that the sunsets in Fira were among the most glorious in the world. It was suggested that to enjoy them to their fullest, we should have dinner at one of the restaurants cliff-side. A jewelry shop owner pointed us to an eatery down the way and, as it was getting dark and we were famished, we thought, why not sample all that Santorini has to offer? When we arrived, the restaurant was all but deserted. We did not think that odd because, as I said, this was the off-season. A waiter who was scuttling about told us to take any table we wanted and he would be with us shortly. When we mentioned we were on our honeymoon, he smiled and told Mira how charming she was, and then he said something that struck me as odd: 'Such a beautiful bride. What a shame no other man will have her.'

"Sensing my wife's discomfort over the remark, he apologized, claiming it was just an old island saying and perhaps between our two cultures, the saying had been misinterpreted. To make amends, he escorted us to a table by the railing so that we could take advantage of the spectacular view. And then, as if to make further amends, he went to fetch us a bottle of wine 'on the house.'

"It was hard to know where we made our first mistake. Was it in telling this boor that we were newlyweds, or going to this restaurant instead of staying in our room, or coming to this god-forsaken island altogether? In any case the waiter returned minutes later with two glasses of wine and left us to look over the menu. You know how when something does not feel right, you get a sense of it deep in the pit of your stomach? I say to you now… never ignore that feeling.

"Covered in dirt and dust from the day's sightseeing, I left Mira so I could wash up before we ordered, while she stayed at the table until it was her turn, for there was only one bathroom. As I made my way to the toilet, I noticed a small room to the left, a storage room. Its door was closed but I could hear a strange noise inside, a kind of scraping. Again, I felt that sense of something 'not right.' This time I listened to my heart and pushed open the door, expecting to find a dog or a cat trapped inside. Instead I was startled to find a man lying in a pool of blood that was oozing from a large gash in his throat. The sounds I had heard were those of his feet kicking involuntarily against the door as the lifeblood poured out of him. I was frozen to the spot, not knowing what to do next, when I remembered that I had left Mira alone. I confess I forgot all about the dying man to run back to my bride. When I returned to the main room, I saw to my horror, the cursed waiter clutching her from behind and pressing one long rakish fingernail to her throat like a dagger. The look on Mira's face as she stared at me, I will never forget it. How could this be, that on the turn of a dime, our honeymoon had become a nightmare? The madman sneered, daring me to attack. I would not disappoint him. Enraged, I leapt for him, but as I did, his filthy nail pierced Mira's throat. He grinned like the devil himself and latched onto her neck, drinking her spilt blood like it was nectar. I froze, hoping he would stop his insane attack, but instead he picked Mira up in his arms and dragged her to the railing that backed onto the cliff. I shouted at him to leave her alone! I begged him! I told him I would give him anything, but the look on his face told me that she was what he wanted, and he would accept nothing less. With uncontrollable fury I charged at him, but he was so fast! With almost no effort at all he leaped atop the railing with Mira in his arms while she pleaded for me to save her. I forged ahead, pushing chairs and tables aside to get at him while he taunted me with an insane cackle. I was barely three feet from him when I tripped over a chair and stumbled. When I looked up, they were gone! Frantically, I fought my way past the rest of the furniture until I reached the railing. I confess I was terrified to look over, certain of what I would find. Ultimately, I forced myself to peer beyond the barrier and down those hundreds of feet to the rocky shore below. But when I did, there was nothing! No bodies, no sign of either of them anywhere!

"This, to me, was a surreal moment! Where could they have gone? The only thing I could think of was to run into the streets and call for help. Shopkeepers peered out from their doorsteps, but no one would come to my aid. Each person I went to shut their door in my face. I was out of my mind searching for help. It was dusk, the streets were empty, and no one would answer my cries. I even threw a rock at a window hoping to attract the police. Finally, I heard the sound of footsteps—two officers came trotting down one of the narrow laneways. I tried to explain what happened, but I was so desperate with fear that I could barely make up a coherent sentence. At first they looked at me like I was drunk or crazy. Then I led them to the restaurant and showed them the body in the storage room. The attitudes of the officers changed the moment they saw the dead innkeeper. They now took me seriously, but instead of going to search for my wife they made me tell my horrific tale again and again. Only after I satisfied all their questions did they let me take them to the spot where Mira disappeared. The senior of the two asked me to remain with the other while he went back into the storage room. I waited in nerve-wracking silence beside the junior officer who was ordered not to say a thing to me. When senior returned a few minutes later, he had the look of having performed some awful, but necessary job. His face was drawn, almost lifeless, as if whatever he had done had drained the humanity out of him. I also noticed there was blood on his shirt cuffs. By this time my patience had run out, and all I wanted to do was to hunt down the madman who stole my wife. Instead, senior insisted on bringing me to the local police station, claiming it was 'for my own safety.'

"There, he made several phone calls, speaking in his native Greek, a language totally unfamiliar to me. You can imagine how this only frustrated me more. When he finally finished with his last phone call, he informed me that he was putting together a search party to find my wife and her abductor. Finally! Even though I was half out of my mind with worry, I thought, at least a call to action! I insisted upon going along with him, but he said, 'Absolutely not,' and he and his patrolmen escorted me back to the villa. He explained that the cobblestone streets alongside the cliffs could be treacherous at night for those not familiar with the town, and then added that he wanted to put all his efforts into finding Mira instead of having to worry about my safety. Additionally, if there was any news of my wife, they wanted to be able to find me without having to search the entire island. Reluctantly I gave in. When we arrived at the villa, senior gave me some strange advice before he went off on his investigation: if someone were to come to my door, I was not to open it on the first knock. I was to wait until the second knock. I learned the reason why later. I also learned later why he did not want me along on the search party.

"I waited in my room all night, frantic for news of Mira, but afraid to go out for fear of interfering with the search and not being available when word came. If I found out that they lost Mira because of my mis-step, I would never have forgiven myself. So there I sat afraid to do something and afraid not to. That is what Hell is, I can tell you.

"When daylight broke, there was a knock on my door. Remembering the officer's advice I waited until the second knock before opening it to find the senior of the two and three villagers standing there with pitiful looks on their faces. In a voice filled with sorrow and frustration, the officer told me that as part of their search they went down the donkey path to the shoreline where they found remnants of Mira's clothing. They were positive that this deranged man and Mira had plunged to their deaths on the rocks below where the tide had swept their bodies out to sea. When I asked what proof they had, they said they had my wife's shoe. I insisted upon seeing it to confirm it was hers, but they said it had already been sent to the mainland as part of the evidence for the investigation. None of this made sense. When I looked over those cliffs after Mira and her abductor disappeared, I would have certainly seen the bodies on the rocks below. The officer suggested that perhaps I struck my head in the struggle and fell unconscious. Even if that were true, would it have been long enough for the tide to sweep the bodies out to sea? As for the shoe, how could they know it was Mira's if they'd never seen her before, if the only one who could identify this shoe was me, and I was not allowed to see it?

"Exhausted and at the mercy of these fools, I began to feel my heart turn to dust. My wife, my bride of less than twenty-four hours had been murdered by some lunatic. Who was this animal? Was he a local? Was he a stranger? Why would he attack my sweet Mira? So many unanswered questions.

"The officer said they would contact the ship to pick me up, and that it would be best to leave the island as soon as possible. But I stubbornly held to the notion that they were wrong, that this was all a mistake and that Mira would miraculously come back to me. Be careful what you wish for.

"After the four men left, I decided to conduct my own search. I walked down the donkey path myself and scoured the rocks on the beach for any signs of proof, but I found nothing. No clothing, no blood, no trace of anything. The officer said the water probably washed away the blood. When I looked up at the restaurant that was perched hundreds of feet above, I could see that the bodies would have fallen far short of the waterline. I walked back up the path and went from shop to shop asking the villagers if they had heard or seen anything that might help me. If anyone had any information, they were not talking. What they did convey wordlessly was fear, fear for their own lives. I learned soon enough that these people were not cowards; they were wise. Mira's disappearance was only the beginning."

CHAPTER 15

Lazslo continues. "By the following afternoon, after a sleepless night, I was exhausted. I returned to my villa to find two men waiting outside my door. They looked to be in their 60s, with lines and creases deeply etched in their faces, a testament to their arduous lives. Anatoly, the more talkative of the two, introduced himself first. He was older, taller, with a gray bristled beard that covered most of his weathered face. Kostas was shorter, squatter and could be easily picked out of a crowd by the scar that ran from the top of his bald head, over his left eye, and down his cheek, a scar he wore as proudly as a medal. They had been waiting for me, and claimed to have information about last night's abduction. Abduction? My heart leapt at the hope that Mira might still be alive, that whoever took her only wanted money and would return her to me. Surely the ship's captain had enough money to pay this bastard off. They asked if we could talk privately in my room, so of course I had no choice. I brought them inside, anxious for any word of my wife.

"Anatoly began by telling me that the police were holding back information and would probably deny everything they were about to tell me. He also said that they themselves had nothing to profit by telling me the truth, yet I would have a difficult time believing their story. I didn't care; I was desperate for any hope. Anatoly continued while Kostas watched me closely. This is the truth as they told it to me.

"Yes, Santorini was famous for its romantic sunsets, idyllic weather and its beaches, but it was also known in local circles as a unique burial ground. The main reason Santorini was chosen for this 'honor' was that the island had proved both difficult to reach and difficult to leave, making it ideal as a cemetery of sorts. The second reason was due to the volcanic nature of the land, the igneous rock was hard to dig into and… and harder to dig out of. For these reasons and more, some of the island locals had become experts in burying those that would not stay dead, the 'Vrykolakas.'

"That dreaded word caused me to laugh and shiver at the same time, for I was not a stranger to this term, having heard it since I was a boy. Many countries tell stories of the undead, mostly to scare young children into obeying their parents. As far as I can remember, there was always someone who knew someone else who had a friend who saw such a Vrykolakas, but nobody I met actually encountered one himself. That is, until I met these two. As they continued I learned that it was their job to slay the demon, bury it, and keep it buried. And what exactly was the nature of this being?

"They explained to me that when a person died, if he or she was a very bad person, an evil spirit would take over their body and re-animate it again to wander the land killing others. Some legends claimed that the fiend would climb onto its victim's chest as he slept and wait until the poor soul awakened. Frozen with fear, the victim could only lay there helpless as the demon slowly smothered the life out of him. Other legends spoke of the demon needing a constant supply of blood from the living in order to keep it in its animated state. The only way to stop the Vrykolakas was to cut the body it inhabited into pieces and bury the parts separately under the volcanic rock. This would prevent the corpse from ever merging and rising again.

"Two days before, one such Vrykolakas had been brought to Santorini for a slaying and burial. Great pains were taken to keep it imprisoned, but before the death sentence could be carried out, the revenant escaped. Word spread across the island, putting all the locals on alert. This demon, they told me, is what killed the restaurant owner and stole my bride. Anatoly paused to let his explanation sink in. When the men realized I was taking them seriously, they informed me that the worst was yet to come: Mira would return within two nights as a Vrykolakas herself! I was speechless. How could I believe them? And yet, how could I not? If I dismissed their story as superstition, I would be shipped off the island the next day by the authorities, never to learn the truth about my wife's fate. If I accepted their rendition in the context in which it was told, the next time I saw Mira she would be a demon like the one that turned her. Did I say that was the worst of it? No, Mira would have to be caught so that she could lead them to the other, and then both would have to be slain. I was to be the bait.

"Night was drawing near and these men needed a decision. If I clung to the wisdom of the real world, then everything these men said was nonsense. If I allowed that the supernatural had somehow intruded into my life, well, that way led to madness. Then I remembered something the police officer told me the previous night about not opening my door on the first knock. The old Greeks looked at each other and nodded. Obviously this was something every child on the island knew, and explained to me that, according to folklore, the Vrykolakas needed to be asked in before it could cross a person's threshold. If no one answered on the first knock, the demon would go on to another house. That's when it struck me that the officer's advice actually supported the extraordinary story these two men were telling me, and I can tell you it made my mouth go dry. I had no choice. That night, when it grew dark, I prepared myself to answer the door on the first knock.

"As the lazy Mediterranean sun dipped into the honeymoon harbor of Santorini, I was busy making preparations to slay my undead bride. The dark descended around my villa like the dimming of theatre lights signaling some macabre passion play. So many wretched fears crossed my mind. Would Mira really come to me as a demon and try to kill me? And if so, would I have the courage to murder her? I knew that if I didn't hold on to some glimmer of hope, I would lose my mind. Then a merciful thought came to my mind: if there was a devil that could bring such an abomination upon us, then mustn't there also be a God? Both Mira and I were God-fearing Christians, so it stood to reason that if we put our faith in the Lord, He would save us. But when I suggested this to Anatoly, he just laughed."

"I knew a man who herded cows. Lightning struck one day, and the cows stampeded. Caught in the midst of the rout, the man prayed, 'Save me, Lord, and I will serve you for the rest of my life.'"

"And?", I asked.

"And now this man serves the Lord a fresh glass of cow's milk every morning—in heaven."

I considered the message in Anatoly's little anecdote and supposed there could be no harm believing in both God and the Greeks. I watched as Kostas and Anatoly began their preparations. At every door and window they fastened a string of beads similar to the ones the women from my village wore around their wrists. Laced between the little white beads was one large blue bead on which was painted a small dot known as the 'evil eye'. Ironically, the evil eye was considered good luck. These charms, they claimed, prevented demons from entering houses through any window or doorway they guarded. When the two men were finished, theoretically, the only way a demon could enter my villa now would be through the front door. And we would be waiting for it.

"But if you're expecting Mira to knock on the front door in the first place, why lay beads everywhere else?"

"One demon may be at the front door to distract us while another enters from behind," explained Kostas.

Anatoly added, "This is not an exact science. There are many types of demons—revenants, vampires, succubae. We need to protect ourselves in as many ways as possible."

Silly superstitions, *I thought! Yet, watching the process made me contemplate two grim outcomes. Either Mira would not return, which would prove these men fakers and I would have to leave my wife on this island forever, or she would return as they said, and my worst nightmares would come true. I was a nineteen-year-old bridegroom, far from home with no family to lean on for support. What was I to… a knock on the door! Oh, God, I was not ready for this. Please let that not be her.*

"Laszlo."

I knew that voice! It was the voice that spoke my name so often in laughter and in love. Maybe she managed to escape from that madman and by luck, found her way home. These two men are frauds, I said to myself. Probably an elaborate ruse to get into my house and steal what little I had. I ran to the door and opened it to find my wife looking as healthy as when I'd seen her last.

"Mira, blessed be God! I was so afraid. What happened to you?"

Overjoyed, I hugged her tight, wanting to protect her against every evil that ever existed.

"Forget about the other night, Laszlo, it was a bad dream. We're together now. Let me in, I'm cold."

I did as she asked and closed the door behind us.

"I want to forget," I said, "but that maniac, he had his hands on your throat, there was blood, I saw you both on the patio, and then disappear over the..."

"I know. Shush," she said like a mother comforting a frightened child.

"How? Where did he take you? If he set you free, why didn't you come back to me yesterday? Where have you been all this time?"

"No more questions, Laszlo. Take me to our bed. Lay with me."

Mira pulled me to her and pressed her lips to my neck, kissing me deeper and deeper, filling me with a passion I'd never known before. The power of her embrace...I became dizzy, oblivious to everything around me until the next thing I knew, the two Greeks rushed out from the adjacent room where they had been hiding and pulled Mira off me. Anatoly bound her wrists with twine while I heard myself telling them, "No! You've made a mistake!"

I tried to stop them, but I was suddenly overcome by a light-headedness. I wasn't sure if what happened next was real or if it was due to my frenzied mind, but I saw Mira's eyes roll up in her head and heard her spew forth an unrecognizable gibberish. The whole effect made the room swirl and my limbs give way. The next thing I felt was the crack of my head against the tiled floor as I dropped like a stone, and suffered a blinding shock of stars. Through the haze I heard the sound of the two Greeks reciting incantations, and Mira wailing like a banshee. I don't know how long it was until my head cleared, but when I looked up again, Mira was standing there in silence, eyes unfixed and expressionless.

"*Mira!*" *I cried.*

"*This is not Mira. She is your wife no longer! She belongs to him,*" *shouted Kostas.*

"*Who? The man who stole her from me?*"

Anatoly, the more gentle of the two, tried to explain.

"*Not a man. A fiend, a demon. To call it anything else would underestimate its power. Get up, Laszlo.*"

"*Yes, but we need to help her. What can we do?*" *I pleaded as I got to my knees.*

Kostas raised me to my feet and looked me in the eye, the tissue around his facial scar pulsing with anger and frustration.

"*Are you a half-wit, man? I tell you she is beyond!*" *He began to shake me by the shoulders until Anatoly noticed the* wound on my neck and stayed his friend's hands. "Fool, we warned you. Thank God the skin was not broken."

Anatoly calmed himself and spoke to me in slow, measured tones.

"We are trying to make you understand that your wife is gone from you forever. The Vrykolakas has taken her soul. Her body stands before you, but her mind and everything that made her Mira, has been bled out of her."

"Bled?"

The thought sickened me, but I was still not willing to give up. I tried to convince them that if there was a God, then He must know how to defeat the devil, and He would tell me because it was not God's way to desert his people during their time of need. Which way to the nearest church, I wondered?

The two old men argued back and forth in their native language while Mira remained transfixed, until Anatoly turned to me.

"What you are asking, Laszlo, has never been done. The only thing that may work is to slay the fiend who did this to her. Perhaps his hold on her will die with him, and after that there may be a way to redeem her, but there is no guarant..."

"I will kill him myself," I vowed, "I will run a knife through his chest and cut out his heart out if I have to!"

"Oh, that will be the least of it," chuckled Kostas." Not only will you have to cut out his heart, but cut off his head and then his limbs and burn the rest so that the demon *can never walk this earth again. Can you do that, my young bridegroom?"*

I brought myself up to my full height and looked the old Greek in the eye.

"Is that all I have to do?" I asked.

Kostas smiled for the first time and gestured to Mira.

"We'll need her to lead us to him."

I looked woefully at my wife standing there like a sleepwalker. Would that I was dreaming myself.

"The sooner this business is done, the sooner I will get my wife back."

Anatoly looked closely at her and searched for any light in her eye while Kostas went into the other room and returned with a satchel.

"What's in the bag?" I asked.

"There's little time to explain, and I have no patience to teach you the ways," replied Kostas. "Be quiet, and do everything we tell you. And then stay out of the way."

The two Greeks led Mira outside, each holding an arm. I heard them whisper back and forth.

"If we find him, she will not idly stand by."

"Then we'll do whatever must be done."

The men walked Mira out to the front lawn and let go of her. She did not move until after Kostas mumbled several ancient phrases and Anatoly struck her hard on the face.

"Go bitch! Tell your master he has no power here!"

That's when a spark came into Mira's eyes, she hissed like a snake, and ran off into the hills.

"Don't lose her!"

"The three of us spread out and followed as best we could. The two old men turned out to be excellent trackers, spry for their age. They needed to be, for Mira was not only fast but seemed to float ahead of us, her feet barely touching the ground as she made her way effortlessly through gullies, wooded crags and knolls. I, on the other hand, tripped over every rock and branch in my path, but fought to keep up knowing that I would be left on my own if I lagged behind. Mira led us up one hill and down the next, and then suddenly, I lost them all. Frantic, I pushed ahead until I came upon a clearing. There she was, standing before some ancient stone structure. The building stood about three stories high and over 100 feet long, made out of large cement blocks. No windows, no doors. Anatoly and Kostas were a few feet to my left, hiding behind a thicket."

"What is this place?" I asked.

"Shhh. The Necromanteion," answered Anatoly, "An ancient burial place."

Kostas pulled out a rope from his satchel and lassoed Mira where she stood. Feeling the tether around her, she struggled to get free.

"Careful! She's not a steer, you know!" I shouted.

"Take this and hold it tight," ordered Kostas.

He handed me his end of the rope while he tossed his partner a second rope that Anatoly threw expertly over her. Pulling both ropes taut prevented Mira from attacking any of us. Then we forced her back and tied her off to a tree. Mira was in a frantic state now, pulling at her bindings and spewing venom while I tried to convince myself this was all for her own good.

"Mira, it's Laszlo. I am with you."

"Shut up and stop thinking that she is your wife!" ordered Kostas.

"What do we do now?"

I had only to look at Anatoly to know my answer. I followed his gaze up to the roof of the funereal structure to see the fiend who stood there glowering at us. Slowly, Anatoly reached into his satchel and pulled out a small crossbow. At the sight of the weapon, the demon hissed and crossed to the far side of the roof, out of sight.

"Gird yourself. He could attack from any direction," warned Anatoly as he handed the crossbow to Kostas and pulled two hatchets from his bag. I was a little more optimistic.

"Or maybe we scared him off and he will just go awa…"

The words hadn't left my mouth when there came a sound from behind us that could only be described as a hellish screech. The fiend flew at us out of the night sky like a *winged beast, knocking me to the ground and slicing open my shoulder with one of his razor-like fingernails. Kostas swung his blade, finding its mark in the demon's chest as it passed over us, but it was not enough to stop him. Picking myself up from the ground I watched the two Greeks position themselves back-to-back to defend each other from the fiend's next assault. But neither of them was prepared when it attacked from under the ground. It wrapped its wretched hands around Kostas's boots, and tried to drag him into the hole from which he emerged. With the demon's body almost immersed in dirt, there was no target for Anatoly to aim his crossbow.*

"*You said this island was made of volcanic rock!*" *I cried while holding my wound.*

"*Necromanteion…underground catacombs!*" *he shouted feverishly.*

"*Kostas tried to wrench himself from the grip of the fiend while Anatoly kicked at the demon's hands. All the while Mira ranted on about burying us all in The Pit. I felt like I was in the middle of a madman's nightmare.*"

At this point in the story, Laszlo paused in his retelling. He had never put the horror of that night into words until now, and in doing so, it had come bitterly alive for him again. That much was obvious to Emylene who noticed how his hands shook when he brought the coffee to his lips. To settle his nerves, Laszlo let his eyes roam the restaurant for a few moments, making every effort to confirm that he was truly back in the here and now.

So helpless and frail he looked, that for the first time, Emylene felt a pang of sympathy for the old man. Yet, she was so enthralled by his grim tale that she couldn't wait for him to continue. Would his story end well, she wondered, like "Hansel and Gretel" where the evil witch was pushed into the oven, or badly like "Red Riding Hood" where the wolf devoured the heroine?

"Laszlo, what happened next? Tell me."

Laszlo placed his mug on the table and in slow measured tones, forged on.

"As I said, the demon's hands were locked around Kostas's ankles. I grabbed my hatchet and began chopping at his wrists until finally the demon's head emerged from the ground, screaming in agony. That's when Anatoly pulled two more ropes from his bag. Kostas kicked free and each man drew a noose around the demon's head, anchoring it to a nearby tree. The fiend pulled and tugged against its bindings, but without its hands, which I had severed, it was helpless. Kostas grabbed the other hatchet, raised it over his head, and beheaded it with one powerful swing. Then he told me to leave, that they would take care of the remains."

"They killed the vampyre, then?" Emylene asked.

Laszlo nodded his head, yes, and continued.

"They gestured to their satchel. Inside was a rope that smelled of garlic. When I put it around Mira's neck, her strength left her immediately. I untied her and dragged her away. The further away we retreated from the killing ground the more passive Mira became, and I knew that if I could only get her off that cursed island, she would be well again.

"Somehow we found our way back to the villa. I grabbed whatever belongings I could carry and we headed down the donkey path to the harbor. But it was almost dawn and Mira was becoming agitated again. People with this affliction…"

"Vampyres," corrected Emylene.

"*People*! My wife was not a monster! She was the victim of one!"

Laszlo's sudden outburst startled everyone in the restaurant, but he no longer cared who heard him.

"*You* of all people should know the difference. I did what I had to do to save my wife!"

Laszlo had a point. All this should have been familiar territory to Emylene. She had been raised on the myths of the vampyre ever since she was a child, a race whose esthetic had been adopted as the paradigm for the modern Goth. But a myth was not to be taken literally. To give credence to Laszlo's story was to believe that vampyres actually existed, in the same way one would take the stories of the Bible as literal truth. Although many of Emylene's ilk revered the undead, none had actually claimed to know one personally.

Now she asked herself whether she was prepared to take this man at his word. As fantastic a leap of faith as that might be, she also had to consider the fact that she had just spent the last sixteen months of her life inside a black and white charcoal sketch. And that the very last image she remembered was Poinsettia's sharpened bicuspids with the revelation of her being 'the real deal.'

"I get it. You were still hoping that he hadn't turned her, right?" she said to appease Laszlo.

The old man took another sip of his tepid coffee and continued his story.

"The sun had risen by the time we set foot on the stony beach. Mira was moaning and suffering over her skin, which was puckered with lesions and boils from the sunlight. I spotted a fishing hut by the water and hid her inside. We waited there until our ship sailed into the harbor later that morning and their skiff paddled to the dock. By then Mira was weak from the trauma and had no fight left in her. I signaled the men, covered her with a dusty blanket I found, and led her onto the boat that took us back to the ship. All the while I prayed that we were leaving the nightmare behind."

CHAPTER 16

The retelling of this story was taking its toll on Laszlo, and Emylene noticed how his shoulders began to sag and his eyes turn sallow and gray.

"When we climbed aboard the steamer, my shipmates crowded around, anxious to hear every detail of our honeymoon, but I told them that Mira had fallen ill from the food so I hurried her back to our cabin. News of Mira's illness traveled quickly, and the ship's doctor came to our room to look in on her. By then her skin had smoothed and Mira had settled into that now familiar sleep-state of hers."

"Perhaps the honeymoon was too much for her," smirked the doctor.

But I could see, as he took her temperature and pulse, that he felt something was definitely odd. He recommended bed rest for the next day or so, and then he left.

"You didn't tell him about the attack at the restaurant, her disappearance, the fiend, none of it?"

"How could I? I loved Mira! I wanted to spend the rest of my life with her. As far as I was concerned it was all a bad dream. We were back on our ship now, back on our home. Rest for both of us and a return to normal life was what the doctor ordered, and that is exactly what she would get."

Emylene stared into the eyes of this pathetic man as though she was seeing him the first time. Up until today all she saw was a bitter, old war horse soured by failure, maybe even touched with some form of insanity. But now what she saw was the remnants of a young groom pledging his undying love for his innocent bride, a man who would walk through the gates of hell to bring her back. Not a hopeless romantic, she thought, but a 'hopeful romantic.'

Emylene reached across the table and took one of his hands in hers.

"Go on, Laszlo, please," she whispered.

Laszlo took another drink and proceeded.

"For a time Mira would sleep through the day, not a calm sleep, but one punctuated with quick, shallow breaths. It was like the tiny engine of her heart was being worked so hard that I feared her next breath might be her last. I sent for the doctor again who suggested various herbs and medicines, but nothing made her better. Then one night I was on deck with some of my shipmates when Mira appeared. Our friends crowded around, happy to see her looking completely recovered. They asked what had transformed her and she answered that it must have been the healthy sea air. Someone brought out a guitar and they all took turns dancing with Mira. She laughed and sang with such high spirits that everyone, including me, presumed she was back to her old self. But there was something else, something different about her. Mira had always been a modest girl, raised by a strict Roman Catholic family. Tonight she had a wanton look in her eyes, a heavy blush in her cheeks and a fullness in her lips. The last time I remembered seeing that look was the night she returned to me at the villa.

"Instead of being comforted by Mira's return to health, it threw me into turmoil. I told my friends that Mira was still fragile, and that she needed rest. We left the deck as they scoffed at me, claiming I was a jealous groom who wanted to keep his beautiful bride all to himself.

"Of course, she fought me first and even cursed me with words that I had never heard come from her mouth. But I dismissed her tantrum as the result of the horror she had been put through over the past few days. Yet, even as we approached our cabin I feared the worst—that of finding some dead, drained body lying on the floor. To my relief, the room was empty and I lied to myself again, thinking it was me who was ill and not her. Until she spoke."

"I told you I was fine. The doctor came 'round to see me earlier and gave me an elixir. Now stop putting such a damper on my fun and take me back on deck!"

"Where is the doctor now, Mira?"

She shrugged and looked away like a child having been caught in a lie. That's when panic overtook me. I locked her in our cabin and began to look for the doctor. When I couldn't find him, I went to the captain and reported him missing. A full-scale search was made, but I knew they wouldn't find him. I had to face the truth, that Mira killed him, drank his blood, and tossed him overboard after she was done.

In the coming days Mira's hunger came back three-fold, and I knew she would have to drink again. I told the captain that the illness she picked up on Santorini had not left her system. I begged him to return us to Croatia where she could get proper medical attention. Without a doctor onboard he had no choice but to oblige.

At this point in the story Emylene stopped Laszlo, leaned in, and asked the question that was uppermost in her mind.

"You said Mira would need to drink. How did she survive the rest of the voyage without blood?"

"Through sickness and in health, yes? I gave her my mine, just enough to keep her alive."

To prove this to Emylene, Laszlo pulled up one of his sleeves and exposed a number of scars, evidence of ancient puncture marks that crisscrossed his forearms. Emylene shook her head in bewilderment as he proceeded with his morbid tale.

"We sailed back up the Adriatic Sea until we finally reached our home port of Dubrovnik. The weather there was much more severe than in Greece, with snow blanketing the roads and hills. I said goodbye to the captain who wished Mira a speedy recovery and return to work. Then I rented a car and began our drive to my village while practicing how best to introduce my family to my beautiful new bride – whom I had locked in the trunk. The roads were so poorly maintained and packed with snow that we didn't arrive until nightfall. Not wanting to take any chances I fastened the garlic rope which I had kept from the island, around her neck and led Mira straight into to my parents' house. You can imagine the look on their faces when I led my bride into their home like a pack mule. Mira remained passive the whole time I told my parents about our ordeal. It must have seemed to them that I was the crazy one. To their credit they didn't doubt me, and suggested the best thing would be to go before the village elders that very night. One of them would surely know what to do. A glimmer of hope.

"When we arrived at the town hall an hour later, I presented Mira to them and repeated my story as they sat grim-faced. When I finished, they put questions to Mira, none of which she would answer as she had remained in her somnambulant stupor. However, it didn't take much to prove my story. When one of the old men took a knife and cut his hand, Mira went into raptures. They had to hold her down while she whined and hissed for the blood like a petulant child."

"Please... one taste only. Not so much to ask. Why do you torture me like this? I have done nothing to you. Give me what I need. Bastards! I will kill your women and eat your babies! Feeeeed meeee!"

"That's when one of the elders used the word, 'Vrykolakas'."

An hour had passed since Laszlo began his story, and though his back was stiffening and his eyes were clouded, he forced himself to finish. For her part Emylene sat transfixed, too deeply involved in the story to ask him to stop.

"As I said before, this was a word known not only in Greece but throughout Europe. In Armenia they are called 'Dakhanavar.' In Italy they are known as 'the Stryx.' In Bulgaria—'Krvopijac."

It was also a subject familiar to Emylene who was eager to share her knowledge with Laszlo.

"In South America they're called 'The Asema'. In Haiti it's 'Loogaroo' and in Trinidad it's 'Sukuyan'. Every culture has a name for them. Isn't that amazing?" She chimed in.

Laszlo smiled to himself. He hadn't made a friend in years, but here he was sitting in a diner bonding with a nineteen-year-old Goth over vampyres. He stretched his neck to the left and then to the right like a runner loosening up before his final hurdle. Now, he took himself back one more time.

"What should I do, what was the cure?" I begged of the elders.

Not one of them had an answer. They had all heard of the legend, but none had ever seen a Vrykolakas in the flesh. The folklore in my country followed the same pattern as I'd heard in Santorini: after the soul separates from the body an evil spirit enters, possessing it. This restless spirit is compelled to transform every living being it encounters into its own likeness. As time goes on, the monster becomes more audacious and blood-thirsty, filled with a lust to devastate whole villages if not stopped.

The elders did agree on one thing, however, that Mira was no longer human, and there was no way anyone knew for bringing her back.

They decreed that she would not be allowed to stay, nor would she be allowed to leave. Mira would face the same fate as the fiend that infected her; her head and her limbs would be severed, and her body burned. Watching these men hold her down and put shackles on my wife broke my heart. I was convinced there had to be another way. I tried to reason with the council using the argument that had now become my mantra: If God could allow such creatures to exist, there must also be a salvation for their victims, a way to protect the innocent ones like Mira, who was the most innocent of all.

But the elders rejected my argument and, for the safety of their village, shut my wife away. It took four men to carry her off. They would wait until morning to execute her, not to give me hope for a reprieve, but because she would be at her weakest and they could carry out their execution without risk to themselves. Cowards!

I returned to my parents' home in utter despair. Later that night, my uncle and aunt came to me. They knew of no cure, but my aunt Daphna, a gypsy, knew of a place where Mira could dwell until a cure might be found.

Emylene sat up ramrod straight.

"The sketch!" she said.

"Yes. My uncle drew the picture himself, a rough portrait of a piece of land you know only too well." Laszlo pressed his fingers to his forehead and continued his story.

"Our village was so small that we did not have a proper jail. Instead, they locked Mira in a barn and stood watch. But the winter nights in my village could be torturously cold, and even with ground fires, the guards had to go warm themselves in a nearby hut every half hour. Knowing this, my father sent two of his field hands to relieve the first set of guards an hour into their watch. With their help, my father and his brother brought Mira to the field where the rest of us were waiting. The farm was about a kilometer from the village, and about 150 acres in total. During the warm months my family grew crops—wheat, barley, and oats while our livestock grazed in the rolling hills. Growing up I remember thinking that you couldn't find a piece of land closer to paradise. The winter was a different story. The wind and the cold were merciless, and the only way we could make a wage off the land was to chop trees and sell them for firewood. It was those winters that drove me to find a different life, a better life. That was why my family chose to bring Mira to the farm. No one in their right mind would risk their lives to follow us out here on this night.

"When my father and the others arrived, they had Mira swaddled in a horse blanket and riding harness to keep her from attacking them. It took all four of the men to tie her to the great cypress while my uncle hastily drew his sketch. The rest of us stood huddled together to ward off frostbite and waited for Aunt Daphna to prepare the spell. The first thing she asked for was a small blood sacrifice. I volunteered, but my blood was tainted from the many times I let Mira feed on me while we were at sea. To her credit, Daphna sliced the palm of her own hand and let a sampling of her blood flow onto the canvas. Then she began her spells. The wind suddenly picked up and Mira, sensing a threat, began to wail like a she-devil. It didn't take long, but I can tell you that when it happened, the transmigration was instantaneous; first Mira was standing before me, and then she was gone, leaving only the blanket and harness on the ground, lying in a heap. It was like a magic trick you would see in the theatres of the great European cities. But that didn't compare to what I saw next; Mira in the drawing itself, staring back at me with a look on her face that said, after all the indignities that have been perpetrated on me, now I must suffer this! Then, from out of nowhere, came an agonizing howl as if nature itself was voicing its protest against this unholy abomination. The deed done, we all pledged our silence and trudged back to our houses hoping that the matter was settled. I can tell you, that night I did not sleep a wink, haunted by that look on Mira's face.

"The next morning, as you could imagine, there was chaos in the village when the town elders realized Mira had escaped. To protect my family, I confessed that I drugged the guards and set my wife free. As expected I was ordered to leave my village and never return. I accepted my exile, and did not speak about my family's help that night to a soul."

"But you took the picture, the canvas. How did they let you leave the village with it?" asked Emylene.

"I told the council the sketch would be the only reminder of my homeland that I would never see again. They didn't think twice about it. The problem wasn't in getting away with the sketch. The problem was in leaving before my aunt could tell me how to bring Mira back from where she'd been sent. For they escorted me out of the town within minutes. When I arrived in America, I wrote home, but they told me Daphna died. Suicide, they claimed, shortly after I left. I couldn't believe it! The only key to rescuing Mira had died with my aunt. Still, I swore that I would find a way to bring her back someday. I kept the sketch in my shop and searched out fellow countrymen, hounding them for any clue about the magic, but they wanted nothing to do with it or me. This was a new country, they said, the old ways were nothing but ignorant superstitions. Years went by and I lost hope. That is, until you showed up."

Emylene put her hand to her mouth in one of those 'Omigod' moments.

"When I first came into your shop, you thought I had the answer, how to get your wife back. And then the next day when I came in dressed in my bride of Dracula wedding gown…"

"…you don't know how terrified I was. It felt like it was happening all over again."

Emylene's heart tugged for Laszlo as she remembered that moment and put herself in his shoes. Her selfish act of teenage defiance had caused him to relive the most calamitous night of his life.

CHAPTER 17

The restaurant manager was getting edgy. It was after six o'clock and these days he was used to closing up early, eager to get home to his wife and children. Emylene and Laszlo were his last patrons. The only way to pry them out of their seats was to give them the bill and send them on their way.

"We're closing up now. Doris isn't feeling too good, so here ya go."

Emylene pushed her seat back to stand up. "'I could use some air anyway," she said.

"Wait here," Laszlo said as he fished some money out of his pockets.

Laszlo understood the girl's need to refresh herself. In fact, he was grateful she hadn't gone screaming out of the restaurant long ago. He walked up to the counter to pay his bill. But when he turned around, Emylene had left the premises and was sauntering into the street.

Dusk had covered the skies with a red, streaky haze and with it came an awareness of something in the air like a tantalizing smell, sweet and irresistible. All across the city, storekeepers tallied up the profits for the day in their cash registers, construction crews washed the grime from their bodies, and stock traders signed off on their closing tickets.

It didn't matter who you were, what you were doing, or where you were from, no one was immune to the call. What did matter was how strong-willed you were. Only the most tenacious would make it home to hunker down safely with their families for the night. The rest would find themselves venturing out to quench their thirsts across town.

Laszlo had trained himself to ignore the craving, but Emylene was totally unprepared. When he rushed out onto the sidewalk, she already had her nose pointed in the air like a hound sniffing an irresistible odor.

"What is that?" she murmured.

"Exactly what we need to avoid."

Laszlo hooked her arm with his and guided her eastward against the flow of traffic.

"It doesn't feel scary."

"That's what she wants you to think."

"Mira?"

"Yes."

"So, what's your plan?" she asked.

If nothing else, Emylene took him seriously now, and for that he was grateful. But, her question demanded a diplomatic reply. What she was really asking was whether he intended to slay Mira or save her?

"We'll talk about it later. For now we need to get a little further out of reach."

"That's not an answer."

"It's not safe to talk about it out here."

"Laszlo, don't bullshit me. Whatever is going on over there, that bitch is responsible. I need to know, are you going to stop her or what?"

Laszlo's hesitation only frustrated Emylene more. As far as she was concerned adults were always trying to keep the younger generation in the dark, like the truth belonged to them alone. It was the way of the world, she thought. The old kept secrets from the young because it was their only weapon against losing their grip on society, and preventing the young from taking over. Whether it was a parent or a teacher or the government, the older generation was scared shitless of losing control, and even more frightened about their past mistakes coming to light. It was the same power struggle Emylene had had with her parents, so why expect Laszlo to be any different? In a fit of pique she turned and walked away. Laszlo swore under his breath and hurried up to catch her before he lost her for good.

"You don't want to go that way, believe me," cautioned Laszlo.

"Don't tell me where I want to go."

"Emylene, listen, I never lost track of you, not from the day you left my shop."

"Which makes me wonder… you went through *a lot* to bring me back."

"Yes, because, besides me, you're the only one who knows the truth about Mira."

"So, what? So you wanted a friend to tell your sob story to?"

This was not Emylene talking. This was the beginning of the sway, the influence of Other-Town.

"A disease is taking over this city. It's like a cancer and I can't stop it, not alone."

"Bullshit! I know what you really want—you want your precious Mira back! You have no intention of slaying her, do you?"

"I wasn't sure if it was you who found a way to bring her back, or whether she escaped on her own, or my ancestors who reached out to us, but Mira is as much a victim as…"

"Oh, boo-hoo! Poor Mira and poor you! You're not the only one who suffered, ya know. That girl killed my boyfriend, Stelio, and then stole close to two years of my life!"

Defiant, Emylene continued down the street under the assumption that it was her anger that was driving her, unaware that she was subconsciously being pulled toward Other-Town by another force entirely. It wasn't long before she found herself caught up in the hustle of the street, people wide-eyed with excitement, as if they were on their way to a Beatles reunion or a motocross death race. The closer she came to Other-Town the more she felt a palpable buzz in the air, short-circuiting her thoughts and reaching deep into her loins until all she could feel was an over-riding erotic urge that threatened to take over her entire being. A feeling Laszlo knew all to well. Just a few more steps and she'd be there.

"Emylene, one more step and you'll never see your parents again! I guarantee it because you will have become one of them!"

Laszlo's croaking plea must have taken hold somewhere in her because she stopped dead in her tracks right at the edge of the demarcation line. Gazing through half-stoned eyes, she peered across the street at what earlier today was a ghost town. Now the area was alive in strange and wonderful ways! Buildings were lit with a seductive liquid neon, and music filled the air with fat, juicy beats. Even the pavement was alive with thousands of sparkling, crimson tendrils, an illuminated pathway welcoming everyone to a Mecca of sensual mayhem.

"They named it 'Other-Town', you know, to make it sound bland, almost harmless. But that's not what you're feeling now, is it? Look…" said Laszlo.

He pressed his toe hard on the ground, and the tendrils oozed playfully under his boot like a school of dancing minnows.

"Pretty, aren't they? Do you know what that is? That is the blood of the victims who crossed over and never came back."

Just then, four brash youths pushed their way past Laszlo and Emylene, acting like they were on their way to Spring Break.

"Let me go! I don't need your help!" argued Emylene.

"Of course you don't. Maybe those boys will help you."

Emylene watched the youths enter the first bar they saw, lured by the music.

"They are acting on the same impulses you feel now. It will seduce them and then it will feed on them. Some will return, some won't. Those who make it back will find themselves a little weaker the next day, like that waitress back at the restaurant. They'll laugh it off, call it a hangover. Except this hangover will never be over. After the first encounter they'll be compelled to return again and again until they have been used up and their lifeblood becomes part of the flow you see beneath your feet. Then those tendrils will stretch a little further to take more of the city until, inch by inch…. Emylene, I told you about the Vrykolakas back in the old country. What you see before you is different, worse. This is not one demon, but a town full of demons, built to ensnare its victims and grow with each conquest. You and I are the only ones who can stop it."

Emylene pressed her toe onto the glittering tendrils. Like everyone else who touched them, she felt a slight tickle, and became giddy.

"I'll make you a deal, Emylene," he continued. "I will do everything I can to help you find your parents. In turn you will do everything to help me find my wife. And I promise, if I can't cure her, I'll kill her. Emylene?"

No reply. Laszlo was not getting through to her. The tendrils were becoming so magnificently overpowering now that if Emylene's life had slipped away then and there, it would have been all right with her. But, something pulled her back. It might have been Laszlo's promise or the chanting from a group of Cowled Men in a distant land or a chilling breeze coming off the snow drifts on a cold, Croat farm. Whatever it was, it imbued Emylene with enough resolve to pull herself back from the edge. The light that had gone out in her eyes briefly had returned.

"Good girl," said Laszlo.

The two stepped away from the brink and Laszlo silently congratulated himself. After all these years of searching he had found the answer, or maybe the answer found him. No matter. If this girl had the magic to extract his wife from the shadow world, then she might also have the power to cure her.

"Enough for today. You need to rest. Tomorrow we'll return."

CHAPTER 18

As Laszlo and Emylene elbowed their way against the crowds that surged toward Other-Town he allowed himself a small joke. They reminded him of the proverbial lemmings diving off a cliff, these people, and Laszlo couldn't help but picture them with giant rodent heads jumping head-long from a mountain top, into the maw of some bloodthirsty deity. The old man had given up trying to warn his fellow citizens a long time ago, after they dismissed him as a kook. If he was honest with himself, he couldn't really blame them. He used to act exactly like one of those idiotic doomsayers standing at the corner of Paradise and Purgatory, warning the world that if it didn't repent now, God would send a plague to wipe it out. At times he thought it would be so much easier just to follow the crowd, one more lemming a-leaping. But he couldn't, especially now that Emylene was back.

When both were far enough away that the pull in the air had dissipated, Laszlo looked for a cheap hotel where they could hunker down for the night. It was nearly nine PM when the duo strode up to the front desk of the Excelsior Hotel. The Excelsior may have been the talk of the town forty-some years ago, but 'shabby' would have been a compliment for it these days. As soon as they entered, Michael, the greasy-looking manager lifted his glazed eyes up from the computer screen and clicked on a spreadsheet to cover the sites he was surfing.

An athlete in his youth, Michael dreamt of competing in the Mister Universe competitions. But a stint in a professional weight-training program proved that he didn't have what it took to make it in the big leagues. Failure and laziness soon turned his once heavily muscled abs and pecs to generous rolls of fat. Fortunately, an uncle with influence arranged to get him the night manager's job he had held for the past three years at the Excelsior. Now all Michael dreamed of was holding onto this position until his uncle died and left him an inheritance. He took one look at the approaching couple and played his favorite 'name the degenerate' game: she was a crack-head turning tricks to pay for her next fix, and he had pawned his last gold filling to cozy up to something warm in his dying days.

"Welcome, folks. How long will ya staying with us?" asked Michael.

"A week or so. How much?" returned Laszlo.

"$80.00 a night. For $125.00 I can arrange the bridal suite, ha-ha-ha. Includes one king size bed, free wireless internet, and continental breakfast. I can also arrange satellite T.V., too, for another eight dollars. All the adult movies you can…"

Laszlo pulled out a wad of bills and laid it on the desk, counting off four twenties.

"Hate television. Like books."

"I love books too," Michael answered. "Green Lantern,

Justice League, Spider Man. Ha-ha-ha. We'll need a credit card for security."

To this request Laszlo counted off four more sets and handed $560.00 in cash to Michael who provided him the key. The two guests then turned and walked to the staircase.

"Call if you need any extras," added Michael, hoping to see more of both Emylene and Laszlo's money roll. When his guests disappeared up the stairs, Michael clicked off the spreadsheet and went back to his two great loves: porn and online comics.

The old Croat and the young Goth treaded down the musty second floor hallway to Room 208. They didn't expect much and were not disappointed when they entered to find a simple dresser, sitting chair, and a king size bed. Since Laszlo paid for the room, Emylene insisted he shower first, but he insisted right back. It was not a point worth debating, so she accepted his offer.

She didn't know that Laszlo had something else on his mind. A half hour later, when Emylene emerged from the bathroom, she found a string of beads taped around every door and window.

"And the question for $400, Alex, is…?" she asked.

"You would have known if you were listening. What are 'evil eye' beads!?"

Then Laszlo gestured to a dish where he'd laid out a few crackers and a peanut butter spread.

"Hungry?"

"Mmm, peanut butter—good source of protein," she commented.

"And if we're really lucky, our vampyres will have food allergies."

Emylene took two crackers and ate them more as a gesture of friendship than hunger. She still hadn't gotten back her appetite. Laszlo pulled a nightshirt out of his knapsack and disappeared into the bathroom, before turning on the shower. Emylene sat on the bed, finally alone with her thoughts. So many images and fears and bubbling up inside her. So many unanswered questions. Closing her eyes, she tried to focus on the moment, hoping it would sooth her… the bedspring under her thighs, the water running in the other room, the mixture of hard cracker and soft peanut butter in her mouth. Things she experienced all her life, but was only appreciating for the first time. She heard the water in the shower stop. She listened to Laszlo leaving the stall, drying off and changing clothes. Normal, she thought. What she wouldn't give for one day of normal. A moment later Laszlo appeared freshly showered and dressed in his long plaid nightshirt.

"The crackers were a good idea, Laszlo. Next time, maybe some apricot jam? When I was living on my own, it was mac and cheese, peanut butter and apricot jam sandwiches—the best."

"My favorite was KFC," mused Laszlo.

"I was never much of a meat-eater," returned Emylene.

The innocuous banter helped put them both at ease. They were still little more than strangers, two misfits thrown together into the most improbable of situations.

"So, you said you'd help me find my parents. We start at the crack of dawn?"

"The safest time to venture into Other-Town is during the day when the sun is highest and the inhabitants are at their weakest. Even then…"

After a short pause, she asked, "So, like, where exactly did Other-Town come from?"

Laszlo knew Emylene would grow angry and distant if she sensed he was withholding, so he decided to be direct this time.

"From you, after you, because of you."

"Excuse me?"

"It started right after the fire, the one you 'died' in. Your people claimed a few jackasses set the fire to threaten the local Goths and chase them out of the neighborhood. You, my dear, became a martyr and they used your 'death' as their big excuse. But instead of staging a riot, or remaining hidden away in that filthy basement club of theirs, they did something completely surprising. They invited the city in. I see the look on your face. How did that happen? Why would people even come? Because Pall Bearer's Paradise had something everybody wanted and no one could resist. It started out small, by hanging some pretty lights, playing popular music, and giving away free drinks. Everybody loves a free drink, am I right? But the key was the 'entertainment.' You know those karaoke bars where drunken insurance agents pretend to be singers? Well, when those agents and hospital workers and shop owners dropped by your club to perform, somehow they all sounded like professionals. Don't ask me how. And that was only the beginning. If you wanted to be a preacher, a flock would gather around and listen to you like you were Jesus telling the Sermon on the Mount. If you liked to gamble, you could play any card game and walk out a winner. You can imagine it didn't take long for word to spread about a place where anyone could shine like a star. Soon it became more popular than going to the baseball game, the race track or the movies. I wasn't so easily taken in. You know how when something sounds too good to be true…I started asking questions. Your Goth friends said the idea came from their new princess."

"Poinsettia?" asked Emylene.

"Only now she called herself 'Mira'. Can you imagine how I felt when I found out? After forty years she was back! I wanted to run to her, but something inside me said, *"Not so fast, Laszlo. Was this the girl you married or the demon she became?"* She was here, you were gone, and that cursed sketch I thought had perished in the fire along with you was now hanging above the bar in that club. It didn't take much to figure out that she found a way to switch places with you. Then there were the rumors; some of the people who came to party didn't always return. Soon people stopped coming to the area by day. Local shop owners lost business and closed down. Families who lived there for years moved out."

"All this was happening and nobody did anything about it?"

Laszlo put a cracker in his mouth and spoke to Emylene in the same way a frustrated teacher might try to explain the most rudimentary social lessons to his dullard student.

"Why would anyone complain when they were given everything they wanted with no consequences? It was like partying with a whore at night and passing her the next day on the street with your family without having to worry about a wink or a nod."

"Such a pig," Emylene shot back.

"It was this pig who walked into that crypt yesterday, took that picture off the wall, and brought you back."

"Which was the least you could have done, seeing as it was your wife who put me there in the first place. What do you want, a medal?"

"Insolent child. No wonder your parents threw you out."

"They didn't throw me out! I left! And how would you even know?"

"Because I made it my business to know after I sold you the picture, after you disappeared, *princess*."

Furious, Emylene stood up and marched to the door.

"Stop calling me, princess! Ever since I was a kid they called me a princess. I am not a princess, and I never asked for this. This is all your fault. Why is this even happening to me?"

"Why you, why me? Emylene, I can only tell you that if you walk out that door, I promise that neither you nor I will ever find out the answer to that question."

Laszlo must have struck a chord because she hesitated, just for a moment.

"They didn't lie, your parents. You were the one who brought my wife back. That was no simple trick. You may not be a princess, but I believe you are special and that whatever you are going through, what we're *both* going through, is for a reason."

Emylene's shoulders relaxed a fraction and she listened as he continued.

"I told you about the revenant, how it returns from the grave to terrorize the living? It would have no life of its own if it didn't suck the life from others. That's what Mira did to you and almost succeeded. But make no mistake, *she* is the blasphemy. You are the real thing!"

Emylene wanted to believe Laszlo more than anything. The truth was, she had nowhere to go and right now, no one to go to.

"You know, it occurred to me…" he said, "Maybe you're not a Goth princess after all. Maybe you're more like a 'lady in waiting' and your time is now."

"Such a charmer," Emylene remarked.

Laszlo smiled. He was getting through to her at last.

"Those tendrils on the ground last night, they grow a little every day. Soon they will take over the entire city and Mira will have won. Will you help me stop them?"

Emylene didn't say yes, but she didn't say no either.

"Emylene. Don't make a decision now. Rest. Tomorrow we'll talk some more."

The truth was that Laszlo was old, and some of the things that needed to be done were beyond a man of his years. Emylene watched the old man climb into bed, looking exhausted. She stood there in silent debate, then turned off the light, and took a spot at the farthest edge of the bed, on top of the sheets, which made Laszlo chuckle.

"You don't have to worry, I have no interest in you… that way."

It wasn't a sexual threat, real or imagined, that kept Emylene from slipping between the bed sheets, so much as it was her having grown accustomed to sleeping on a forest floor for the past sixteen months. Bed sheets and a mattress, the flicking of a light switch, drinking coffee in a restaurant, all these things still felt foreign to her, and only served to remind her of how detached she had become from her own world. To make things worse, scraps of memories came bubbling to the surface leading her to worry over the whereabouts of her parents and the inevitable confrontation with her nemesis.

Whether she was a princess or a lady in waiting like Laszlo suggested, she couldn't help feeling that her whole life up until this point had been a lie, and no set of clean white sheets or fluffy pillows, or rah-rah pep-talk from some stranger could make her feel better. Her first night back… down she went, down into the murky depths of sleep.

CHAPTER 19

If Emylene felt unsettled that night, the morning brought an even more perplexing feeling: that of hope. She couldn't put her finger on why exactly, but it would come to her, this rare and mystifying sense of optimism. And then she opened her eyes…to find another eye staring back at her, not one attached to a head, but to a necklace lying three inches from her face.

"It's yours, for good luck," came Laszlo's voice from across the room.

Emylene looked up to see him standing by the bathroom, dressed in a clean white undershirt and a towel draped around his waist. With his hair slicked back and his face freshly shaven, he looked more like 'human race' than 'human waste.' Laszlo was even smiling now, rare for him. Her eyes skirted over his pasty, string-bean body, and couldn't help but notice the intricate tattoos inscribed from his wrists to his ankles, an odd site for a man who was closing in on seventy. But, really, what was there about him that *wasn't* odd? In addition to the tats, he wore evil-eye bracelets on each limb, and one large necklace around his spindly shoulders.

"Superstitious, much?" she asked.

"If not for these, those revenants would have ripped the flesh from these old bones long ago."

"What time is it?" Emylene queried as she got up on one elbow.

"Ten o'clock in the morning. I've been out and back already. You must have needed your sleep, but now it's time to get up. There are some clothes in the bag I bought for you. I expect no girl likes to wear the same thing every day for sixteen months, not even a Goth."

Emylene sat up and reached for the large brown bag on the chair next to her, out of which she pulled a pair of blue jeans, a madras top, socks and panties.

"I guessed your size from the clothes you had on. Also, your shape is pretty much like Mira's."

"Not exactly my style…but thanks," she offered.

"Don't forget the charms."

Emylene nodded as she padded past Laszlo into the bathroom with the new clothes draped over her arm.

"You know the history behind the evil eye?" he asked as they conversed through the closed door.

Emylene dropped the new duds on the toilet seat and took a moment to look closely at the charm in her hand. It was a large blue bead with an eye painted on it, surrounded by smaller white beads, the same as Laszlo had placed at all the entrances of the room the previous night.

"No, but I have a feeling you're gonna tell me," she answered as she stripped off her old clothes.

In the adjacent room Laszlo dropped his towel and slipped on a pair of brown corduroys.

"I was in Ephesus, Greece once and there, as in a great many other places in the old world, is a carving of the Medusa at the entrance of a temple. People who don't know better take it as a sign of evil unto those who enter. But they would be wrong."

"I know who Medusa is, I'm not an dunce," replied Emylene, "She's a gorgon with a head full of snakes."

"Right, but how did she get that way?"

Emylene had some vague recollection of the myth from studying it back in high school, but she wasn't going to let Laszlo know how ignorant she was about ancient history.

"Every kid knows that from grade school. I wanna know if *you* know," she shouted back.

Laszlo smiled and played along.

"Okay, you tell me if I have this right, Miss Emylene. Medusa was a woman of incomparable beauty whose downfall was conceit. She bragged of being even more beautiful than the Goddess Athena. You don't taunt the Gods. One day, while in her temple, the Sea God Neptune appeared and ravished her."

"Ooh-la-la," Emylene cooed playfully through the door.

"When Athena heard this, she became jealous of Neptune's 'affections' towards Medusa. Outraged, she turned her into a monster, as you say, with snakes growing out of her head."

"So far so good."

"Thank you. Thereafter, any man who came to court Medusa would instantly be turned to stone if he looked into her eyes. In this way Athena got her revenge. So, knowing your mythology as well as you do, you've also heard of the classic Greek tale, *The Odyssey*?

"The journey of Odysseus, right?" Emylene surprised herself.

"Right, the only person to defeat Medusa. And the way he did it…"

"I know, I know! By tricking her into looking into a mirror and when she saw her own image, she turned to stone."

"Very good. So what was the lesson the Greeks took away from this story? They carved the likeness of Medusa in all the entrances of their homes and public buildings hoping that any evil spirits trying to enter would be warded off by staring at evil itself and turning to stone."

Emylene looked at the bobble in her hand with a mixture of respect and puzzlement.

"This one looks like it's staring at me."

"That's right. The charm is worn like an eye so that when evil looks upon itself, it is destroyed. But this is not strictly a Greek superstition. These beads can be found throughout Europe, from Italy, to Turkey, to Israel. Every culture has some form of evil eye."

"So… what you're saying is, everybody in the world is aware of the existence of these demons or revenants except a certain second-gen Goth princess?"

"Being 'aware of' and 'believing in' are two different things. And, the proper term for them is 'Vrykolakas,' undead beings that survive by taking life from the living. Demons, succubae and vampyres are a sub-species that have their own peculiar habits and methods of killing."

Emylene emerged from the bathroom dressed in her new outfit, looking more like a teenage sophomore than a Goth princess, and it made Laszlo chuckle.

"What?" she asked.

"The first time you came into my store you looked like Mrs. Edward Scissorhands. The next time I saw you, the bride of Dracula. Today…Barbie."

"I wouldn't be talking if I were you, Mister Rogers."

Standing there in his canary yellow shirt and brown cords, Laszlo looked like he might be more at home playing chess at an old folks home than hunting Vrykolakas.

"So, this evil eye is actually a good luck charm…" Emylene mused, "Makes as much sense as anything else I've heard lately. I'm ready, let's go."

Laszlo gestured toward the bed where he had placed another four bracelets.

"We go nowhere until you put all of those on, little lady. Rule number one, never underestimate evil."

"Yes, sir." With that, Emylene held out her arms and allowed Laszlo to fasten the charms around her wrists and her ankles.

"Alright, let's kick some Vyrk butt!" she shouted.

"No kicking any butt on an empty stomach."

"Mister Rogers has so many rules."

"The name is Birij, Laszlo Birij."

Emylene smiled, thinking this was the nicest exchange they'd had since they met.

"Emylene, I wanted to ask you something. When you were in the world of The Cowled Men, did you see others?"

"Other what?"

"I don't know how to put this: is this a place you might call heaven, and if it is, did you meet anyone of my family?"

"No," was all she answered.

Laszlo accepted her reply for the moment and motioned that he needed to relieve himself. Without another word he entered the bathroom and shut the door behind him. This would be the perfect time, thought Emylene.

"Meet ya down in the lobby."

Emylene raced out of the room, taking the stairs two at a time until she reached the main floor. Michael was there behind his desk.

"Hey," she said casually.

"Hey yourself," he replied, instantly perking up.

"Mind if I use your computer a sec'?" asked Emylene in an almost coy tone.

"It's for company business," he replied with a feigned air of authority, but then relented. "You'll have to come around."

Michael eyed her closely as she opened the gate to his domain. He took one step back leaving just enough room for her to squeeze between him and the computer. As she did he breathed in her essence and let his mind race. This was a big favor he was doing her and now she owed him. What could he get out of it, he wondered? Meanwhile Emylene was busy tapping in a Google search.

"So what's your name?" she asked.

"Michael. But everybody calls me Michael. Ha-ha-ha," he laughed.

"So Michael, do you mind?" she asked, gesturing for some privacy.

Playing it cool he drifted over to the side of his desk and shuffled a few papers while a dozen sordid scenarios played out in his mind. Emylene knew she wouldn't have much time so she quickly Googled "Santorini." A list of a dozen sites immediately popped up. She clicked the first one and skimmed over descriptive phrases like, 'secluded Greek island'…'built from undersea volcanoes'… 'ideal vacation spot or honeymoon destination.' Then she did a second search, this time adding the word 'vampyre'. Up came half a dozen more sites. She clicked the first one and read, 'Forget Dracula, forget the Carpathian Mountains. For centuries the island of Santorini has been known as the most infamous burial ground for vampyres.' This was amazing, she thought! Emylene had never heard of the island before, yet apparently its history was as rich and relevant as any other familiar to her culture. If this much of Laszlo's story was true, she reasoned, could everything else he told her also be true? She wanted to read on, but the creep of a manager was creeping over to start up some kind of creepy little romance.

"So what's the deal with you and…"

At that moment Laszlo came loping down the stairs. Emylene clicked out of the site, opened the gate, and joined Laszlo by the front door.

"You're welcome," snapped Michael, annoyed at being abandoned so abruptly.

"Yeah, so thanks," she returned brightly. "Have a great day."

"Thanks for what? What were you doing?" asked Laszlo as they sauntered out the door into the morning sun.

"Nothin'."

"You were checking out my story, weren't you?" Laszlo smiled. "Poor girl. You're about to find out how real this all is."

CHAPTER 20

It was one of those brilliant, "glad-to-be-alive" mornings. Traffic edged easily along the avenues as drivers headed to work with nary a beep or a honk. Citizens of all sizes, social and economic backgrounds hustled past banks and brokerage houses that were nestled alongside parks, theatres, and little league baseball diamonds. There was no crime or poverty to speak of. Not even a vagrant could be seen on a street corner hustling for handouts. Generally speaking any man, boy, woman or girl could walk down these avenues day or night without a worry in the world. The city was a model urban paradise. Of course, it wasn't always like this. There was a time when brothels, gambling dens, crack houses, grow-ops, and shootings flourished as they did in every other city. But not since Other-Town. Now, there was no need. Everything to satisfy one's cravings could be found over there, and for free!

"We're not going to kick any butt today," said Laszlo matter-of-factly as they trotted down the sidewalk.

"But you said…" Emylene protested.

"Today we just get a feel for the place. One mistake could cost us everything. Already they know too much about me."

"But..."

"No buts... demon or otherwise."

Emylene and Laszlo scarfed down a couple of bagels and juices he purchased from a local grocer as they made their way west. When they reached the demarcation line, they stopped to survey the empty street ahead of them. The glittering tendrils from the night before lay dormant now like stagnant, chalky streaks dried up by the heat of the day. The only movement came from a few newspaper broadsheets that blew aimlessly along the desolate sunbaked pavement. Last night it was Mardi Gras. Today, there was a feeling in the air of awkward regret mixed with impending disaster.

"Lemme guess—more rules."

"It's daytime and most revenants are dormant, but you never know for sure. So, we walk down the middle of the street away from doors and windows. Stay close, don't lose sight of me even for a second. And remember, no matter what you see or hear, it's a lie."

Laszlo took the lead as he stepped out into the road and made his way down the center of the avenue with Emylene following closely behind. The only sounds to break the eerie silence were the crunch of pebbles and broken glass beneath their boots. The streets appeared empty, but that didn't mean they were alone. Both could feel a presence lurking behind every window and darkened recess they passed.

"Think happy thoughts," suggested Laszlo.

"Funny you should say," she answered, "'cause I woke up with all these happy thoughts this morning."

"Tell me," he said as he slowly proceeded, carefully scanning both sides of the street.

Emylene did as he did, peering into various shops, trying to suss out what kind of dangers might be laying in wait for them.

"Poinsett…I mean Mira, was right about one thing. She made me see that my upbringing as a Goth was totally bogus. I mean, it's not like my mother raised me on a bottle of blood. And I didn't go around biting my classmates. But being Goth kinda made me feel superior to everyone, like I was in on something they weren't. At least that's the way my parents made it sound, anyway. Looking back, I realized that everything I did and thought was to please them, like every other kid in the universe. So how different was I, really? Even running away from home was more of a typical act of teenage rebellion. But when Mira showed up and actually did some of the things I only dreamed about, I realized that she was the one who was hardcore."

"And now, after what you've been through?"

"I'm thinking maybe my youth wasn't such a waste. Maybe it was a kind of preparation, a training, and that all my life experiences have given me what I need to deal with whatever waits down this street….that, or I could be totally full of shit."

"I like that. I want to see if we can get back into the club…"

The attack didn't come from one of the storefronts as expected. And it wasn't so much an attack as a strategically-planned ambush that quickly escalated into chaos. It began with an anguished cry that rang out from the second floor of a building a dozen feet to the left of them. The cry was followed by a body being pitched through the glass window and landing on the ground, steps from the interlopers. It lay there in a broken heap, arms and legs contorted in painfully arched angles. Incredibly, the still-conscious man turned his emaciated face toward Emylene.

It had been almost two years since she'd seen him last, but even in this twisted position Emylene recognized her old friend.

"Thrall!"

The poor man was lying broken in front of her with his limbs splayed across the sidewalk, his lungs gasping for air. Her first reaction was to run to his side, but before she could make a move Laszlo grabbed her.

"Wait!" he ordered.

"I know him! He's my friend!"

But Laszlo would not release her.

"Who did this to you, Thrall?" she called.

"They did…when they found out I wanted to help you. Your parents, they're here…prisoners," he warned.

"Where, in Other-Town?"

He nodded as best he could.

"I can help you find them," he offered.

"Laszlo! Help me get him outa here!" shouted Emylene.

Laszlo made no move to either let her go or help the victim. Instead he looked upwards. Nasty, scuffling sounds came from behind the window Thrall had been pushed through, sounds that giant insects might make as they marshaled their forces.

"Wait. The show is just beginning," he replied as he directed her back to the twisted body lying in front of them.

Waves of heat were building like an aura around Thrall, and a ghastly steam emanated from under his black cloak, his body cooking from under the clothing. The victim let out a high-pitched wail that startled Emylene, causing her to jump back. Then two other cloaked figures ran out from one of the recessed doorways to drag Thrall back out of the sunlight and into the shadows. Laszlo clapped his hands at the entertainment and put a supporting hand on Emylene's shoulder.

"That was all for you, *babika*. Remember, nothing here is real, everything you hear is a lie. Your friend, Thrall, is a Vrykolakas and he'll tell you whatever you want to hear."

"No, not him. He was trying to help me. He knows my parents, where they are…"

As they argued, a number of dark figures standing behind the windows and doors began to emerge from their hiding places, pasty-faced demons dressed in black cloaks with red, penetrating eyes that stared maliciously out from under their hoods.

"Time to go, Emylene!" whispered Laszlo.

"I thought you said the daytime was safe."

"In theory."

As soon as they turned to make a break for it, one of the Vrykolakas charged at them from across the street. But it wasn't long before the sunlight seared its exposed flesh and drove him back into the shadows. Another dashed out and came close to Emylene this time, until it, too, had to turn back. As she and Laszlo made their retreat, more black-clad wraiths joined the assault, calling out her name in a chilling chorus of "Emyleeeene!"

With about thirty yards to go, a dozen Vrykolakas attacked from both sides, trying to cut off the two intruders. A cacophony of demonic wails filled the air, disorienting the two. But, the most harrowing diversion of all came from a single voice.

"Emylene…" The woman's voice didn't have a blood-curdling resonance like the others. This one was soft and familiarly haunting, and it made Emylene turn toward to the female huddled pathetically under the awning of an abandoned shoe store.

"Mom?" Emylene gasped as she slowed to face the specter.

"Don't leave me again," it pleaded.

"I didn't. I was…they sent me away…"

The momentary distraction was all that was needed for one of the Vrykolakas to reach Emylene and rip the evil-eye charm off her neck. Laszlo pulled a junior sized baseball bat from his belt, and whacked the creature in the skull, knocking it to its knees. Then he grabbed Emylene by her arm.

"It's not your mother. At least not anymore. Come!" he shouted.

The rest of the hooded demons were almost upon them now, their blackened fingernails reaching out with a single deadly purpose. Emylene did as she was told and ran with all her might. When she crossed the demarcation line, she turned around to find the old man a dozen feet behind her, surrounded by four Vrykolakas.

"Laszlo!" she called.

The old Croat had his bat out and was swinging away to play for time. The wraiths were desperate to get their hands on him, but they were also unable to withstand the daylight. It wasn't long before their skin steamed, puckered and peeled to the point that they had to run back to the safety of the shadows.

"Run, you bastards!"

Satisfied, Laszlo turned and waltzed across the line to safety, twirling the bat in his hand like Babe Ruth after hitting a homer.

"Are you crazy?" asked Emylene, catching her breath.

The combination of seeing her friend, Thrall, in such a morbid state, encountering a demon-version of her mother, and watching Laszlo risk his life was too much for Emylene. There was freaking out and then there was teeth chattering, eye-popping "FREAKING OUT!"

"I knew what I was doing," he answered like a scolded child.

"I don't care! Don't ever leave me like that again!"

After the few minutes it took to get their breaths and their senses back, the odd couple made their way eastward to 'the land of the normal' where families shopped for bread and fruit, women went for manis and pedis, and kids walked their dogs.

Along the way Emylene's thoughts wandered back to her old teacher, Miss Hartman, with whom she'd had some wonderful arguments. Miss Hartman used to say that people invite certain things into their lives whether consciously or unconsciously. Emylene had always been inquisitive and passionate about the darker aspects of human nature. But what could she have done to have invited this living hell upon her? And then a wild thought came to mind. Could Other-Town be the physical manifestation of that dark wish she and her friend,

Nostra-dame, toyed with all those years ago? Could these experiences be likened to 'dipping her toes into the Pool of Oblivion?' Damn Miss Hartman!

"Laszlo, can I ask a stupid question? If that place is so heinous, why doesn't somebody close it down or nuke it or something?"

"People talk about doing just that all day in their offices. Then they go over there at night to party and the talk is forgotten."

"Partying is one thing, but that over there…"

"Other-Town serves one other very important purpose. If you've noticed, there is no crime here. No robbery, no rape, not even a break-in. It's like all the ugliness of the city was swept off the streets and locked up in that sector. Which is a nice, tidy concept, except that the sector keeps growing."

Emylene continued in silence. Adrenaline had kept her mind and body functioning until now, and the impact of what she had just experienced was starting to kick in, making her body shudder.

"You're going into shock. I'm taking you back to the room," he ordered.

Laszlo hoped that after she rested she'd feel better. What worried him most was Emylene's frailty. Could she be counted on to do what needed to be done in the next forty-eight hours? He watched her stand there, unable to stop her teeth from chattering, unable to stop the trembling of her entire body. Surprisingly, though, she willed herself to speak.

"If that was my mother, if my parents are..."

"I also told you whatever you saw out there, likely was a lie."

"And if not?"

"Then they're part of it now and there's nothing anybody can do."

Laszlo knew exactly what she was feeling because he experienced the same thing that night in Santorini when he lost his bride.

"You didn't give up on your wife...so...how do you expect me to give up...on my parents?"

Her anger and determination were acting as a stabilizing agent. Good. The more she focused on the quest, the more centered she'd become. But did she have the fortitude to endure what needed to be done regardless of her parents' fate?

"Emylene, I've been watching Other-Town for months now. Every living being within that twelve-block perimeter has been turned by Mira and her spawn. "

"I don't care about her or them or anyone."

"Well you have to! This is not about your parents anymore!"

Laszlo spoke with such absolute assertion that it took Emylene by surprise.

"The sickness grows, and soon no one will be safe no matter where they hide. Sooner or later everyone will perish. The only person who knows what this is and how to stop it is me. I am cursed with this knowledge and because of it I can't walk away. I need to know that if your parents are beyond our help, I can still count on you."

Emylene took a breath. She never had to think about the big picture before. The world always managed to turn on its own with or without her. All she ever had to deal with was her life and her problems. The little Goth straightened her shoulders and drew herself up to her entire five foot four frame.

"So what's the plan?"

"We go back to Other-Town, kidnap one of those wraiths, and force it to tell us how to get to Mira. She is the key to it all."

"When?"

"Tonight."

Emylene put on a brave smile, but she'd experienced Other-Town when it was supposedly dormant. Tonight would be altogether different. Tonight she would walk into the belly of the beast when it was awake and hungry and it would take all of her strength, courage and smarts to survive. Laszlo watched her start to tremble again, as doubt and apprehension saturated every pore of her body. Then, he watched her tame that fear and calm herself.

"Tell me what I need to know," she demanded.

Laszlo smiled at the feisty moppet, remembering the first time she entered his store. Maybe she was up to the task after all. He suggested they have lunch and Emylene agreed, as long as they could eat at a health food restaurant. She figured that if they were going up against an army of undead, a stomach full of organic foods and antioxidants would prove as potent as any of Laszlo's beady-eyed lucky charms. They found a little bistro called Carrot Tops and sat for the rest of the afternoon, plotting the details of how to prepare for the coming night.

CHAPTER 21

Sunset. Other-Town was calling. Its signal was as palpable as a high voltage buzz from a power line. Laszlo, dressed in his army-style greatcoat, and Emylene, in her Barbie outfit, stood at the demarcation line where, in front of them, the little crimson tendrils swam like neon tetra fish beneath the translucent pavement. Across the street, throngs of people weaved in and out of the shops with blissful looks in their eyes. At first glance it all looked like good, clean fun, but as soon as Laszlo and Emylene stepped onto those tendrils, a salacious shiver worked its way up through their bodies, and nestled deep into their groins. The only thing that kept them from giving into their urges was the awareness that this libidinous pull was born out of evil. The key was to be ever vigilant. Those who ignored it were lost as soon as they set foot on the grounds.

Emylene and Laszlo stood amongst them now, people of all ages roaming the crowded streets, alone and in packs, each one drawn here to fulfill a deep, personal need. No one was immune: youths, middle-aged and the old aged. One teen, a little too drunk for his own good, shouted to three girls who passed by.

"Hey, girls! Let's see 'em!"

The girls smiled, ready to oblige until they were beat to the punch by a granny who sidled up to the boy and flashed hers instead. Then, she planted a big wet one on the kid's lips and everyone went their merry way. Good times!

Laszlo suggested they wander around awhile to get a feel for the district. Watching the transformation in the visitors who entered the various storefronts was astounding. Dowdy women in apparel shops tried on designer clothes and stared into mirrors to see fabulous versions of themselves. Teenage girls reached for free samples of bracelets and rings that were being offered at the door by slickly-groomed salesmen, with promises of exquisite gold and diamonds inside, all for the asking. Down the block, outdoor cafes provided tables of beautiful women who beckoned to lonely men looking for comfort and companionship. Up above on the second floor, big band music filled the air as 'Fred and Ginger' couples glided elegantly past one window and into the next.

"Where are all those nasty creatures we saw earlier today?" asked Emylene.

"Right in front of your eyes, but the music and the lights bedazzle, makes everybody see what they want to see. Emylene, I asked you earlier about the place you dwelled in before I brought you back. You said it's not heaven, but The Cowled Men, my ancestors, were there. So I have a question: when I die, do you think I might go there too?"

"I don't know. It's not like anybody ever talked about it."

"I ask because I would hope that the good I am doing here might be recognized, that when the time comes, I will be rewarded and be reunited with my people."

Emylene heard the plaintiff tone in his voice and felt sad for the old man. She knew the answer to his question, but had pledged never to reveal any of the secrets of that place. So she just shrugged as if to say, "I know how you feel".

Passing a karaoke bar, Laszlo and Emylene heard a businessman belting out an old standard to a crowd who swooned like bobby-soxers. Next door, bells rang from slot machines paying out another big win.

"Every desire man can conceive of, every wish granted."

"It's Vegas on wheels!" remarked Emylene, her eyes wide with amazement.

"You've been to Las Vegas?"

"No. But I've seen Chris Angel do his show from there on T.V."

A sultry woman dressed in fishnets and a satin miniskirt spied the two and sashayed over.

"Company, lover? One woman, two? Three? Something for your friend?"

Laszlo waved her off as they passed.

"You don't answer or say anything, understand? You walk away. The trap is sprung as soon as you make your wishes known. Show any interest in any of these revenants and you'll see their true nature quick enough."

Walking another five paces, they noticed a man in his early thirties standing in a doorway. He was nattily dressed, sporting Hollywood-good looks, and he eyed Emylene appreciatively as she passed.

"Now there's a face that could launch a thousand ships! What's your name, sweetheart? The world needs to know who you are and I'm the guy who can make that happen. I'm going to make you famous."

Emylene snubbed the huckster as easily as Laszlo did the woman a moment ago.

"This is the best they got?" scoffed Emylene.

"Emylene Stipe!"

The familiar-sounding voice came from behind her in the crowded street. It belonged to a woman waving at the little Goth, but the face did not jive with the voice. Although Emylene recognized the timber and the texture in the hailing of her name, she did not recall ever seeing this person before. With long, russet hair that flowed luxuriously down to her shoulders, in another age this woman might be referred to as a dish or a dame. She wore a three-quarter length chartreuse colored off-the-shoulder number that drew the eye to her shapely calves. Standing there in three-inch stiletto pumps, this femme fatale could have walked right off the pages of a pulp fiction detective novel. Emylene had to look past the 'physical' to recognize her former employer.

"Ronald?"

With a brimming smile, her old boss strode up and gave the bewildered Emylene a big hug.

"Omigod, Emylene! It *is* you! They said you died in the fire! Where the hell have you been? What happened to you? Tell me everything."

"Well, gawd, Ronald, I guess I could ask you the same thing," sputtered Emylene, trying to wrap her head around her employer's incredible makeover.

"Oh, don't look so surprised," he purred. "You must have sensed something way back when, with me running the family business for years and hating every minute of it. After that wretched fire burned the store to the ground, I was ready to give it up, and I mean take a fist-full of pills and walk right into the white light. But the weird thing was, the fire actually freed me from the trap I was in, and gave me a chance to start over. What you see now is the real me. Before, that was the costume. Anyway, you should have contacted me, Em…your parents will be so thrilled to see you."

"You've seen them? Are they all right? Like, normal?"

Laszlo felt it was time to step up.

"Oh, Ronald, sorry," interjected Emylene, "This is my friend, Laszlo."

Ronald took a moment to run his eyes up and down Emylene's friend before he spoke, judging whether or not to trust him.

"They're fine. They moved into a duplex a few blocks from here," Ronald began, "After the fire they'd come around to see me. I guess because in those days I knew more about you than they did…so sad. Anyway we became great friends, bonding over our mutual loss of little old you. We'd meet for tea and talk for hours. They were wonderful, and so supportive of me. Will they ever be happy to…"

"Really?" she interrupted in an accusatory tone. "Because I saw my mother yesterday, here, during the day… so don't lie to me!" Emylene's face soured, picturing her mother's altered state.

"Your friend, Laszlo, probably knows what tricks can be played here but, honestly, I've seen them, Em', they're fine."

Emylene breathed a heavy sigh of relief and noticed an energy in Ronald's rich, brown eyes she hadn't seen before. Back in the day, they would pass each other in the store, one of them was generally preoccupied, the other was pissed off over something. Could it be that Emylene hadn't clued in to her boss's true nature in all that time because she was such a self-absorbed, little twit? The little Goth chastised herself and admitted that—with all the turmoil that her departure from this world caused her—re-emergence was rewarding her with new insights every day.

"Great! When can you take me to them?" she chirped.

"I suppose we could make a date sometime."

Laszlo broke in again, having let the banter go long enough.

"What's wrong with right now? I mean, if Emylene's parents live so close…?"

"Well, I was waiting for a friend, but… you're right, this is much more important. Besides, it's always best to keep your date in suspense, isn't it? Now, I can't guarantee your folks will be home, but we can try, can't we?"

Ronald led the way through the crowded streets.

"Listen, Emylene, I don't want you to think I come here a lot," Ronald continued, "it's just that here, I'm accepted. You know yourself what it feels like to be different. Anyway, Other-Town is quite safe if you know how to navigate the district. Your folk's house is just off the main drag. Takes one to know one, don'tcha know."

Laszlo piped up as he followed a step behind the young people.

"I thought you said her folks weren't in Other-Town."

"What I said was, 'a few blocks from here'. Emylene, I see you have a new look, too. Finally rejected the black, have we? I remember thinking, what a waste. You had so much more going for you, more than anyone else in my staff. Always had a way with the customers."

Emylene thought that it was easier being with her old boss now than it ever was! Of course, they were no longer boss and employee, and Ronald seemed so much more relaxed in his new persona. He babbled on as he made a right turn, and moved off of the main street. The city proper and its downtown office buildings could be seen just a few blocks north, but the area from here to there was dimly lit. There were less revelers, less lighting, less action. Ronald stopped and turned to his friends.

"Not far from here. Your folks always liked to live on the edge," he chuckled. "But I suggest we pick up the pace. It gets a little iffy around here, don't you know!"

"I do," answered Laszlo as he pulled a green plastic bag from underneath his great coat.

"What's that?" asked Ronald suspiciously.

"A feather boa. Do you like?"

Laszlo untwisted the tie at the top of the bag and pulled out a length of rope that he whipped around Ronald's neck. The very touch of it brought Ronald to his knees, draining the life-force out of him.

"Laszlo, what're you doing?" Emylene demanded while Laszlo maintained a firm grip on the rope.

"It's only a piece of rope with a little garlic rub."

And to prove it, Laszlo rubbed the end of rope all over his own face to show Emylene it had no effect on him.

"Doesn't bother me. How about you, Emylene, does it bother you?"

Laszlo pressed the rope to Emylene's face, while Ronald began coughing and hacking.

"I have allergies. Now take this filthy thing off me!" he cried.

Instead, Laszlo yanked the rope harder and pulled Ronald along the street like a beast of burden.

"So revenants do have allergies. This way!" Laszlo demanded.

Laszlo didn't have to tug very hard to get Ronald to obey him. Emylene remained silent until she could get a better read on what was happening, until she could get it into her head that her former boss was a mincing, cross-dressing Vrykolakas. Laszlo led Ronald to the nearest vacant store and kicked in the front door. Two years ago this place had been a tidy little barber shop, complete with old-style barber chairs and a wall of floor-to-ceiling mirrors. Laszlo led Ronald to one of the dusty chairs, seated him and tied him securely to it so that he was facing the front window.

"Back in a minute. Whatever you do, don't listen to what he says, don't go near him." Laszlo said as he hoofed to the back of the store, out of sight. Emylene stared at the revenant sprawled out in the barber chair. It returned her gaze defiantly.

"Emylene, I am not what he says I am. I don't know what his deal is, but the man is either crazy or a liar. I can prove it. Take this off my neck."

Laszlo reappeared from the back room and to Emylene's surprise, turned on all the lights in the shop.

"What did you do that for?" she shouted. "Now the whole town will know we're here!"

"He tried to tell you I was lying, didn't he? Look in the mirror, Emylene."

Emylene turned around to face the mirror on the opposite wall and saw a reflection of herself and Laszlo... and an empty barber chair. It took her breath away.

"Sit on his lap," ordered Laszlo.

"I beg your pardon?" she sputtered.

"We are deep in the heart of revenant territory. If you don't want to draw suspicion from any of his kind who might be passing by, this needs to look like a party. And then, with the right encouragement, Ronald is going to tell us what we came here to find out."

Besides acquiring information, Laszlo had another motive for having Emylene get up close and personal with the demon. He needed her to understand the nature of the beast so that she'd never again doubt what she was up against. Reluctantly, Emylene hiked up her skirt and climbed onto Ronald's lap to face him.

"That's it, get a good close look," said Laszlo.

The first thing Emylene felt was Ronald's bony torso beneath her legs.

"Not a lot of fat under there," he continued. "They don't gain a lot of weight on a liquid diet."

Emylene studied Ronald closely, and reminded herself that she was sitting atop an undead being. She tried to treat this as a science project, but it felt more like she was giving her old boss a lap dance. Yechhh! She quickly pushed that thought out of her mind and concentrated on the task before her. The first thing she noticed was his pale, smooth pallor, with nary a wrinkle on his brow. Perhaps, in their search for eternal youth, all those cosmetic companies and plastic surgeons were on the wrong track. Perhaps the undead had the answer all along, and it began with avoiding direct sunlight. That much, Goths and vampyres could agree upon. Next, Emylene noticed how small Ronald's pupils were in contrast to when she had seen them earlier—a reaction to the garlic or perhaps the florescent bulbs, or the shining light of the truth? And, the corners of his mouth were turned down, making him look pitifully sad. Emylene wondered if that might be a telltale sign of his tortured existence.

"Ronald, I'm so sorry," she whimpered.

"Don't you feel sorry for that monster," shouted Laszlo, "Touch his head!"

Emylene reached out tentatively with the back of her hand and pressed it against his forehead.

"Cooler now than when you hugged him a few minutes ago, isn't he? You know why? Because he fed just before he met you, the blood of his last victim warmed his veins, a trick to gain your confidence. You know how he did that? He lured some innocent person to her death, a young girl maybe, like you. Promised her jewelry or a chance to lose weight without having to diet. Then, when her eyes were turned to the mirror to imagine how she might look, he sunk his fangs into her neck and punctured her skin, gorged himself on her blood…"

"Stop it!" shouted Emylene.

But Laszlo had no intention of stopping. He had to make Emylene realize the danger that Ronald and his kind posed to the world.

"Look under the bulges of his top lips."

Deadly, elongated bicuspids lay just under the flap of Ronald's graying lips, teeth that belied his pernicious nature.

"He is a predator, Emylene, and we are the prey. Get that into your head."

True enough. This was no longer Ronald, former cross-dressing owner of Lamereaux Textiles. This was a devil that would use any means to trick its victim and bleed it to death. Emylene pulled away and looked at Ronald with an entirely different attitude now. The garlic was having a debilitating effect on the vampyre who could no longer hide his true nature. His head lolled from one side to the other and he moaned a low-pitched growl. Satisfied that Emylene was now onside, Laszlo found a radio and turned up the volume. Then, he turned the chair away from the front window so that no one who might happen to pass by could see the vampyre's sickly condition. To complete the scenario, Laszlo started dancing indulgently around the barber chair to the beat of the music, acting like this was the kind of party he'd requested.

"Where is Mira, revenant?" Laszlo sang.

The ruse was over and the vampyre knew it, but the game was not yet done. Ronald smiled weakly and played his last hand.

"Emylene, your friend is misinformed. Other-Town is not here to hurt you. It is here to fulfill your dreams. Anything you want."

"At what cost?" smirked Laszlo.

"At what cost? Where in *your* world does anyone get anything for free? You think I'm cursed with some kind of disease, a freak or slave to my thirst. What if I am enlightened? You used to be one of those worker bees not so long ago…all year long slaving for a lousy wage and a two-week holiday, the rest of the time spent scrimping and saving to make rent, to pay bills. You're the ones who've been slaves! Ever heard of something called 'Tax Freedom Day?' June 6th this year, I believe…working for the government for five months before you get to keep one freakin' dime for yourself. Who are the real vampyres? Oh, I know what you'll say, 'at least we get to follow our dreams.' 'Dreams' is all they are. Why do you think they're called that? I was like you once, someone who had to hide who I really was just to make a living to keep the doors open. If that doesn't suck… But now, no money problems, no threat of eviction, no lack of food, no more hiding. Let them worry about that over on your side. Let them worry about growing old, getting sick, getting turfed out by their families when they become senile, sent to some warehouse for the dying. Not me. Know why? Because *this* is the land where dreams actually true and nobody dies!"

"Very compelling argument," noted Laszlo. "But if it's so much better here than there, why do you need to trick people into coming? Why all the lights and the music and the magic? What happens to you in the daytime? Where do you go? Down to a cellar to lie in the filthy dirt? Not so free then, are you, Vrykolakas? We're done here!"

Ronald had a feeling that his time was nearly up, but it was the nature of the Vrykolakas to inflict as much pain upon its prey as it could. If the revenant couldn't do it physically, it would do the next best thing.

"I'm ready to die. But, before I go, my last wish is for you to know the truth, Emylene. After all, we once were friends. Your parents are dead."

Emylene recoiled at the devastating news.

"Liar!" shouted Emylene.

"Tell the truth, vampyre," demanded Laszlo, "Or I'll sever your head from your neck before you can utter one more lie!"

"Did I say 'dead?'? Sorry, my bad. They're more like… like me."

"Liarrrr!" screamed Emylene again.

Ronald's lip curled into a diabolical sneer.

"Why would I lie? You saw your mother with your own eyes earlier today. Mira turned them, she and your father,

Theo, *asked* her to. *Begged* her to. Now they're one big happy family and *you're* the outsider. But I can help you, Emylene. I can bring you back into the bosom of your family. That's what you really want. That's why you're here."

Ronald found what he was looking for. Emylene's most heart-felt desire. She was alone and desperate, and of the three of them in that room, he was the only one who could grant her wish. The revenant lifted his head ever so slightly and nudged closer to her throat.

"Let me help you." He wet his lips and drew them back in a half-smile. If he could manage to take just a few drops of her blood, it might give him enough strength to wrestle his way out of those cursed ropes. One more inch and… that's when Laszlo pulled his knife from his coat and stuck it into Ronald's mouth, deep enough to pierce the soft palate. Emylene screamed and jumped off the demon's lap while Laszlo kept the vampyre at bay. Ronald laughed maniacally as Emylene shivered with the knowledge of how close she'd come to being bitten.

"Do you see now how cunning they are?" barked the old man.

There was only one thing left to do. Laszlo withdrew a larger blade from under his coat, drew his arm back, in preparation to behead the demon.

"No!" she screamed.

"You know what he is, Emylene, he won't change. We let him go and he'll kill again."

"I don't care. He was my friend once!" she screamed, stepping in Laszlo's way. If the old Croat had learned anything about Emylene over the past few days, it was that if he carried out this execution against her wishes, he'd alienate her for sure. He glared at Ronald who summoned all the sympathy a walking corpse could. Frustrated, Laszlo sheathed both his blades. Then he turned off the lights and hustled Emylene toward the back of the store as she shouted.

"Ronald, if you're in there somewhere, I'm sorry."

Laszlo shook his head in wonder as they made for the door.

"You think it was an accident that you ran into him? You were set up, played, from the moment we arrived. That's what Other-Town does. Finds out what you want, offers it to you, and makes you pay with your life. And now that they know, they'll use it against you every chance they get."

Cautiously, Laszlo opened the back door onto an alleyway and listened. The lane and the nearby rooftops looked clear, but he waited another twenty seconds just to be sure, before he and Emylene stepped outside.

"Anything?" whispered Emylene.

"No, that's the problem. If they're about, we won't know it until it's too late. Move!"

Laszlo and Emylene slunk down the pitch black laneway watching for signs that might betray the presence of predators. They didn't get very far. There, in front of them, stood one dark figure blocking their way. Laszlo turned around, expecting to find others behind him and he wasn't disappointed. Three more black-cloaked figures blocked their retreat. Slowly he reached for the scabbard in his belt.

"Door on the right, when I say," he whispered to Emylene.

Four more revenants leapt from the adjacent roofs to join the one in front, eight in all. Laszlo nudged Emylene over to the door and she tried the doorknob. Amazingly, it opened.

"Where do you think I went when I left you at the barber shop? Inside!"

Knowing that vampyres could cover ten paces for every one of a human's, Laszlo was prepared for their surprise attack with his surprise escape. He pushed Emylene through the door and locked it against their charge. But, the two were far from safe.

"Go, out the front," he ordered. "Stay close to the shadows, keep off the main street, and run north as fast as you can!"

"What about you?" cried Emylene.

A fist was thrust through the wood door with superhuman strength, sending a shower of splinters in every direction. Without hesitation, Laszlo lopped off the hand with a single stroke of his scabbard.

"Emylene, I can't protect myself when I'm worried about you!"

"How can I leave you here?" she whimpered.

Two more hands smashed through the door and grabbed Laszlo on either side of his shoulders.

"Is this what you're after, demon?" Laszlo cackled as he placed the revenant's hands on his own throat, making direct contact with the evil eye pendant. The hands sizzled and made the Vrykolakas on the other side of the door howl with pain. Then Laszlo clenched the handle of his scabbard with both hands and thrust the blade back through the door, into the chest of the demon. The attack ceased, but he knew it was far from over.

"I'll hold them here while you go! Meet me back at the hotel!" Laszlo cried.

Emylene remained where she was, afraid to leave the old man to his fate.

"Why are you still here?" he shouted.

Emylene knew Laszlo was right; this was the only way if either of them was going to escape. She uttered an awkward goodbye and stumbled through the dark shop as waves of guilt and nausea washed over her. Jogging to the front of the store, she passed a large Plexiglas case that in its day was used to display daily baked goods. Not so long ago the store was filled with smells of fresh bread, pastries, and children's happy voices. Now the air reeked with the smell of rotten food, and the only visitors who came to feast were rats, maggots and vampyres. What a world!

Emylene crept to the front door of the dilapidated shop feeling like a coward, but knowing she'd be more of a hindrance to Laszlo than a help. She peeked out into the street, which appeared to be empty for the moment—not that she could be sure of anything at this point. The only thing she did know was that if she listened a moment longer to the struggle going on behind her, she'd go crazy. Emylene said a silent prayer for Laszlo, opened the door, and sped off. Stealthily she made her way north, hugging the buildings and darting in and out of the shadows the way Laszlo had instructed her to do. Behind her, Other-Worldly howls pierced the night and she feared her protector had been overpowered. The comfort and safety of the big city lights were visible to the north now, and Emylene's feet felt as light as feathers as she raced along the pavement. That is, until she glimpsed four figures approaching the intersection about twenty feet ahead of her: two college boys and two females. Emylene skidded to a stop and pressed herself up against the nearest wall, trying to control the panting of her breath. The raucous laughter of the four ceased when they came to the intersection. The females stopped and sniffed the air, sensing her presence, but the frat boys were anxious to get on with their party.

"C'mon, ladies, we had a deal," said one of the boys as he slipped his hand into his date's blouse.

"Don't worry. You will have everything you desire and more."

The females pressed their bodies into the men and teased them with sensual open-mouthed kisses.

"And none of this 'love' stuff, alright? We're taking turns, Danny and me, switchbacks and everything."

"All that you desire," repeated the second female.

'Succubae', Emylene thought to herself, demons that feed on humans through sex. She'd heard of them but assumed they were a mythical a creature like the vampyre—that is, until now. Apparently, the two males were sufficient enough a meal without having to add Emylene to the menu. They ignored her and continued to escort their prey down the street. They would find some rank cellar where unspeakable sexual needs would be met for a payment rendered. What was it that made men take such risks? Was sex such a driving primal force? Was danger itself the aphrodisiac? Or the assumption that youth thought itself so damn invincible? Those questions and more occupied Emylene's mind as she continued north until the crimson tendrils under foot tapered off and she was back on her side of town again. As her breathing slowed she gave herself a moment to ponder the experience of these past few hours. A childish vision of Death as a romantic partner was the first thing that popped into her head. When Stelio was taken from her, Death became a shadowy thief in the night. Looking into the eyes of Ronald tonight, she realized that Death was a vicious bird of prey whose sole purpose was to steal life from the living. In that moment, when he leaned in to latch onto her throat, Emylene understood how precious her own life was to her. That, she owed to Laszlo. But what about Laszlo? Where was he? Had he escaped and would he meet her back at the hotel as promised? Was he even alive?

CHAPTER 22

"Touch it. Come on, you know you want to."

Laszlo stood defiant in the small dimly lit chamber. Measuring eight by thirty paces, it was not much more than a prison cell constructed out of cinder block and poured concrete. Judging from the malodorous air and scrapings of dried blood encrusted in the cement, he assumed he wasn't the first hostage to face his fate here. He just hoped he had better luck than his predecessors. Surrounding him were the eight revenants that had ambushed him in the back alley an hour earlier. He rather expected this outcome. In fact he counted on it. For the moment he was curious about them, to interact with them. A 'Jane Goodall' for the undead. Vrykolakas had keener senses and greater strengths than humans. Laszlo wondered if it was because of the pure blood diet, or if Satan imbued his minions with a supernatural strength before he let them loose upon humanity. These particular revenants were newly-minted, which meant that they were drones, not much more than slaves to their thirst. They would have drained Laszlo dry if a higher authority hadn't ordered him left unharmed. Still, there was no telling how long it would be before their basic instincts kicked in. He knew he was being held here for a reason, so while he waited he conducted a few experiments. Besides, they needed to be taught a lesson.

"Come on, touch it!"

He egged on the one closest until it grabbed him by the shoulder, and quickly pulled away as if his hand had been scalded. Laszlo laughed tauntingly and pointed his finger at the next demon in line.

"You, how about a thigh?"

Laszlo lifted his leg to the second revenant that reached for it, and was repelled in the same way as the first. Then, with a warrior's cry, Laszlo ripped off his shirt and dropped his pants displaying his naked body which was covered in tattoos of blue, white, and purple 'evil eyes'. They wound around his limbs and torso like chain mail, and converged over his heart in one giant tattooed eye that glared menacingly at his hosts. Laszlo charged another revenant that tried to side-step the old Croat, and avoided being burned by the cursed charms.

"C'mon, demon, what are you afraid of? You're already dead," he jibed.

Laszlo was enjoying himself now, becoming the aggressor, chasing the monsters around in the tiny cell and threatening to burn them at will. The scene looked like some macabre video game, the kind that would give a fifteen-year-old endless hours of enjoyment. Not so much fun for the demons. But this was more than some wacked-out game of terror tag for Laszlo. This was payback.

"Now, which one of you gutless wonders threatened me at your little hideout the other day? Which one of you said he'd kill me a thousand times? You? You?"

Laszlo separated one revenant from the rest of the pack and boxed him into a corner. The fiend shuddered when the tattooed madman pulled him into a vicious hug and branded the demon's skin. The poor vampyre screeched with such an unholy wail that it was hard *not* to feel sorry for the demon.

"Enough!"

The female voice carried the authority of a gunshot that caused both the living and the undead to freeze.

"Leave!" she ordered.

One by one the Vrykolakas left the chamber, cowed and obedient. Laszlo turned to the door, recognizing the voice he hadn't heard in over forty years. In his dreams, he had imagined a dozen different scenarios of how and where this meeting might take place. In none of his fantasies did he ever envision this moment with his pants down around his ankles. Yet, here he was, and there Mira stood, looking exactly as she did all those years ago. Staring into her implacable eyes it was impossible to know what she was thinking. Did she recognize him? Did she still feel for him? When he spoke, would she hear the loving resonance in his voice or would she be callously indifferent?

"Mira, I've missed you."

CHAPTER 23

Emylene yanked open the door of the hotel lobby looking like the last survivor from a Freddy Kruger movie. Laszlo had given the hotel manager a week's advance to pay for the room, so Emylene wasn't expecting any hassle when she returned. Then she remembered Laszlo had the only key, and realized she'd have to deal with the dweeb at the front desk to get the spare. When Michael saw her enter the lobby alone, he naturally assumed Emylene had dumped the old dude for him. She shuffled up and prepared herself for his insinuating tone and annoying habit of punctuating every remark with a laugh.

"Partying a little late tonight, are we, ha-ha-ha-ha? Your friend couldn't keep up with you, I'll bet, ha-ha-ha-ha-ha. Listen, I got a key to the penthouse on the top floor. The mayor used to keep his mistresses there, ya know. Best view in town. You like red wine or white, or maybe you like to mix it up a little? Ha-ha-ha-ha-ha?"

"Damn, where's my key?" she mumbled absent-mindedly, "Every time Dad comes to town on one of his lectures, he ends up going out for drinks with his buddies at the fraud squad."

"That guy's your father? He's a cop?"

"Retired. Mom won't let him back in the house until he goes for anger management classes, so he has to stay at hotels. Do you have a spare?"

Michael meekly handed over the spare key and Emylene made her way upstairs, chuckling to herself ha-ha-ha-ha-ha. The exchange actually lightened her mood. Just speaking to another human being after having endured the night's perils brought a feeling of normalcy, even if the guy was a degenerate. Then she thought, after what she'd been through, words like degenerate, depraved and perverse would never be used so lightly by her again.

Safely locked inside her room Emylene stripped off her clothes and flopped onto the bed. The things she'd witnessed tonight! The greedy crowds in Other-Town, her old boss who had become a cross-dressing vampyre, the attack in the alleyway, it was still so vivid that she needed to close her eyes to soothe her frayed nerves. She took a few cleansing breaths and opened her eyes again, looking for anything to calm her mood. She fixated on the red L.E.D. lights from the fake mahogany wood radio on the bed stand. What time was it? 3:20 AM. Good. She reached for a pillow and tucked it beneath her head, luxuriating its softness. Better. Then she spotted the clothes that Laszlo bought her, strewn all over the chair - and the memories of the night's debacle began to roil inside her like curdled milk working its way up to her throat. Her eyes darted around the room nervously in search of anything that might repel the urge to upchuck, and saw the string of evil-eye beads around the doorway. That's when she could hold back no longer and vomited in the waste paper basket by the bed. She should never have abandoned Laszlo! It was such a cowardly thing to do, an action not just beneath that of a Goth princess, but of a fellow human being. In that moment she despised herself. Poor Laszlo. She wondered, had he succumbed or, God forbid, been turned? Maybe, against all odds, the crazy old Croat survived. Thinking back, she remembered he had said something about a Plan B. Not so for poor Ronald, clearly beyond all hope. One thought led her inexorably to another, until she came to the sad conclusion that, in a world like this, her parents could not possibly have survived. She shook her head reminding herself how, as a teenager, she couldn't wait to get out from under her parents. Now, all she wanted to do was find them and tell them how much she loved them and feel comforted by them in return. But it was not to be, Emylene told herself. Time to face the ugly truth that they were ultimately lost, and there was no Plan B for her.

So lost was she in the sturm and drang of it all that she barely heard the knock at the door. Could that be Laszlo? Had he found his way home? Then she remembered he had a key, so why would he knock? Maybe it was that greasy, low-life hotel manager. Ignore it. Then something else came to mind: Laszlo's story about the night Mira returned to him, and the warning by the old Greeks about not answering the door on the first knock. Emylene padded to the door and listened for any clue as to who it might be.

"Who's there?" she demanded.

No answer. She dropped to the floor to see if there was a pair of shoes under the threshold. No shoes, but there definitely was a presence. To confirm it, she gently pressed her hand against the hollow melamine door. Whatever was on the other side pushed back! Nervously, she fingered the beads Laszlo encircled the entrance with.

"Go away! No way you're getting in here!"

Still no answer. She knew that whatever she said would not make this thing go away. Anxiously, she looked around for an escape. The window! She was on the second floor, she could jump, no problem! That's when she saw it—the window was already open. And that's when it dawned on her, that the knock on the door was a diversion. The real threat was already inside! Suddenly, she felt light-headed as though all the oxygen was being sucked out of the room. A pressing on her chest made Emylene's lungs burn. She couldn't run out the front door with whatever was waiting on the other side, so she lurched to the bathroom only to find there was barely a gulp of air left in there as well! Lights were growing dim… no way out…should've taken the sleazy hotel manager up on his invitation. Then she had a crazy idea. She reached for the television remote, turned on the T.V. and pumped up the volume to its max before she fell back onto the bed and awaited the inevitable. Through her haze she thought, what a cheap, humiliating end: succumbing to a suffocating delusion in some fleabag hotel. *Knocking on the walls.* Funny, this wasn't how she expected her life would end. What she hoped was to wage war for her life, to fight and struggle for every last gasping breath. *Knocking and yelling.* Perhaps even a plea to be good if she lived. But now a different feeling was coming over her. Whatever this was, it didn't feel like death. It felt like she was being wrapped in some kind of sensual cocoon, a helpless fly caught in a fleshy, carnal web. As she stared helplessly at the ceiling above her, she even thought she imagined a dark figure materialize and slowly descend, to feast on her with lascivious pleasure. She clenched the sheets and awaited her fate, but as menacing as this entity seemed, there was also something familiar about it. The closer it drew to her the more Emylene sensed it probing her, unearthing a deep desire she had kept hidden for years. It even 'spoke' to her and reassured her that if she would reveal her deepest, darkest wish, it would reward her. What did it want? What was that deeply hidden, bone-crunching need? To be with Stelio!

    A phrase from her youth suddenly popped into her head, *petite morte*, the French term for orgasm. It was pressing down on her now, enveloping her, promising to whisk her away to Nirvana. If this was death, bring it on! Come on...take me. Emylene was about to give herself completely to it when… *pounding on the door.*

"Go 'way," she managed to moan.

"Miss? Hey? This is the hotel manager? We been gettin' complaints about the noise. Would ya turn down the T.V.?"

Michael had been notified by several guests about the blaring volume of the television inside Room 208. It was the best excuse he could have imagined to make contact with Emylene.

"I got a key and the authority to use it!" he shouted.

Let him. Emylene was beyond caring as she drifted farther and farther from reality, and closer toward this sensual annihilation. Michael used his passkey and opened the door to find Emylene naked on the bed, eyes glazed over, and semi-conscious.

"Whoa, girl, you're not OD'ing, are ya?" he asked.

No response. The girl was gone, floating around somewhere in another dimension. This scenario was more than he could have hoped for. In all his fantasies, and he had many, this was his favorite—coming upon a semi-conscious young beauty in one of his hotel rooms. If she was over-dosing, would she even care if he 'helped' himself?

Michael took a few steps closer and watched her chest gently rise up and down. This was the moment he had dreamed of, and it made him feel like the most powerful man in the world. His fingers itched to touch her and his heart began to pound like a jackhammer. He could do anything he wanted to her right now, and probably get away with it. Or he could save the damsel in distress and become the hero of his own fantasy. His eyes glided from Emylene's blood-red lips down the length of her slim torso. All the while an angel sat on one shoulder and a devil sat on the other, both demanding obeisance. Finally, with his mind made, he turned her hands palms up. No track marks on her arm. He opened her mouth. No pills inside, only the distinct smell of vomit. She was not self-destructive, she was sick, and she needed his help. "Wake up, wake up. You all right?" he asked.

He shook Emylene until her eyelids fluttered open and she began to focus. As soon as she did Michael threw a sheet over her to cover her nakedness. Tonight, he would be her hero! Coming to, the first thing she noticed was the time—3:59. She had been out for almost half an hour. Secondly, she noticed the all-consuming specter had left, leaving the greasy hotel manager in its place. Which was worse, she wondered. Emylene apologized for the ruckus, and asked for a drink of water. Michael nodded as if he just heard her say, *thanks for saving my life,* and trotted into the bathroom to fill a glass.

"You were passed out. I saved you," he added, just in case.

Alone for a moment, she tried to get her bearings to make sense of the nightmare. Then she heard the tap water running and thought about the manager again. The dude seemed different now than earlier, genuinely concerned for her safety. And he covered her up, thoughtful. Michael returned and offered Emylene the tepid glass of water. After taking a sip she made a feeble excuse about having an iron deficiency and said she'd be all right, thanks to him. All she needed now was rest. Before he said goodnight Michael shut the window, locked it, and told her he'd look in on her at the end of his shift. After he left, she made sure every entrance was not only secured but protected by an evil eye. Emylene had known boys who were shy with women and often put on macho fronts to hide their insecurity. Maybe he was one of those, or maybe he was just scared to get on the wrong side of her 'father.'

Feeling secure for the first time, Emylene took stock of her situation. The entity that tricked her at the front door and snuck in through the back window was not death. She was certain of it. Death would not have to trick her; it would just have taken her when it was ready. This led her to wonder what kind of pernicious spirit had the power to overcome her the way it did. As Emylene laid her head down to sleep she vowed to be smarter next time.

The morning sun broke through the paper-thin blinds much too soon for Emylene's liking. Her head felt like it was being punished for some kind of drinking binge the night before. As she came around, she cursed the sunlight and, just for a second, worried whether she had been violated in more ways than one last night. She checked herself for bites and other tell-tale signs of last night's visitation, and sighed with relief in the knowledge that she was both still human and a virgin. And alone. Laszlo was still missing. Safe for the moment, she recalled the experience that held such a fascination for her—two parts terror and three parts erotic. Maybe that's how a virgin felt her first time. She hoped she'd get the opportunity to find out one day. For now, she was just happy to be alive, and to celebrate, she would get up and shower. After that, everything was up for grabs.

Emylene glanced at the filthy clothing lying on the chair and knew she had come to a crossroads. Realistically, what could she do against the legions that appeared to be amassing against her? If she was truly alone now, without parents and without Laszlo, how much longer could she outwit these forces? But what was the alternative, to turn and run? No. She would persevere if only for Laszlo's sake. His sacrifice last night confirmed that life was worth holding onto, and it instilled in her, purpose and determination, qualities she thought had abandoned her long ago. But how to proceed? Everything she had done up until now had proven fruitless. She remembered two of Miss Hartman's favorite epithets that were starting to make more and more sense: The definition of crazy: *Doing the same thing day after day and expecting different results;* and *""How do you expect anything to change if you don't change first?"* What better way to make a change than by starting with a change of clothes? Which brought Emylene to her next problem: money. Laszlo always had cash on him and he planned on coming back; ergo, there must be some money in the room somewhere. Emylene climbed out of bed and began rooting around, tossing everything in the air from clothing to bedding to cupboard drawers. Nothing. Where else? The bathroom! She scampered in and went through the few sundries that Laszlo left behind until she found it: a wad of tightly-rolled bills hidden underneath a flap in his toiletry bag, nearly 600 dollars! Emylene was not a thief, nor was she about to run out on Laszlo with his stash, so she peeled off 100 dollars and wrote the sum down on a piece of toilet paper which she left in the bag as a marker. Then she showered, put on the clothes she had worn the night before, and tromped downstairs to change the world.

Before leaving the building, Emylene also left a handwritten message for Michael, assuring him that she was fine and would thank him again when she saw him next. Funny, how one can be so wrong about people, first impressions and all. Stepping outside she tried to get her priorities straight. If her parents were truly gone, then Laszlo was the only person alive who could help her put a stop to the madness. But where was he, and was he still alive? She had no idea. If worst came to worst, she would have to return to Other-Town by herself. But first, that change of clothes.

Emylene sauntered past shops filled with pleasant customers and happy proprietors. Everyone seemed to be so placid, as if all aspects of moodiness and ill will had been washed away by an early morning rain. Yet, in spite of this city full of contentment and happiness, she had never felt so alone and un-nerved. Not even in the shadow world of the sketch had she felt so abandoned, for The Cowled Men were always there to give her comfort. She thought about that now, the place where time didn't matter, where life was not ruled by a clock or the circadian rhythms of sleep or the need for food. The world inside the sketch was a constant. Poinsettia knew it as a dreadful place populated by horrible forest dwelling killers. But if that was *her* experience, it wasn't Emylene's. This gave her encouragement, for as much horror as she had recently experienced, she had also experienced good, maybe enough good to conquer the other. Suddenly, she was struck with the revelation that last night was not an attempt on her life, it was an attempt to pervert her from her purpose, to throw her off the track, maybe even to rob her of her courage. And that really pissed her off!

In the past, Emylene would never have been caught dead in a Super Mega Valu Store. Those big-box outlets reminded her of mausoleums, and their elderly greeters dressed in ill-fitting smocks looked like crypt-keepers. Not that the young Goth princess had anything against mausoleums and ghouls, but the place and the people working in them just made her feel bad about her life. The poor elderly; it seemed that after a certain age, all mystery and adventure evaporated in one's life. You began each day with a pill or two, stood on your feet for eight hours waiting on people who treated you as if you had one foot in the grave already, and then finished your shift with a plate of fish sticks and milk. Two more pills before eight, and lights out. The only thing to break up the monotony was the occasional trip to the doctor. Then Emylene realized it was not them, it was her. *Nothing changes until you do.* She looked again at some of the venerable faces in the store and considered that these people had all confronted fears and demons of their own at some point in their lives. They came out on the other side for the better, whereas her trials were just beginning. In a way she envied them, and wondered what words of wisdom they might impart to her. She was even tempted to ask one of them where the aisle of 'hope and redemption' might be, but she didn't.

    Instead, Emylene meandered down the aisles on her own past the specials on chocolates and batteries toward the ladies' department in search of an outfit she hoped would reflect her new upbeat mood. Picking her way through the crowded racks, she found a white blouse, yellow skirt and a tan belt, an ensemble that screamed, "Have a nice day, even if it's your last!" She carried the outfit to the change room, dropped her old clothes in a heap, and put on the new ones. Gazing at the new 'Pollyanna' image of herself in the mirror she took a moment to fantasize about how her life might have been had she grown up in an alternate universe: Chip, her steady boyfriend, would arrive for their regular Friday night date and knock on the door holding a bouquet of flowers. Theo and Vandy (who would have made their livings as a professional stock broker and lawyer, respectively) would invite Chip in for a drink, and they would discuss which university looked best on his resume' after he graduated with his MBA. Then Chip would reach into his pocket and pull out an engagement ring with a diamond the size of a large kidney stone. He'd propose to Emylene right there in front of her parents who would burst into tears of joy and make wonderful toasts to the happy couple. They'd all sit and discuss the wedding plans: the date, the reception hall, and even the color of the invitations. Emylene would ask Chip who his best man would be and he'd reply, "Who else, the man who saved you from that pack of Vrykolakas, Laszlo."

Emylene stared at her alter-ego in the mirror as a tiny saltwater tear dripped down her cheek. She wiped it away with the rest of her fantasy, stuffed her old clothes under her arm, and headed to the cash register. *Get real*, she thought. *Your problems don't disappear and the world doesn't change just because you buy a new dress.* In line behind the other customers, she remembered she hadn't removed the tags from the new clothing she was still wearing, so she began to twist and turn in an effort to get at them. She managed to get almost all of them off before she arrived at the cashier.

"Sorry, I wanted to wear these out and forgot about the tags," she said off-handedly to the check-out girl. "Didn't want ya to think I was.... Jesus Christ, Mother of God!"

Not Mother of God, mother of Emylene! Vandy Stipe stood behind the cash register, staring back at her daughter, slack-jawed and flabbergasted.

"Emylene?" Vandy blinked several times to confirm this was not an hallucination standing before her, and then her legs buckled. Emylene reached over the conveyor belt to try to prevent her mother's fall, and both found themselves with their legs splayed in the air, holding onto each other for dear life. Neither was sure whether to laugh or cry. The other patrons in line were not at a loss for words though.

"Are you two alright?" asked one customer.

"Cause if you are, could you move it along?" asked another.

"It is you, isn't it?" Vandy whispered again, afraid that speaking out loud might frighten the vision away.

"Yeah, Mom. Is that you?"

Both women regained their footing and rushed around the conveyor belt to hug each other. Vandy clasped her daughter so close to her bosom that Emylene was in danger of being drowned in the over-sized Super Mega Valu Store smock.

"I thought you were dead!" cried Vandy.

"I will be if you don't ease up!"

Vandy relaxed her grip and stared her daughter in the eye.

"Where have you been all this time?"

"Lady, if this is going to be a long story, can somebody open up another register?" asked one of the customers.

Vandy tore off her smock and tossed it at the customer.

"Guess what? It's 'help yourself' day!"

With that, Vandy took a firm hold of Emylene's arm and marched her toward the front door past one of the greeters.

"Mom, I didn't pay for the…"

"Malcolm, meet my daughter, Emylene," said Vandy as she pulled out her phone and started texting.

"Vandy, you know the rules; no texting on your shift," cautioned Malcolm.

"I know. I'm messaging Crystal that you caught me texting and I'm firing myself. So long, Malcolm."

Vandy handed Malcolm the tags from Emylene's new clothes.

"And tell Crystal she can take these outa my pay."

Malcolm stood there looking befuddled as he watched the two women exit the store and stroll into the beautiful sunny morning.

After the initial shock of their chance meeting began to wear off, neither Emylene nor Vandy knew quite what to say next. Awkwardly, Emylene slipped her hand into her mother's as they wandered down the street in silence until she finally spoke.

"So the last time I saw you wearing a Lululemon outfit I thought that was scary. But seeing you now in a Super MegaValu Store smock…"

"And you in this lovely summer's day frock. You look like a refugee from a Disney movie."

They giggled as much to ease the uncomfortable moment as to confirm the sound of one another's laughter. Then it was Vandy who could hold back no longer.

"Emylene, where have you been all this time?"

Emylene hesitated, remembering the last time she spoke her truths to Vandy. Nervously she wondered whether this conversation would end in another break or a healing this time.

"You ready?" she asked.

In preparation, Vandy pulled out a cigarette and lit up. Then mother and daughter continued to stroll while Emylene recounted everything that happened to her from the day she stormed out of the Stipe house to last's night's terrifying encounter.

"…and that's the last I saw of Laszlo."

When her mother didn't reply immediately, Emylene felt the familiar sting of rejection, and cursed herself for making the same mistake. Did she honestly think anything would change? She was so engrossed in her inward thoughts that she nearly missed hearing her mother's reply.

"Once upon a time, Emylene, I would have written this off as another one of your attention-getting antics. But after what I've seen and heard, not anymore."

Now it was Emylene who couldn't believe it! Her mother's tone and reaction *had* changed. Completely! Gone was the sarcastic edge and the hair-trigger judgment. This was a miracle, and for a moment the image of a Cosmopolitan magazine cover headline popped into her head that read, *How Vampyres Brought Me Closer to Mom.*

"Thanks, Mom. You have no idea how much that means to me. Now I have about a million questions for *you*, starting with… where is Dad?"

Vandy hesitated, lit up another cigarette, and after one long drag, pointed west. The look in her daughter's eyes almost broke Vandy's heart, but Emylene had told her truth and now it was time to listen to her mother.

"It was late that morning when we heard the news about the fire that killed you. Your body was never found, but the authorities said the heat was so intense and the rubble was so extensive that they might never find your remains. Still, we needed closure, so we had a service for you. Thrall insisted on helping. I think he always had a crush on you, you know? In fact your father and I secretly wished one day…anyhow, we let him arrange the music and he picked a very nice selection from *Heaven Will Burn*. We purchased a plot at the Rosedale Cemetery and bought a headstone engraved with your name in the language of our ancestors, the Ostrogoth. Everyone in the community showed up and, since there was a casket but no body to bury, people brought articles that reminded them of you—a velvet glove, spiked dog collar, a dozen Bacarra roses. They were all placed in the coffin, which we lowered into the grave. So beautiful. You would have loved it."

Emylene listened as her mother recalled the many heartfelt tributes. She felt especially blessed, for how many people could say they were there to hear first-hand about their own funerals? The aftermath, however, was not as pleasant. Her mother went on to explain Theo's descent into depression after losing his only child. Although Theo was never a demonstrative man, he nevertheless doted on his daughter in his own quiet way.

"You never knew this, Emylene, but the day you moved out, your father cried."

Vandy went on to explain that Emylene's moving out was something Theo eventually overcame, but her death was not. The morning after the fire, Vandy felt like her heart had fallen out of her chest. Theo, on the other hand, simply turned as cold as the granite marker on his daughter's grave. Vandy hoped that bringing him to the cemetery for visits might help him deal with the loss, but the tactic failed and Theo withdrew into himself until he became almost unreachable. The only person to whom he responded was Poinsettia. Maybe it was because both girls were so close in age, or maybe she had a knack for drawing him out. Vandy wasn't sure which, but having Poinsettia around seemed to help, and for Theo's sake, Vandy let the girl move in with them. But it wasn't long before something about Poinsettia began to rub Vandy the wrong way. And then there was 'the incident'.

One night a teenage boy was brought into Pall Bearer's Paradise, a cocky street kid who had been bullying one of the Goth girls in the neighborhood. 'Mira', as Poinsettia now referred to herself, said he needed to be taught a lesson, so she ordered that he be tied to a chair. Then, she had one of her people cut him on the arms and catch his dripping blood in a chalice. She told the boy that the only way he'd get out alive was if he drank his own blood.

"People have blood fetishes," continued Vandy, "It's none of my business. I've always been of the mind that you should be free to do what you want; it's your body. But after that night, I began to see how Mira was turning our content little community into an aggressive cult with a big accent on blood. Your father and I fought about it a lot. He said it was a natural progression from 'playing at being' to actually 'being.' He called it a metamorphosis; I called it 'twisted'. Of course, by then I knew that Mira had her hooks in him, but I couldn't make him see that. In fact, he wouldn't let me say one negative thing about her. Anyway, that's what split us up. Meanwhile rumors began to spread that you were murdered by a bunch of rowdy rednecks who were trying to run all the Goths out of the city.

"That's a lie! It was Mira. She did it," cried Emylene.

"I don't doubt it. But the rumor thing was a smart move

on her part, made you a martyr to the cause. Wasn't long before she demanded more blood rituals and ceremonies, claiming it was 'our time' and that our lifestyle should be celebrated, even brought into the mainstream. Everybody out there was a poseur, she said. We were the one true religion. She became obsessed with turning us into some kind of social/political force. I told Theo that we should just 'get the hell out of Dodge,' but he begged me to stay, that we were figureheads to the movement, and we couldn't desert the flock. Well, it was time for me to get out while I still had both my figure *and* my head. I left one night and moved to Queen East. On my own for the first time, I had to make money, so I sort of morphed into this."

It took Emylene a good few minutes to take everything in: the guilt of abandoning her parents without a word, of feeling responsible for her father becoming so depressed, and adjusting to the consequences of her departure.

"So, you're telling me Dad is one of *them* now?"

"I haven't seen him in eight months, hon', but I know he's with them, works as a kind of emissary to the city. There's no doubt in my mind. But, Emylene, listen to me. This is not your fault."

Emylene could have let the news defeat her, but instead her eyes blazed with newborn determination and resolve.

"We need to find out for sure. We need to go there and find him."

"Sorry, Em', not me', I'm never going back! As far as I'm concerned he made his coffin and now he can lie in it. I did everything I could. And also…if he's turned, I just couldn't deal with that. You know, I look back now and I see how stupid I was. For years I wore the black, feeling like I knew more than everybody else about life, death and everything in between. But when Other-Town sprang up and I saw the kind of depravity it could lead to…I won't go back there, not even for Theo."

In the past, Vandy's stubbornness would have provoked Emylene into an argument, and there would have been a contest to see who could jam each one's point of view down the throat of the other. Now, there was a silence between the two; only this time it was not a brooding, angry silence but a healthy, respectful one.

Emylene accepted her mother's position and, like a miracle, her mother gave back in kind.

"*You can't change the world, you can only change yourself…*" she remembered Miss Hartman saying. But what miracles happen when you do! The women continued walking in tandem for a block or two until they came upon a derelict standing on the corner with a cup in his hand.

"Now there's something you don't see every day," remarked Vandy as they passed the nervous-looking vagrant.

"What? A bum begging for money? What world do you live in?" asked Emylene.

Just then, a police cruiser pulled up, and the vagrant ran like he'd seen the devil. He was fast, but the cop was faster, jumping out of the cruiser and chasing him down without any trouble whatsoever.

"Hey, buddy, where ya going? You hungry? Come with us. We'll get ya fed."

The bum was arm-wrestled into the back seat of the cruiser, which quickly drove off.

CHAPTER 24

City Hall in downtown Toronto was composed of three buildings that included one short central rotunda in the shape of a flying saucer flanked by two tall office towers. It was an architectural marvel in its day, but its day had long past. The mayor's office was on the fifth floor, and for security reasons was not noted on the elevator directory. Anyone who had business there would be directed by an underling.

A closed-door meeting was being held in said office by two high-ranking individuals. One of whom was the mayor who sat behind his great oak desk, wearing a traditional three-piece pinstriped suit. The other person was a pasty-faced Goth dressed in a high-styled black velvet evening coat, Edwardian ruffled shirt, black leather boots, and a gold razor dangling around his neck—Theo Stipe. It was an odd sight, to say the least, these two.

"Are you insane?" snapped the mayor as he wiped rivulets of sweat from his balding pate.

Theo smiled as he always did when faced with the politician's bluster. He was used to these outbursts that he had regularly put up with over the past year. His reaction was to leisurely puff on his cigarillo, and reply in a soft, friendly voice.

"Really, Mayor, you rule the entire city. What's a few more feet?"

"I know you, Stipe! First it's a foot, then a yard, then a whole block! You don't get it, do you? Every time Other-Town asks for an extra inch of pavement I get deluged by angry taxpayers claiming that they're being pushed out of their homes and businesses."

"That's nonsense. Nobody has to move. They can join us any time they want."

"Figuratively or literally?" snorted the mayor.

Theo couldn't help but smile at the mayor's remark. Every growing city required the requisite 'blood, sweat and tears' of its citizens to flourish, and nobody knew it better than the mayor who had upped commercial and personal property taxes three times during his term. Other-Town was no different, except that Other-Town needed real blood to make it grow.

"You have to admit, Mayor, that conditions in your local neighborhoods have become a lot safer since Other-Town came to be. Crime is down, the homeless problem you had a year ago is all but obliterated. Even the teenagers are behaving better."

"Because people in this city are terrified that they'll disappear into the night if they *don't* behave!"

"Fear is a great motivator, is it not? And let's don't forget, in return for being model citizens, those same people get to visit us at night to have their needs met."

This was true. The general electorate was as two-faced as their politicians when it came to the popular vices: gambling, liquor, and prostitution. At work, at home, at church and even in the daily newspapers they ranted and raved about how social decay would lead to the fall of their fair city. But it was the language that was the problem. This 'social decay' they spoke of was just another term for the basic needs of human nature, fundamental ingredients of which society was too ashamed to admit. It had existed for as long as man lived in communities, and would continue as long as man walked the earth. The solution that Theo and Other-Town proposed was simple: lift the veil of hypocrisy and allow the constituency to satisfy their needs openly and without guilt. After all, hypocrisy was akin to deceit, which was akin to lying, and lying was immoral... was it not? Following that logic, Other-Town was probably the more honest of the two societies. If only everyone admitted what they wanted, no one would have to lie anymore. And wouldn't that kind of honesty bring them closer to God? What religious or political leader could argue with that? But the mayor was still stuck on the small stuff.

"I'm telling you, Stipe, it's not just a night on the town that people object to. Your little cult is riddled with all kinds of messy problems. We're forever getting complaints of disappearances and rumors of occult monkey business going on over there. Plus, you attract a lot of negative attention from the outside, and it's starting to make waves."

"Then invite the outside in! Let us give them a taste of what Other-Town can offer and I promise we'll solve their problem the same way we've solved yours."

The mayor didn't have a ready-made reply for this, which meant it might actually be worthy of consideration. Now was the time for Theo to close the deal with a carefully-worded incentive.

"Elections are around the corner. Another eight months. You have a lot to crow about, Mayor…and a lot to protect."

The mayor brooded a moment before he made his pronouncement.

"You tell that little witch of yours, that this is the last time. One block only!"

"In all directions," added Theo.

"And I don't want to see your pasty face in this office again!"

Theo stood up and smiled graciously, knowing he'd be back in a month or so with the same request, and they'd have the same conversation ending with the same result. They both knew it.

"Leave the way you came!" barked the mayor.

Theo nodded as he strutted to the back door of the office.

"See you tonight, Mayor. Same table?" smiled Theo.

Theo was on his way out when the mayor asked, "Stipe, let me ask you something: how do you manage to get around in the day when the others can't?"

"I'm blessed."

With that, Theo let himself out and closed the door behind him. The only evidence of their meeting was the perspiration still beading on the mayor's brow.

Theo rode the private elevator down to the parking garage. As always, the chauffeur was waiting next to the limo with blacked-out windows. When the elevator doors opened and Theo appeared, the driver opened the car door and let him inside. The driver then climbed into his seat and drove out of the building. Neither said a word to the other.

Twenty minutes later the limo pulled up to the outskirts of Other-Town. Theo let himself out and walked along the deserted streets unhindered, until he came to the familiar alleyway that led to Pall Bearer's Paradise.

CHAPTER 25

"Mira, I've missed you," Laszlo said softly.

Laszlo gazed longingly at his wife. He had aged, but she still possessed the look and figure of a young girl.

"I'm sorry... I got old..."

Even worse, he realized he was standing there naked. Embarrassed, he hurried awkwardly to put his clothes on.

"I...I tried to keep myself in shape for you, but..."

And then Laszlo ran out of words—or the words ran out of him. In his wildest dreams he never imagined greeting his wife while scrambling to put his pants on.

"It's no matter, Laszlo. Come with me," she replied with serene calmness.

Mira smiled and held out her hand. It was cold to the touch, but he took it anyway. Then she led him out of the cell and into an adjacent hallway where they ascended a set of narrow stairs that led to a door. The door opened before they reached it, as if it anticipated the couple's arrival. When Laszlo entered the next room, he found himself back in somewhat familiar surroundings.

Pall Bearer's Paradise, I should have known," he said.

"The same, but different...," replied Mira,

"...as is everything."

She was right. Laszlo looked around to see a very different version of the club he broke into just a few days ago. That day it was a dark, foreboding tomb that reeked of death, a home to threatening creatures with beady red eyes. Now, the place looked more like an ultra-hip nightclub filled with an upscale crowd that barely seemed to notice or care less about him. He looked around at the revelers dressed in an updated, hyper-version of Goth wear—basic black accentuated by vibrant streaks of fluorescent make-up and hair gels—a combination of near-death and glow-in-the-dark. Males and females reclined in plush booths, sipping exotic drinks and gyrating sensually to the heart-thumping, hedonistic music. Mira watched Laszlo take it all in.

"You are thinking that this was not what you saw when you were here last."

Laszlo looked surprised at her remark.

"Yes, I was here," she continued, "You were never in any real danger."

Mira smiled at him. Was that genuine warmth, or a carefully crafted response? Careful, he told himself.

Laszlo was prepared for a blood-lusting Mira, a demonic Mira, and even a vicious, unrestrained, maniacal Mira. But for 'endearing Mira' he had no defense, and he cursed himself for the resolve he felt slowly melting away.

He pressed his fingernails hard into the flesh of his palms to remind himself of the danger he was still in.

"I'm not stupid like the rest of them who come to Other-Town. I know what goes on here. You give people whatever they want and then rob them of their lives drop by drop, until one morning they wake up and can't bare to look at the sun anymore or realize they have a thirst they can't quench."

"So dramatic, Laszlo, and so *morbid*. Look around. Do you see such creatures?"

"Back in the cell I just left?"

"Like all species there is a maturation period. When they first turn, they are like babies. The next time you see them they may be at one of these booths with better manners than you. This is why I brought you here, Laszlo, to see for yourself the great misconception you've been under."

Mira gestured for Laszlo to escort her through the club. They came to a small table where two females sat drinking Bloody Marys. Laszlo picked up one of the glasses, dipped his finger into the liquid and put it to his lips. Alcohol.

"You were expecting blood?" laughed Mira.

Laszlo placed the glass back on the table and moved on. After he passed by, one of the females picked it up and licked the spot where Laszlo handled it. Then she downed the drink with a most delicious grin on her face.

"We enlarged the space since Emylene's day," Mira commented as she continued the tour. "We had to, to support our ever-growing community. Once people realized the delusion they were under and what life could really be like, they flocked to us."

"Delusion?" he queried.

"That your life is the righteous way and that ours is deviant, when actually the opposite is true. The truth is your entire society was conceived under false principals in order to enslave you. Yours is the twisted vision. Look no further than when you wake every morning. Which of you really *likes* to get up and go to work? How many of you love it, and how many resent it? The truth, now. How many build up so much pressure and angst through the day that they need to release it afterward at gyms, or through drink, or drugs or worse? It seems to me that the day is filled with anxiety, and the night is there to release it. Am I wrong? You go out at night, you feel romantic at night, you make love in the night. The truth is, night is right. It's as plain as… what's the word I'm looking for…ah, yes 'day'…plain as day! You think I am trying to brainwash you, Laszlo. We're not evangelicals, we don't go door-to-door asking for donations or soliciting converts. People come to us freely after they've discovered the trick that's been played on them. You, yourself, came to me of your own free will, admit it."

"I do."

Laszlo put his hand on her dead chest.

"But within this breast no heart beats."

Then he brought her hand to his warm chest and her eyes lit up like she was receiving a shot of adrenaline.

"Now it's your turn. Don't lie to me, Mira. This is what you want but you can't buy for any price. Oh, you can get a taste if every once in a while, when you press your mouth to a warm throat and suck the life out of it. But then it's gone and you're hungry again. You're an addict, that's the difference between us."

Mira let her hand rest on Laszlo's chest to feel his beating heart, while he read the want in her eyes.

"We all have addictions of one kind or another," she whispered as she drew herself close to him. "Otherwise you wouldn't be here."

Laszlo pushed her back and said what he'd been waiting to say for forty years.

"Mira, if there was a way to bring you back…"

"There is no way, and I wouldn't take it if there was. Neither would you if you knew what I've experienced."

"I saw what you experienced! I saw you being ravaged by a blood-sucking Vrykolakas on our wedding night! I saw the life fade from your eyes and heard you screaming for mercy while I was just a few feet away, unable to save you! These are not people, these are monsters!"

To prove his point, Laszlo strode up to a vampyre who was engaged in conversation, and struck him hard across the face. The revenant ignored Laszlo's insult, and returned to chatting with his companion. Not satisfied, Laszlo pushed the demon into a group of others, jostling them all. He steeled himself for the reprisal, but the group just walked away.

"If you're looking for a fight," Mira said, amused,

"You'll have better luck in one of the taverns on your side of the city. We are not an aggressive people or demonic as you may think. We live much like our predecessor Goths who were simple, passive and knowledge-seeking."

"What do you want, Mira?" he asked out of exhaustion and despair.

"I want *you*, Laszlo. I have since the day we were separated."

"I want you, too! That's what I've been saying…"

"…we can be together as we were meant to," she completed, as though reading his mind.

"But I'm old now and you still look like you did the day I married you."

"That's the miracle! I can make you young again and we can evolve into something better, more natural."

Mira knew she had reached him on some level. He just needed time to think it through.

"You don't have to answer now, husband. Come to me when you're ready. Bring Emylene if you want to. Tell her that her father also waits for her here. We can all begin our lives over."

With that, Mira led Laszlo to the main door.

"No one will harm you, you're free to go and free to return whenever you please. Just don't keep me waiting too long."

CHAPTER 26

Laszlo's mind was on fire. It was a lie, he told himself: everything about Other-Town and everything Mira claimed, such as being better off now than she had. How could she know, how could she compare? She hadn't been herself since that night in Santorini. As Laszlo made his way down the hallway toward the alley, the morbid details of that awful night came flooding back to him; finding the innkeeper lying in a pool of blood, running into the restaurant to witness that hellish fiend making off with Mira. After having endured all that, how could she possible know her own mind? And yet, she spoke with such eloquence and resolve. The more he thought about it, the more it puzzled him. Was it an accident—the two of them in the wrong place at the wrong time all those years ago, or were they pawns in some larger plan?

When Laszlo emerged from the alley into the night air, the lure of Other-Town was all around him: the music, the raucous crowds, the party atmosphere. He passed one storefront after another watching people enjoying themselves, satisfying all manner of appetites. Most of them would wake up tomorrow, curse their dreary jobs only to return the next night. Was Mira right? Were people literally slaves to their work? Had he and everyone else been brainwashed into thinking that working eight hours a day for five days a week at something they hated was the better way? A tune by Usher drifted through the air, one he'd heard over and over again on the radio,

> So we back in the club
> Get that bodies rockin' from side to side
> Thank God the week is done
> I feel like a zombie gone back to life

Only now did he pay attention to the lyrics. Other innocuous song titles from popular music came to memory, *Working Nine To Five*, the old Loverboy tune *Everybody's Working For The Weekend, Take That Job And Shove It*. He was hard pressed to remember any songs that glorified the work week. Other signs of daily strife were abundantly apparent if anyone bothered to look. Civil strikes, poverty, drug abuse, recession…where did it all go wrong? Worse, could Other-Town have gotten it *right*?

As Laszlo continued walking, he noticed the crimson tendrils playing under his shoes and, for the first time, he thought, "They *are* kind of pretty, aren't they?" He crossed over the demarcation line where the crowds thinned and the sounds and sights of Other-Town faded, and all that was left was nagging doubt.

It was 4:00 AM when Laszlo made it back to the Excelsior Hotel and climbed the stairs, dog-tired. He pulled out his key and unlocked the door. Without bothering to flick on the light he went to the toilet to empty his bladder, and ran right into Emylene's mother who was just getting up from the seat.

"Get that thing outa my face!" yelped Vandy.

"Get your face away from my...who the hell are *you*?"

Vandy hopped aside and pulled up her pants, as surprised by Laszlo as he was of her. Upon recognizing the old man's voice, Emylene awoke, jumped out of bed in the adjoining room and hurried to the bathroom door, just as Laszlo was relieving himself.

"Laszlo, you're back, thank God! I was so worried."

"Now, so am I," Vandy said.

Emylene followed her mother's gaze to the toilet where she noticed the black urine splashing the bowl.

"Do you mind?" cried Laszlo as he pushed both women out of the room and slammed the door in their faces. The ladies looked at each other in astonishment. It wasn't possible! It was just too big a coincidence. What were the odds? A flush was heard, followed by the sound of running tap water. A moment later, a somewhat flustered Laszlo opened the bathroom door to find both women staring at him in wide-eyed amazement.

"I am not a freak," he said, "It's a condition called..."

"Alkaptonuria. I know, I have it too," stated Emylene.

Laszlo stared at Emylene with wide-eyed astonishment.

"That condition of yours is as rare as *shit*, you know…" remarked Vandy, "…Sorry… bad choice of words. I don't have the gene, but my husband carried it."

"Laszlo, meet my mother, Vandy," remarked Emylene.

Laszlo put his hand out to shake Vandy's. When the gesture wasn't returned, he took his hand back to cover the awkward moment.

"Something's going on here," she pondered. "The condition is common in only two areas of the world; the Dominican Republic and Slovakia. I checked it out when I learned Theo had it, and you're sure as hell no Dominican."

After all he had been through in the past twelve hours, this newest shock was beginning to take its toll on Laszlo.

"Lady, can we do this in the morning? I've just been through a night from hell."

He looked at both women, begging for a reprieve. When he realized he wasn't going to get one, he just plopped himself down on the edge of the chair, put his head in his hands, and began to explain.

"My name is Laszlo Birij. I was born in the village of Sisak in Croatia."

"Sisak? How far is that from Bratislava?" asked Vandy.

"About two hundred kilometers. You are familiar with Croatia?"

Vandy's brow furrowed, worried about the direction this conversation was taking.

"What is it, Mom?" asked Emylene.

"You know your father was born in Bratislava, Slovakia. What you don't know is he had family in Sisak. Another thing you don't know, your last name is not Stipe.

"Too many negatives for this time of night. *Please* simplify," begged Emylene.

"Most people who came from Europe over fifty years ago could barely speak English. They arrived at the immigration office and gave their names, but the officials were so over-worked that they made up names to make life easier for themselves. Your father's name, before it was changed, was Stropnicky."

"My aunt's name was Stropnicky! Daphna Stropnicky. Laszlo replied incredulously. "That would mean your husband and my aunt were cousins!"

Emylene marveled at the amazing coincidence.

"Most people are related through blood. We're related through urine. How perverse is that?"

There was a moment of silence in the room. Pieces of a great cosmic puzzle were dropping out of the ceiling and all three needed a moment to digest this new-found information.

"This is all starting to make sense in a bizarre sort of way," said Laszlo. "How Emylene would have the ability to bring Mira out of the sketch. Not only did she inherit the black urine from my aunt, but her powers, as well. So when you said you were a Goth princess…"

"Ostrogoth Princess to be precise," interjected Vandy.

"Ostrogoths? I am only aware of the Visigoths."

To which Vandy explained, "Like many peoples, the Ostrogoths began as one tribe, Goths, back in the fourth century. Years later they split up. The Visigoths settled in Eastern Europe and the Ostrogoths remained in Germania. My husband was named after Germania's most famous king, Theodoric.

It was then that Emylene was struck with an epiphany.

"The other morning when I woke up with that sense of optimism, just before I found you again, Mom, I didn't understand…*this* whole thing is not a coincidence or a mistake or even an accident. It's fate. The three of us were brought together in that bathroom for a reason: to stop Other-Town and to slay Mira!"

Laszlo slumped into his chair like a modern day Oedipus being forewarned of the tragic fate that awaited him. He, too, had considered the events of the past few days as being cosmic in nature. But, if that was true, a much grimmer question faced him… if two people had diametrically opposed fates, which one would prevail? If Emylene believed her fate was to slay Mira, and Laszlo believed his fate was to save Mira, which was the truly fated outcome? And if the two were friends, cousins and allies, would fate require them to be adversaries in the future? Would fate require one to kill the other? Damn fate!

"Laszlo, are you all right?" asked Vandy.

Emylene rushed over to the chair to prop up his head with a pillow.

"I'm such an idiot," she said. "This guy just escaped from a pack of wild vampires, and we've been unloading all this on him. Laszlo, I didn't even ask how you are, how you got away."

"Maybe in the morning, when I've had some rest," he replied weakly.

The women nodded their understanding and pulled a set of sheets off their bed to make up the couch for the old man.

As Emylene's mood improved with the knowledge that this adventure might be part of a grander scheme, Laszlo's degenerated. It was as if the universe was closing in on him and he was powerless to stop the events about to unfold. Intellectually, he knew that Mira needed to be stopped, but he always held out the hope that he'd find a way to return her to her original condition. If Emylene's prophesy prevailed, then not only would Laszlo have to stand by and lose his wife a second time, but he might even end up being the agent of his wife's demise. If, on the other hand, he were to triumph and save Mira, would he have to slay Emylene and her mother in the process? This was all too much for one man to deal with in his current physical and mental state. Laszlo closed his eyes and wondered what he would do when the time came to act.

It was almost five in the morning before the women climbed into bed.

"I can't stop thinking about Dad," whispered Emylene. "I mean, I found you, so maybe there's a chance."

"Do you remember the last time you saw your father at the house, Em', wearing those god-awful Nike workouts? After they told him you died in the fire he went back to wearing the black, looking like the man I fell in love with. But that was just a shell. The pain of your absence hung around his shoulders like an albatross, and Mira exploited that pain to the hilt. By the time I left, he was totally under her influence. I don't think there's any question what happened."

"But, what if…" offered Emylene.

"No more 'what if's' tonight, Em'. No more," pleaded Vandy.

Vandy kissed her daughter on the forehead the way she did when Emylene was a child, and both savored the sweet feeling. But nothing could stop the strange notions that continued to swirl through Emylene's head.

Laszlo was born in Croatia and Emylene's father, Theo, came from Slovakia. The common geographical thread between these two countries was the Carpathian Mountains. Bad mojo, the Carpathians. Emylene's mind teemed with questions that would not give her rest until she came to a decision. It was only after she made up her mind as to what had to be done, that sleep overtook her.

The morning light pierced the blinds, waking Laszlo first. He stretched out of his cramped position on the couch, wrapped himself in a blanket, and tiptoed to the bathroom, trying not to wake the still-sleeping women. Watching his dark urine spill into the toilet he was once again reminded of all the strange coincidences that had been revealed just hours ago. What a world, he thought, as he flushed and watched the remains swirl round the bowl and disappear. Why couldn't life be that simple? Why couldn't you just flush all your problems down the toilet? As he washed his hands he wondered if demons ever washed theirs. That brought a rare smile to his face. After drying off, he checked his shaving kit and found the wad of bills along with Emylene's marker. Another smile crossed his face, and he reflected how little he had smiled or laughed in the last few months. The times he did, were due to Emylene. Then he worried what he would do if circumstances demanded that he go up against her in order to save his wife. The argument he was having in his head would have to wait. It was being drowned out by a nastier one in the adjacent room.

"You are not! I forbid it!" shouted Vandy.

"You can't forbid me anything, I'm twenty years old!"

"No matter how old you are I will always be your mother!"

The last thing Laszlo needed to deal with this morning was a screaming match between two sleep-deprived women. Wrapping himself in a towel, he opened the door to find mother and daughter sitting upright, staring daggers at each other.

Laszlo spoke, "I never had children, but one thing I do know is that parents are always right."

"Stay out of it, old man!" said Vandy.

"Yeah, mind your own business!" ordered Emylene.

"At least you two agree on something," quipped Laszlo. "Now, what is all this about before my head explodes?"

Emylene straightened her spine and pumped out her chest, defiantly.

"I'm going to Other-Town tonight to find my father."

Vandy stared her daughter straight in the eye.

"And I said no! You'll only get yourself killed."

Laszlo sauntered into the room, whipped the sheets off the couch, and casually started to fold them.

"Missus Stipe, do you know for sure that your husband is a Vrykolakas?"

"That's the direction he was going the last time I saw him, courtesy of your wife."

"But you never actually saw him in his altered state?"

The only answer Vandy could muster was a shake of her head.

"Cousin, I'm not trying to take sides," he continued.

"Then don't. And don't call me cousin!" she spat back.

"Mom, we *have* to go back. It's called *closure*," said Emylene. "We need it for Dad, and Laszlo needs it for Mira, don't you?"

Laszlo let the silence speak for him. There was no way he was going to tell them he had already met with Mira. That would have opened up a can of worms he was not ready to deal with. For her part, Vandy interpreted Laszlo's silence as weakness, and pressed on with her point.

"You want closure? How's this? I will not risk losing my daughter again, not even for my husband. Knowing what I do, I wouldn't take him back now even if he asked." In defense of her father, Emylene turned on her mother, "Sounds to me like you've written him off. Sounds like you've moved on. What's that about, Mom? Got someone on the side?"

The fragile truce between the women that began yesterday was broken. A challenge had been issued.

"Your father's the one with someone on the side, baby girl! He made his choice and chose that little slut with the blood fetish over me!"

"So that's what this is about? You're jealous? My God, Mom, she's a vampyre. It's not like he had a choice."

"Oh, they always have a choice, dearie!"

"Doesn't change the fact that I'm going after him."

"Then you'll die, and I'll have lost you both! Satisfied?"

Laszlo dropped his towel and stood naked before them.

"Not necessarily."

Vandy gawked in stunned silence, not so much at the old man's nakedness, but at the incredible body tattoos that covered his torso from head to toe.

"It's the evil eye," noted Emylene, and hoping to trump her mother, added. "Do you know the story of the Medusa?"

"Since before you were born, young lady," Vandy returned smugly.

Now that Laszlo had their attention he was going to take full advantage of it.

"Last night after Emylene escaped, eight vampyres had me cornered, but I fought them off. You know how? With these. They fear these."

Laszlo opened his arms wide like a tattooed, senior citizen version of Jesus delivering a speech to his flock.

"Ladies and cousins, demons have terrorized our family for a very long time. I don't know why, only that they will not stop. I propose that if you have the will and the desire, I will lead you to put an end to this nightmare."

Vandy sighed. The naked old Croat was right and she hated him for it.

"I'm not going anywhere until you put on some clothes. And stop calling me, cousin."

Laszlo smiled as he bent over to pick up his robe, in a little less dignified manner than Jesus might have done.

Later that morning, when Laszlo led the two women downstairs past the front desk, Michael was there as usual.

"You're looking all colors of lovely this morning," he cracked to Emylene.

Emylene smiled and walked over.

"Michael, that was so…anyway I just wanted to say thanks again for helping me out the other night. I really appreciated it."

"No prob-lem-o. So maybe sometime we could…"

"Yeah, I'd like that. Catch ya later," answered Emylene quickly as she joined Laszlo and her mother to head out of the building.

"What was that all about?" Laszlo asked.

"I had a thing a couple of nights ago after I got back from Other-Town."

Emylene recounted the episode when the ominous presence stole into their room and terrorized her, and how Michael came to her rescue. Emylene's take on the event focused on the redeemable value of human nature. Laszlo, however, saw something much more sinister in the tale. Looking deeply concerned he muttered, "That was my fault. They marked me when I broke into their lair. Then they followed me here and found you. But worse, they've found a way out of Other-Town. No one is safe anymore. We need to prepare."

CHAPTER 27

Back in the day, the Baker's Dozen Donut Shop was one of the busiest hangouts in the neighborhood. However, it wasn't their baked goods that made the place so popular. At this donut shop you could score a lot more than an extra pastry. In addition to maple glaze, sprinkled, and double-dipped chocolate you could also order a side of hash, crack cocaine and a fist full of bennies. In theory, donuts and drugs may have sounded like a good combination to push to the local youth, but in practice it was a stupid move, for both got the attention of the local constabulary, and it wasn't long before the owners were busted. A month later the shop re-opened as a tattoo parlor under the name Voodoo Tattoo. Contrary to expectations, the location actually gained stature in the eyes of the community because at least this was a regulated business. Still, a hangout was a hangout and as such, it attracted the same annoying kind of teenager looking for a place to act cool on a sweltering summer's morning. They were there as usual, five shiftless punks chilling on the stoop when Laszlo, Vandy and Emylene approached.

"Why don't we just go back to the guy who did your tattoos?" Emylene asked Laszlo.

"Disappeared, not long after he finished me. Nobody knows what happened."

Laszlo ignored the kids and went to the front door of the parlor to scope it out. He peered inside first to make sure that a business license was visible over the counter. Then he perused the interior until he satisfied himself that the studio was both legitimate and clean. Meanwhile, the kids amused themselves by joking about this early morning freak show.

"Maybe somebody lost a bet," said one to another.

"Or maybe somebody was trying to feel young again," joked a second.

"Or maybe somebody was trying to *feel* someone young again," cracked a third.

The biggest of them stepped up to Laszlo with a look that said, 'This ain't no place for you old man,' but Laszlo just smiled. "Hi, Son. Got a tat yourself?"

The kid smirked and pulled back the sleeve of his dirty white tee shirt to show off a death skull inked into his shoulder.

"Nice," said Laszlo who lifted the entire front of his shirt to display his heavily decorated chest.

"Holy shit!" said all the boys in chorus.

With new-found respect, the kid and his buddies stepped back to let Laszlo and the two women inside without any further hassle.

Jules, the young, bald tattoo artist, was already at the counter with his sample books open when the three entered. He had sized up this trio while they were sizing him up:

granddad and his daughter were out to give the hot little granddaughter the birthday present she'd been pestering them for. He'd sell her on a dragon or a pretty little unicorn at the base of her spine, four inches north of the tailbone—harmless enough until she showed it off to her boyfriend. It wouldn't be long until that horny little winged creature would be taking them both to new heights of ecstasy on the hot summer nights ahead. This sale wouldn't be a big score for Jules, but it would start his day off nicely. He rested his fingers on his most popular designs until Laszlo strode up and closed the books on his fingers. Then he pointed to the intricate evil eye tattoos that encircled his own arms.

"Can you do this?" the old man demanded.

Jules studied the tats with a professional eye.

"Evil eye? I can do that blindfolded."

He waited for Laszlo to laugh at his weak joke, but none of the three even cracked a smile.

"Tough crowd," he quipped. "Seriously, something that intricate ain't for these girls, too much pain involved. Not even pretty. I'm an artist. I can do way better than those gnarly markings. I'm thinking maybe a cute little unicorn at the base of your grand-daughter's spine, and for mama-san a butterfly on the ankle?"

Vandy elbowed Laszlo aside and stepped up into the tattoo artist's face.

"What's your name, son?"

"Jules. What's yours?"

"Jules, I had my nipples pierced before you were born. I've done surface weaves and suicide suspensions, and I've been through labor which trumps them all, so don't lecture me about pain. And you can call me Vandy."

"No disrespect, Vandy. I was just sayin'," apologized Jules.

Then it was Emylene's turn.

"No unicorns, no butterflies, Jules. I want the evil eyes just like my friend here, and my mother wants 'em, too, or we'll take our business somewhere else. Laszlo will tell you exactly how they go and where they go and if you don't do it the way he says, then me and my Mom will show you some real pain."

This was exactly the kind of customer Jules hated. He'd spent seven years apprenticing under someone else before he opened his own shop just so that he wouldn't have to take crap from people like this mouthy, spoiled brat. He narrowed his eyes at Emylene.

"This is my shop. I don't have to do anything I don't…"
Laszlo laid a wad of bills on the counter.
"Who's first?" asked Jules.

Vandy unbuttoned the sleeves of her blouse, while Jules stepped over to the sink to wash his hands with germicidal soap. Emylene whispered, "Nipples pierced?" to her mother, who shrugged nonchalantly. Old news. When Jules returned, he led the trio over to a table facing the picture window, in full view of the boys who were still outside on the sidewalk.

"This is not a peep show," snapped Vandy.

Jules smiled as he laid out his tools.

"It's called marketing. Dudes gather round, hopin' to see some blood or a boob or somethin', and then others stop and low and behold, I snag a few new customers. If you're not up for this, then no amount of money you throw at me..."

Vandy looked out the window at the horny little vultures. *This is who we're saving' the world for,* she wondered?

"What the hell, let's give the boys a thrill," she proclaimed as she pulled off her blouse to reveal a skimpy, bone white camisole and lay down on the table face-up.

In today's parlance she'd be called a cougar. In cruder terms, a MILF. By any standard, Vandy had a solid build that most women her age would kill for. Jules began to clean and disinfect the areas around Vandy's arms, legs and chest above her heart. Then he put on clean plastic gloves and opened a fresh pack of sterilized needles. Using the tattoo machine, he began drawing an outline of the evil eyes on her skin.

"They have to be linked, no breaks," advised Laszlo.

"Roger that," he replied.

The outline was cleaned with antiseptic soap and water. Then sterile, thicker needles were installed on the machine that Jules used to add shading. After cleaning the area again, color was injected, and traces of blood were removed with a sterile, disposable cloth. When he finished one tattoo, Jules cleaned it off and applied a bandage over the area before he began the next.

"So, like, is this part of an initiation or somethin'? Rotary club? Family reunion picnic?"

Laszlo looked at Emylene and Vandy who remained tight-lipped. Vandy's threshold for pain was generally quite high, but the needle drilling into the same small patch of skin for so long was beginning to make her grimace. A sad reminder she was not in her twenties anymore. Jules put down his tool.

"Look, mama-san, we're only part way done, and I can see this is bringing you a world of hurt no matter how many piercings you had or babies you pushed out. Maybe it's an idea to spell each other off a bit so it doesn't get too intense— unless that's what you're into.

Emylene and Vandy looked at each other, agreeing that this was indeed a good idea.

So you never said what this is for," Jules remarked.

Laszlo was getting more impatient with the young artist as the minutes passed.

"None of your business," he replied flatly.

The old man had a talent for using the wrong tone at the wrong time. Jules puffed out his chest like a provoked baboon and laid down his instrument in protest. The two of them were itching for a fight.

"Hey, who's hungry?" interjected Vandy. "I sure could use a sandwich and coffee right about now. How about you, Laszlo?"

Laszlo bit his tongue and swallowed the bile rising in his throat.

"And while Laszlo gets us *all* a bite, Jules, would you mind doing my daughter next?"

Vandy's suggestion, soft voice and offer of food did the job of easing tensions enough to allow both men to retreat to their respective corners without losing face. While Jules went off to get fresh needles, Emylene took Laszlo aside.

"What's wrong with you besides you're a grumpy old man?

"I don't like him and I don't trust him," Laszlo replied.

"You don't like or trust anyone."

Emylene thought it ironic that Laszlo mistrusted practically everyone he'd met and yet his entire quest was bent on saving society.

"You and your mother will be all right if I go?" he asked sheepishly.

Emylene smiled and nodded. Reluctantly, Laszlo wrote down their orders, and even included something for Jules.

"Lock up after me," he said to Vandy as he strode to the front of the store. Before Laszlo could open it, one of the teenagers opened it for him. When the old man turned to say 'thanks', the kid gave him a wide, toothy grin, displaying two enlarged vampyric teeth. Startled, Laszlo backhanded the boy, sending the kid's fake teeth flying out of his mouth and onto the pavement.

"What'd you do that for, asshole? I was only playing."

"Play somewhere else—like in traffic!" barked Laszlo. "The Chinese got it right; one kid per family!"

The boy rubbed his jaw and picked up the set of false teeth while his buddies cackled over the incident. Vandy locked the front door as told and watched Laszlo lurch down the block.

"Ladies, we still got a ways to go here, so…," called Jules.

Laszlo should have been pleased with himself. Everything was working out as he planned. In his last conversation with Mira, she mentioned that Emylene would be welcomed back into the fold. The members of the Stipe family were still valuable figureheads, and now Laszlo could deliver two for one. This gave him a little extra leverage to use in his quest to get Mira back. Hell, he should have been ecstatic with the way things were shaping up. But he wasn't.

Wandering down the block, Laszlo recognized the restaurant where he brought Emylene for lunch that first day and decided to order his food from there.

While he waited for his sandwiches and coffees he thought back to the matronly waitress who had served them that day. When the manager brought his order in a large bag, Laszlo asked about her.

"Doris? Called in sick again. Who knows anymore."

"What do you mean?"

The manager opened the bag to make sure Laszlo's order was complete, and then rang in the sale.

"I dunno, people just don't seem right these days. Used to be you'd go to Other-Town for a good time…come back with maybe a small hangover, shake it off…"

Obviously preoccupied, the manager took out one of the sandwiches and started munching on it as he continued.

"…and get on with your life. Lately it's a hangover twenty-four seven, or people go a little cuckoo, or disappear altogether. Did you notice how friggin' bright the sun was this morning?"

"No, but I noticed you eating my food," remarked Laszlo.

The manager stopped in mid-chew as he realized what he was doing. Embarrassed, he put the sandwich off to the side, off-loaded an entire chocolate cake from a tray, and stuffed it into the bag to make up for his faux pas.

"Sorry about that. This hunger came over me so sudden-like…anyway the bill is $34.50. The cake is on the house."

Laszlo paid the manager and left the restaurant, scratching his head.

Back at the tattoo parlor, Jules was working his magic on Emylene who winced as the needle pierced the fleshy part of her upper chest. Her mother sat next to her, keeping her company.

"I still can't get over the coincidence that your friend Laszlo is my second cousin. Emylene, how long have you known this man?"

"A few days, I guess"

"You trust him?" asked Vandy?

"With my life," replied Emylene.

"Bit of an arrogant asshole if you ask me," added Jules.

Both women were suddenly reminded that Jules was listening in on their conversation.

"Well, nobody's asking you," shot back Emylene.

"Hey, don't blame us for asking. We're only looking out for you," he argued.

"What, all of a sudden you and my Mom are a team? And what's it to *you* anyway? Not that it's any of your business, but, Jesus, if you knew what that dude's been through...."

"Honey, everybody has a story that could break your heart," interrupted Vandy. "I just hope he's got your best interests..."

Vandy stopped in mid sentence. Something outside caught her attention.

"What?" asked Emylene.

"Do they look okay to you?" Vandy asked, nodding her head toward the boys standing outside by the window.

Jules and Emylene turned to the small troupe of kids that had been hanging out on the sidewalk all morning. Earlier, they had been cracking jokes and ogling the ladies, but now they stood silently watching the women through the glass window with looks of somber menace on their faces.

"Jules, is there a back room?"

"Yeah," replied Jules, a little spooked.

Emylene gestured for Jules to halt the procedure. She sat up and wiped her brow, then spoke with a voice loud enough to carry outside. "Man, those needles're killing me. Can we stop a minute?"

Slowly, casually, Jules put his needle down and all three moved away from the front window while the pack outside watched their every move.

Making his way back down the block from the restaurant, Laszlo kept playing the incident with the restaurant manager over and over in his head. He glanced at the sun thinking it wasn't any brighter or different than normal. What was the guy thinking? And what was up with him eating the sandwich? That's when he heard the sounds of a female whimpering across the street. A middle-aged woman was crouched in the shadow of a doorstep while a man tried to coax her into the sun. By the way she was shielding her eyes, it was apparent there was no way she was moving out of the shade. Laszlo continued down the block carrying his bags until he arrived at the tattoo parlor and immediately noticed three things: the teenage boys were gone, the girls and Jules were no longer in the picture window, and shards of broken glass lay strewn all over the stoop. Laszlo dropped everything and hurried to the front door to find a hole punched through the window next to the handle. He opened the door, and cautiously stepped inside. His heart told him to hurry, but his head told him to proceed with caution. Sussing out the situation didn't take him long. Ugly sounds were heard coming from down the hall toward the back, animalistic grunts and the pounding of fists against a door. Laszlo looked around for something to use as a weapon. On the table by the front window lay the abandoned tray of needles. He scooped them up in one hand and headed toward the ruckus. Treading as lightly as he could, he edged his way down the hall to find the five teenagers banging and kicking at a locked door. They sensed his presence and turned threateningly toward him, but these were no longer lazy teenage boys with fake teeth. They had fully transformed into the real thing, young Vrykolakas in their most feral and fierce state. Laszlo clenched his fist around the needles, and just as he was about to make his move the locked door suddenly opened, and out came Emylene charging the intruders with a long, jagged pole in her hands. She skewered the first revenant in the chest and he fell to the floor writhing in agony. Laszlo looked at the weapon sticking out of the dying corpse and realized it was actually a lamp stand. Resourceful girl! Jules appeared next wielding a pair of nunchucks, and attacked the nearest vampyre. These were the real deal, handled expertly by the tattoo artist. While the beast tried to dodge the sticks, Laszlo sneaked up behind it and drove the needles into its neck. It wasn't enough to take him down, but it distracted the demon for the moment. Meanwhile, the other three Vrykolakas side-stepped Emylene and charged into the room where Vandy was waiting by the window blind. As soon as they entered, she ripped the blind off the wall, allowing the sun's rays to fill the room and fry the skin right off their bones. The revenants stumbled back into the hallway looking like smoked sausages. Jules and Laszlo shoved, kicked and pushed all five creatures toward the back door where Emylene stood waiting. When they got close enough, she opened the door and herded the demons into the daylight before shutting it closed again. Screams of utter anguish followed until all that was left was silence. Only then did the humans take a breath.

"We've got to go now," said Laszlo.

"But Jules hasn't finished my tats," protested Emylene.

"They'll have to do, the world is coming apart."

"I got some bandages up front," offered Jules as he caught his breath.

Bedraggled and unnerved, the four made their way to the front of the shop where Jules sat the women down and tended to their superficial wounds and newly-tattooed skin.

"Keep those babies covered. Don't pick at 'em and don't get the area wet. If you see any signs of infection, spreading redness, drainage, or puss, see your local doctor and do you mind telling me what the hell just happened?"

Emylene looked at the others who nodded their okay. They owed Jules that much.

"You've been to Other-Town to party, right? Well, Other-Town has found a way to bring the party over here."

"Is that what these evil eyes are all about?"

"Kind of. They're like…protection. You know you're pretty good with those nunchucks."

"He makes a good nurse, too," added Vandy.

"Would you be interested in coming along?"

"Thanks, but I got a wife and baby. If this shit goes down like you're saying they're gonna need me. So number one, these tats are not near finished, and two, they need to be under wraps for twenty-four hours, right?"

"We don't *have* twenty-four hours," replied Laszlo.

"Then, basically, it's been good to know ya."

Emylene and Vandy put their shirts back on while Laszlo pulled out his cash.

"How much do I owe you?"

Jules looked around his shop. "Let's see, two hours on the tattoos, new glass for the door, new door, maybe some bars to go along with it…"

Laszlo peeled off 1,000 dollars from the wad of bills.

"Wow, thanks, man!" said Jules.

"That's not all," added Emylene.

"What, I owe him more?" replied Laszlo, a little annoyed.

"An apology."

Laszlo looked at Jules and reluctantly held out his hand for the artist to shake, then Laszlo looked at Emylene for confirmation.

"Are we good?"

"We're good. Thanks, Jules, go home to your family and don't leave them tonight."

CHAPTER 28

It was a glorious afternoon in the downtown area. The sun was at its zenith, pouring all its life-affirming energy into the world. Flowers in over-sized planter pots adorned the city streets that basked in the sun's nourishing rays, while bees and insects carried their pollen from pistil to stamen, fertilizing the local flora, and regenerating as they had done for centuries. Birds warbled their rich sonorous tunes, filling the air with song. It was a picture-perfect day except for the people retching on the sidewalks and cowering in doorways. The disease that was spawned in Other-Town had crossed over to the city proper. The world was still spinning, but it had tilted on a seriously radical angle.

Laszlo, Emylene and Vandy made their way cautiously along the sidewalks as unsavory-looking citizens gave them wary looks that, if were not overtly hostile, were certainly creepy. The three continued another block before Laszlo spotted a big box hardware store and entered.

"What are we doing here?" asked Emylene.

"Find a shopping cart, meet me in the wood section," replied Laszlo.

"Is he always this bossy?" asked Vandy.

Emylene and her mother spotted a stray shopping cart at

the end of the aisle and appropriated it. Then they jogged up and down the next two aisles, looking for Laszlo.

"Why do they make these places so big? You can get lost in here for a week. I liked the old neighborhood hardware stores, three aisles at the most. They didn't have everything you needed, but you were in and out in ten minutes," complained Vandy.

Frustrated, she spotted an employee wearing a large orange smock and called out.

"S'cuse me. Got wood?"

Vandy chuckled a little at her bawdy joke. Emylene grimaced with embarrassment. The pasty-faced, employee turned, and charged at Vandy, with a ravenous look in his eye. Startled, she managed to wedge the cart between her and the monster while Emylene frantically looked for a weapon. The employee growled demonically and pushed both Vandy and the cart up against one of the aisle shelves, effectively trapping her. He was so obsessed with sinking his gnarly teeth into her jugular that he didn't notice Emylene until she swung a five-gallon can of deluxe latex paint into the side of his head, knocking him off his feet. Vandy grabbed a nearby roll of electrician's tape and quickly wrapped up his hands and legs so that the demented employee was effectively hog-tied. Only then did the two women begin to breath again.

"Of course there *is* something to be said for having everything under one roof," panted Vandy as she and Emylene continued down the aisle with their cart.

They found Laszlo in Aisle 14 searching through the wood bins. As the two women careened down the aisle toward him he picked up a stick - a prime example of what he was looking for.

"Maple. Light but sturdy."

"Great, load up. We got trouble." Emylene replied as she and her mother stopped to gather the wood.

The trio tossed as many stakes into the cart as they could while the women filled Laszlo in on what took place back in Aisle Seven. They also picked up three hatchets and three tool belts before making their way to the counter. Laszlo handed a couple of 100-dollar bills to the check-out girl along with a little free advice.

"Keep the change, sweetheart and buy something nice for yourself, and take the rest of the day off."

Then the trio pushed the cart out into the parking lot and made their way down the sidewalk, avoiding dubious looks and stares from people they passed. Vandy was beginning to feel the itch from her new tattoos.

"Mom, don't scratch. Remember what Jules said," ordered Emylene.

"He also said these things needed twenty-four hours to heal. What if they don't have the power to fend off demons? I just got you back. I'm not going to lose you again."

"With what's going on around us we can't afford to wait even one more day," interrupted Laszlo.

"And how are we three going to take on Other-Town all by ourselves?" asked Vandy.

"Mira, she's the key," replied Emylene. "It's like killing the queen bee and the hive dies, right, Laszlo?"

Laszlo didn't acknowledge Emylene as quickly as she'd liked, which perturbed her. Maybe he was focused on some other aspect of the mission. Or maybe her assumption wasn't correct. He was obviously determined, but determined to do what, exactly? Before she could voice her concern, a familiar, exotic, music came wafting through the air. Other-Town was calling, but this time it was calling in the middle of the afternoon. Unusual.

Laszlo had the two women wait outside a grocery store while he hurried in. Crowds of people were heading westward in droves, in zombie-like fashion. Emylene wanted to warn them, but could tell by the vacant look in their eyes that no one was going to listen. In fact, when Emylene tried to stop one woman, she turned and growled like a rabid dog. Vandy pulled her daughter back, and the two kept to themselves. A moment later, Laszlo emerged from the store with a bag of garlic and a bag of apples.

"I get the garlic, but what are the apples for?" asked Emylene.

"To eat. Let's go. We have much to do."

All three bit into the apples and laughed. They needed both. As juice dribbled down Emylene's chin, she felt it was time to ask Laszlo the question that had been on her mind ever since they met.

"You've been very generous, Laszlo, but can I ask where you got all the money? I mean it's not like you have a regular job or anything."

Laszlo considered his response before answering.

"In the beginning, Other-Town was growing block by block. You could wake up one morning, walk out of your house, and find the other side of your street abandoned, dead. Nothing could stop it. To save themselves, people had to leave their homes and businesses, sometimes in a hurry, so..."

Emylene's back stiffened.

"That's called looting!"

"It's called survival, little girl."

"Maybe that's why you're not..."

"Maybe that's why I'm not what?" asked Laszlo. "Going to be reunited with my ancestors when this is over? I'm not worthy?"

"Not for me to say," was all Emylene replied.

An awkward silence hung over the three as they made their way to their next stop—an army surplus store where they bought two great-coats like Laszlo's, courtesy of Vandy this time. Fifteen minutes later, the trio returned to the hotel with their purchases. As usual, Michael was at his desk, by his computer. When he saw Emylene, he picked up his head and smiled.

"So… you said we'd get together?"

"Tonight's not a good night, Michael. But another time, for sure."

"Yeah, yeah," he snorted before he turned back to his computer. This wasn't the first time he'd been turned down and it wouldn't be the last. Emylene wanted to warn him, but she was being urged to move along by the other two. Still...

"Look, Michael, don't ask me why, but don't go out tonight, okay? Stay home, catch a flick or something."

"You know what, sweetheart, I got a life, too." he snapped.

She smiled sadly, and reluctantly followed the other two upstairs.

Ensconced in their room, Laszlo and Emylene laid the wood stakes on the bed and started chopping the ends into fine points with their hatchets. They passed them to Vandy who carried armfuls at a time to the bathtub and dumped them in. Then, as instructed, she cut the garlic bulbs in half and began rubbing the juice all over the pointy ends. When they were done, the three of them strapped on their tool belts and fitted the stakes into the slots where the tools would normally go. Laszlo had been closed-mouthed most of the time, except when barking orders. Finally, after stewing long enough, he blurted out, "I took what I had to, to survive, okay, to prepare for all this. Maybe I won't be Citizen of the Year, but what we are doing here tonight might get some of those people's homes back one day, so if I borrowed a few things to pay for our little adventure, you can call it stealing if you want. And if my ancestors want to punish me for that, so be it!"

Emylene knew that Laszlo could be grumpy and outspoken, but he was the only man ready to stand up to Other-Town.

"I just want you to know, Laszlo, I think you're the bravest man I've ever met," she replied.

Laszlo nodded his appreciation. The women also knew that sacrifices needed to be made for the greater good, and made no further comment.

"So, to business. When we cross into Other-Town tonight, they will know it, and they will pick their time to attack. Be clear in your mind, there will be blood, hopefully not ours. When you come up against one of them, you use the blunt end of the hatchet and drive the stake into their hearts like so."

Laszlo took a stick and pointed it into the bed.

"It has to be driven through flesh, bone and muscle. Not as easy as it looks in the movies."

To demonstrate, he hammered the blunt end of the hatchet against the fat end of the stake several times.

"That's one dead mattress," quipped Vandy.

All three allowed themselves a laugh, which was enough to soothe the ill feelings that had built up over the past short while. They put their greatcoats on over their work belts and checked themselves out in the mirror—three rag-tag, misbegotten saviors of the world.

It was 8 PM when they set out from the hotel. They weren't sure what to expect outside, anything from a brawl to complete chaos. Michael was not at his post in the lobby. Emylene hoped that he'd taken her advice and hunkered down somewhere. The three stepped outside and joined the crowds surging westward toward the new Mecca, Other-Town.

There was a palpable mix of danger and excitement in the air as if people were on their way to a Sex Pistols reunion or a mixed martial arts event. Random fights between one person or another would break out for no reason. The police could not be everywhere, and did their best to control the packs of feral youths who roamed the back alleys, stalking anyone foolish enough to be out on their own. Amid the whoops and hollers of the torqued-up masses were ever-growing pleas for help and cries for mercy. It was a night about to explode. Laszlo, Emylene and Vandy stuck close together to avoid any confrontations. Getting caught in a fracas now could easily foil their plans before they could be initiated.

Emylene's mind was abuzz with worry; if they managed to kill Mira tonight, would that actually put an end to this madness? Taking out the leader was a classic military move, but there was no guarantee that her followers would fold. And, if Emylene's course of action wasn't murky enough, there was the issue of her father to deal with. What if she *did* manage to find him in all this bedlam and he had been turned, as everyone believed, what would she do? Did she have the cajones to hammer a wooden stake through her own father's heart? It was a dilemma of Greek tragedian proportions.

One thing was for sure, Emylene was not prepared to leave the question of Theo's fate unanswered. She glanced at her comrades who marched silently but determinedly alongside her. Laszlo was a good man, but when the time came, could he be trusted to slay his wife for the greater good? And what about Vandy, the person for whom Emylene was most afraid? She was a mother first and foremost, certainly not warrior material. True, she may have managed to hold her own in the skirmish earlier today, but tonight promised to be a full-out, knock-down, do or die battle. The question in Emylene's mind was, *would her mother survive?* For that matter, would any of them? The only thing she knew for certain was that in the next twelve hours everything would change.

The trio reached the point where the new demarcation line lay. In the space of the last few days Other-Town had grown by a full city block. The familiar crimson tendrils that undulated so seductively in the past seemed to be in a hyperactive state tonight, stretching greedily out to seize the rest of the world. Laszlo reached into his pocket and handed Emylene a slip of paper.

"What's this?" she queried.

"You left me an I.O.U. the other day for some money you borrowed. Here," he offered.

Emylene opened the slip and read what he wrote, 'I.O.U. everything'. She smiled and put the scrap in her breast pocket over her heart. Laszlo stomped on one of the tendrils with his boot, and a gooey red liquid spurted out like blood gushing from a severed artery.

"Now we kick some ass," he said to her.

Across the street, intoxicating music blared and strobe lights beckoned. The carnival of carnivores was beckoning. Emylene and Vandy checked their belts, making sure their weapons were in place. Laszlo pointed the way.

"She'll be at Pall Bearer's Paradise. Do not become distracted and do not split up."

"Wait," said Emylene. "You asked me once, if when I was in that other place, I ever met your family. The Cowled Men made me swear I would never reveal what I knew, but you're more important to me than they are. They are there, Laszlo. They don't blame you for what happened when you brought Mira to their village all those years ago. They have been watching you and they are proud of you."

"Thank you, *babika*," was all Laszlo said.

With that, all three stepped onto the nasty little tendrils and crossed into the zone. The atmosphere was as ripe as the last night of Mardi Gras, making it more difficult than ever to stick together through the teeming, drunken masses. As the trio weaved its way through the crowd, they recognized a few familiar faces. There was the matronly waitress from the restaurant sitting at a café laughing like a hyena as three waiters fell over themselves trying to serve her. Ronald was there all dolled up in a slinky black number, escorting two truck drivers into a beer hall. He caught Emylene's eye and threw her an over-the-shoulder kiss. Further down the street, Emylene noticed Michael entering a flophouse with three teenage girls dressed in Catholic school uniforms. Poor Michael, she thought. Dark visages stared malevolently down at them from second story windows—scouts, no doubt, reporting on the advances of the intruders dressed in greatcoats. Emylene peered into the face of each person she passed, searching for a familiar set of eyes. And then, she heard his voice behind her.

"Emylene?"

Emylene turned to see a figure in a doorway dressed from head to toe in black. It was the image of the man she grew up with, someone she'd loved all her life.

"Daddy?"

Vandy held her daughter back protectively.

"Wait, Em'."

Theo Stipe walked out from the shadowy entrance of the store to meet his wife and daughter. Laszlo braced himself as Theo approached, ready for anything.

"They said you were dead," remarked Theo in a flat, lifeless tone to his daughter.

"I'm not, Daddy. Are you?"

Theo took a step closer. Emylene wanted to reach out and hug her father. Even if he *was* one of the undead she believed he would never harm her. Vandy, on the other hand, wasn't as confident and stepped between them.

"Theo," she said.

Theo nodded perfunctorily to Vandy, but responded to his daughter.

"After you burned in that fire, I had to make a choice."

Emylene started to tear up. Theo used to be the mediator between the two women, often taking his daughter's side. Now Vandy was protecting Emylene against her father or this 'thing' her father had become. The world had flipped over onto its head, and Emylene needed to deal with the fact that Theo was truly lost to her.

"If my father were here now, I would tell him that I don't blame him, but I would also tell him Mira totally lied."

"And perhaps he would answer that, when he lost his daughter he lost part of himself, and the part that was left could not go on." The anger welling up deep within Emylene grew until she was unable to hold back any longer.

"I hate that bitch for what she did! She stole my family from me and turned you into a monster and the next time I see her…"

Laszlo put a comforting arm around Emylene and whispered, "Save it, child. Save it."

Then he looked Theo in the eye.

"You know who I am, demon? Take us to her."

Theo's back stiffened and his lip curled.

"I don't think so."

Laszlo clenched his fists. But all four knew that an altercation out here in the open would benefit no one.

"It's alright. We don't need him," said Vandy.

She pulled a stake out from inside her coat and pointed it in Theo's face.

"You follow us or try to harm my daughter, I will plunge this so deep into your skull you'll see eternity through the other side."

Vandy pointed the end of the stake at Theo as she led her daughter away. He did not make a move against her, but when Emylene passed her father, he discreetly brushed his warm hand against hers, and it reviled her.

"I know that trick, revenant!" she said with disgust.

Laszlo and Vandy waited for Emylene to catch up.

"You did good, ladies," said Laszlo, as all three continued down the street.

"It was easy, that wasn't my husband," she answered. It was not so easy for Emylene.

They continued through the once-familiar neighborhood, dodging partygoers, and ignoring stares from un-friendlies, until they came to the alley that led to Pall Bearer's Paradise.

"Obviously we have blown the element of surprise. So what's the plan?" Emylene asked Laszlo.

"When we get inside, I will tell Mira I came to join her. I will separate her from the others and use her as a hostage to get us all out safely."

"And then?"

"And then I'll put her to rest."

Emylene and Vandy were not convinced this plan would work. Nor were they convinced Laszlo would be true to his word when the moment came. But, since no one had a better plan, they continued down the alley to the entrance of the club. Emylene was right about one thing: their presence was no surprise. Revenants were waiting at every juncture. When the trio arrived at the bronze door of Pall Bearer's Paradise, Emylene led the way. Upon her entrance every head turned to acknowledge her, and every revenant bowed at her passing, as if their banished princess had returned to her throne. Some faces looked familiar, others looked strange and others looked stranger than strange. They stood at the bar or huddled at tables—these pseudo-beings, discussing all things serious and trivial. Looking around, Vandy recognized the mayor who sat across from two lovelies. On the table between them were a half dozen shooter glasses of absinthe and two other silver chalices filled with a dark crimson liquid. Two different drinks, two different societies, one disastrous vision of the future. Vandy and Emylene paused to listen in on the Mayor as he bragged to the exotic-looking femmes.

"You know, I saw Frank Sinatra perform in Vegas once. It was at Caesar's Palace way before your time. He was older then and didn't have the voice he had in his youth, but he commanded an audience like no one else. I remember sitting there with a few buddies. The opening act, some comedian, had just left the stage and everyone was hyped for the main event. Then, without an introduction, without a word, *he* walked onto the stage. The room went as silent a tomb. Coulda heard the proverbial pin drop. Then the band struck up, he opened his mouth to sing, and... magic! But it was later that night that really stuck with me. After the show he would hang out in the lounge with his friends and have a drink. Loved to be out there in the open with the people. I remember seeing him sitting no further than twenty feet way. The lounge was about five or six steps higher than the main floor, and there were two bodyguards on either side of his entourage to make sure nobody messed with him. But from where he was he could see the whole room, and the whole room could see him. That was power, man, that was magnificence!"

Vandy nudged her daughter, making her aware of the two burly men guarding the mayor as he held court. Every once in a while the two vamps would laugh and the mayor would gaze out into the club to make sure everyone was watching him, admiring him.

"Welcome, Princess."

A large male stood before Emylene, someone she had

never seen before. And then, out from behind him, without warning, stepped Mira.

"You should be proud, Emylene. Everything you see here began with you," she said.

"And got twisted into something heinous by you."

"I only took it to its natural conclusion."

Emylene flashed back to the first time she'd met the girl, how shy and child-like Mira seemed then. Now Emylene saw her for what she was, a lethal, heartless Vrykolakas.

"Natural? In your dreams—if you have any, poseur."

"Careful, Emylene. In this place we are the norm and you are the freak," she replied.

Laszlo tensed, afraid that hostilities would come to a boil before he could initiate his plan. In a confrontation he and the two women would have no chance here, no matter how many weapons and tattoos they had. He stepped in between the two rivals.

"Which is why we've come, Mira. When you and I spoke last, we talked about how we could all get along."

"You two spoke before? As in, behind our backs? As in, betrayed?" Emylene fumed.

Laszlo ignored Emylene and continued his conversation with Mira.

"Perhaps there's a more private place we can talk."

"I was thinking the same thing, husband," she replied demurely.

Mira turned to lead the group toward the back, but

Laszlo gestured for his companions to stay where they were. He knew that the deeper they moved into the club the more dangerous it would be.

"I was thinking outside where the air is a little more..."

"'S'cuse me? Can I make a suggestion?" Vandy interjected.

She moved to the bar and placed her hand on a sconce fastened to the wall.

"I know it's a hoary old cliché, but...."

She pressed a latch which triggered a hidden door that popped open. Laszlo hesitated to follow until Vandy assured him with a gesture that she knew where she was going, then led the group into a small chamber. This was the private office that Vandy and Theo had used when they ran the club. After all four entered, the door closed behind them.

"I never knew this room even existed," said Emylene.

"Well, it was *our* place before it was yours."

Emylene recognized the furniture that she had last seen in the basement of her home—the crimson curtains, the antique war axes that hung on the wall, the intricately wood-carved chairs and the grand oak table that was the focal point of the room. She ran her slender fingers across the table she had known all her life. Like the chairs, it bore similar carvings, except these were inlaid on the face of the table instead of on the edges, and resembled a topographic map of some kind. When Emylene was a tot, she would amuse herself by making up stories of the people who dwelled in these faraway places. Seeing these heirlooms here, it was apparent that her parents never abandoned the faith, just went underground with it. For a moment it gave her a warm, nostalgic feeling—until she noticed the large window that looked out onto the club, a window whose opposite side was the glass mirror that hung behind the shelves of liquor, a window that concealed the fact that anyone inside could see the comings and goings of those outside without their knowledge.

"You were here every night spying on me?" exclaimed Emylene.

"Let's save this for another time, shall we dear?" her mother advised with a discreet nod to Mira.

Emylene reigned in her anger, realizing that her mother might have a point. They would have their argument another time, if they managed to live through the next few hours. In fact an argument of that intensity and proportion almost promised to be worth the effort. In any case, before she could satisfy her righteous indignation, she'd have to deal with Mira who was standing at the far end of the table wearing a particularly smug grin. Why? And then she saw it. Emylene followed the contemptuous eyes of her nemesis to the object that lay at her fingertips—a black Bacarra rose.

"What's *that* doing there?" she demanded.

"Sit and all will be revealed," commanded Mira.

On-guard, Emylene remained where she was until Mira took her seat first.

"Sit," she repeated.

Only then did Emylene take her own seat on the opposite end, ever cognizant of the blood-red flower. Aware of the distress in her daughter's eyes, Vandy took her place next to Emylene while Laszlo took his closer to Mira. After everyone was settled, Mira spoke.

"Those stakes beneath your coat must be uncomfortable. To tell the truth, they are to me, as well, especially as I'm so outnumbered."

"I'm not giving them up," snapped Emylene.

"That's not what I had in mind," replied Mira.

Sensing treachery, Laszlo stood up to defend himself, but it was too late. The drapes rustled behind them and an ancient evil materialized. Mira smiled as the concealed figure made himself known. If Emylene was bewildered at seeing the rose, it couldn't compare to the astonishment over what her eyes now beheld.

"Stelio!"

This couldn't be! Mira killed him almost two years ago and yet, here he stood before her, alive! And they looked to be friends, more than friends. So Stelio's death was a ruse! There could only be one explanation; Mira had bewitched him the same way she did her father. The bitch would stop at nothing until she had it all: Emylene's position, her parents, even her lover! Emylene's blood boiled with a rage beyond anything she'd ever felt. She wanted to fling herself at Mira to avenge this pernicious betrayal, but to her surprise, Laszlo made the first move, armed with two stakes at the ready.

"Defiler!"

He ran, not at Mira, but at Stelio who side-stepped him and took the stakes out of his hands with a super-human speed. Emylene was at a loss as to what was going on. The only thing that was obvious to her was that these two men had a history.

"Who the hell are you?" Vandy demanded.

"My name is Stelio Ysplantis," answered the revenant in a rich, sonorous tone.

The way Mira beamed at him now made it all too clear. He wasn't bewitched by her; it was the other way around! And then it dawned on Emylene. She knew Stelio as the Greek haberdasher from Queen Street who swept her off her feet. But recalling Laszlo's sordid tale from the past, it was clear that he was also the same demon who stole his bride over forty years ago!

"I am sorry for the subterfuge," he continued, "but I needed to wait for certain elements to align themselves before I could reveal myself to you. I know what thoughts lie in the hearts of each of you, but before you judge me...Emylene, as a child you used to play at this table, making up stories about distant lands. Let it speak to you now. Let it reveal its truth, after which the outcome of this meeting may be greatly changed from what you expected."

No one trusted Stelio, but no one saw an opportunity to overpower him either. He continued,

"I promise you that when you place your hands on the table, the mystery will be unveiled before your eyes. And I promise you no one will be harmed. If I wanted you dead, I would have seen to it already."

Laszlo, Vandy and Emylene had no choice but to take their seats at the great table, hoping that an opportunity might arise for them to make a move. For now, Stelio was in control. Emylene put her hands on the table first. Then Vandy, Laszlo and finally, Mira. When the master vampyre placed his hands likewise, the delicate carvings embedded in the surface came to life. At first they undulated, and then grew into a three-dimensional world, transporting each person by virtue of their contact. In this way, they experienced Stelio's tale as if they were there in person.

CHAPTER 29

The master vampyre's voice echoed with a resonance, depth and weight of a life that spanned over 200 years.

"I was born Stelio Ysplantis in 1793, second son of Prince Constantine of Romania. I grew up to be a distinguished soldier in the Russian army before retiring to Mykonos, Greece when I was in my thirties. In those days Mykonos was a small island paradise with a sparse, hard-working community who sustained themselves with the meager crops they grew on land, and with whatever fish they caught from the sea. The island was a welcome change for me after the rigorous demands of military life. The constant sun and gentle climate provided a respite where a soul might fall into a slower and more natural daily rhythm, and brought with it an appreciation of simple pleasures. Our only nagging problem was the pirates who attacked the seaside village of Chora every few months. They looted, killed and raped at will, and we were helpless to stop them. Because Mykonos was so poor and could raise no money for defense, I proposed an idea to the town council to protect us: we would rebuild the streets of Chora in a series of meandering laneways that would confuse and confound anyone who was unfamiliar with them.

It took months to accomplish, but the next time the pirates attacked, we were ready. I instructed the villagers to meet the marauders on the beach and then retreat, leading them down the blind alleys that we'd built adjacent to our homes. I watched from the rooftop and knew exactly when and where to ambush them with the garrison of townsfolk I trained. As we slaughtered them, their screams filled the air like music. The sounds of their massacre rose and fell like a symphony, but the real beauty of my plan was that their comrades could hear each and every cry and do nothing about it. When victory was ours, we allowed a few to escape so that they could spread the word that Mykonos was no longer a place to trifle with.

"They called me a hero after that, and gave me a pension on a large plot of land. I loved that island and even tried my hand at farming, but the parched soil was unsuitable for planting. The surrounding waters, however, provided a healthy bounty, so I suggested that we expand our fishing industry by building ships and exporting our catch to neighboring towns along the Mediterranean coast. The idea was a sound one, and by the following year the island began to prosper. Finally, I had time to turn my mind to the more important matters of the heart. Helena, the mayor's daughter, caught my eye when I first arrived on the island. With my success and rise in society I felt confident enough to introduce myself to this beauty. I courted her slowly and leisurely, as was the custom in Mykonos, and soon we fell in love. Unfortunately, our story was not to have a happy ending.

"You see, I was born a Romanian, not a Greek, and because of that, Helena and I were not allowed to marry. I also suspected there was more than a little jealousy on the part of her father who saw me as a rival for his office. She and I remained stubbornly in love, and the mayor began to look for ways to discredit me. Rumors spread about my employing black magic to defeat our enemies and enabling the island to flourish. With those seeds sewn it was not much of a leap to suggest that I also put a spell on Helena to make her fall in love with me. The Greeks are a very superstitious people and, although there was no evidence, the mayor was all-powerful. I was branded a sorcerer and sentenced to be hanged.

"Upon my imprisonment, Helena sought out the only woman she knew who could save me, and together, they hatched a scheme. This woman lived as an outcast in the nearby hills. With her knowledge of the land, she prepared a potion from herbs and medicines concocted from the local vegetation. Helena's plan was to offer my jailors a drink when visiting me one last time, and after they fell asleep, she would free me so we could leave the island forever. But her plan was foiled when one of the suspicious guards only pretended to drink. In a fit of rage the mayor accused his own daughter of treason. They tortured her until she confessed her scheme and then, convinced that she was bewitched, hanged her. Can you imagine my torment knowing my love died trying to save me and there was nothing I could do about it? There, in my jail cell, I swore to avenge Helena's murder by killing her father and every city official who sanctioned this travesty. Fearing more sorcery, they moved up my execution date, and the next day, my death sentence was carried out. Yes, they hung me that morning, but I was resurrected that same night. How, you ask? The woman who aided Helena revived me with another of her potions. Apparently the woman, too, was a victim of the superstitious townspeople. After being branded a witch many years prior, she was excommunicated from the church and sent to live alone in the foothills, a pariah. As it turned out, the villagers had good reason to be superstitious. The woman really was a witch! After she heard about Helena's murder at her own father's hand, the woman was more than happy to help me exact my revenge upon those unjust devils.

"I put my plan into action on the second night of my resurrection. The mayor lived in a large apartment at the top of a hill overlooking the meandering lanes by the harbor, the same lanes I had built to save his precious town. I waited until the candles were doused in his room that night and he went to sleep. All the doors in the house were bolted, and there were no windows on the ground floor where I could enter. I was stymied until I noticed the thick green vines that grew upon trellises, a popular garden affectation of the day. The trellis nailed to the wall was made from the sturdy wood of the olive tree, making it an ideal ladder. With my many years of military training it was not difficult to climb the framework all the way up to the second floor. As I took my first steps, I felt almost weightless. Curious, I thought. The trellis ended several feet short of the second floor balcony, but I was more than determined. I reached out onto the brick and found purchase in the rough mortar. Again, my weight did not seem to be a factor and to my surprise I was able to scale the short distance using only my fingers and bare feet.

"The balcony door to the mayor's bedroom was open, probably the last place he expected an intruder to break in. I found him alone, snoring peacefully in his bed. I made no sound as I crept closer and stood over the murderer of my beloved. I was not sure how I should end his life exactly until that very moment. Then, it came to me. Silently, I climbed up upon his chest. In my weightless condition I realized I could sit there forever and he'd never even know it. At first I thought I would wait until he woke to find me astride him, and then stop his heart with fright. But to kill him in one easy stroke would neither satisfy my revenge nor make him understand why he needed to die. No, this was to be a just retribution. As I stared down at him my rage grew, and with it, my presence on his chest. He squirmed a little, feeling the weight of me on top of him. I slowly bore down until he finally awoke to find me there.

"'Detestable spirit!' he shouted, 'Be gone!'

"'Detestable spirit'? He had no idea how right he was. He closed his eyes and tried to wish me away like a bad dream, but when he opened them again to see me there still, and I saw that he was cogent, I put my considerable heft to bear and began squeezing the air out of him slowly like a python smothering its prey. All the while, I spoke to him, recounting the good that I had done his town and how he repaid me by killing my love, his own daughter. Each time he fought to take a breath I squeezed a little tighter. If he shifted and tried to throw me off, I doubled my efforts. When he became so weak that he could barely gasp for air, I slit his wrists and made him watch the lifeblood drip from his veins, until finally he expired. With my duty done, I sat back to appreciate my work. That's when the female screamed! I turned to find a half-naked maiden frozen with fear in the doorway. She must have been one of the mayor's mistresses who had returned after leaving his bed to clean herself of the lout. I had no quarrel with her, so I just nodded in a gentlemanly way as I dismounted my victim and left the room the way I entered. I was about to climb back down the wall to leave, but the girl began to scream as though it was her I attacked, and her cries were threatening to bring the servants at any minute. From a new-found confidence deep within me I opened my arms and gave myself to the night. Miraculously, I floated to the ground, and upon landing, simply walked away. It was a wondrous feeling, this new power, and I reasoned that God must have taken pity on my plight and made me his angel.

"In the succeeding nights I visited each man on the town council who sanctioned Helena's murder, and killed him in the same manner. I rejoiced in the blood I drew. This became not just my purpose for a life reborn, but my sustenance, as well. I felt myself to be a righteous soul for having re-written such a horrendous wrong. When my work was done on Mykonos, I left the island to mete out justice to other black-hearted villains across the continent. Some called me an avenging angel, others called me 'Vrykolakas.' I suppose it depended on one's point of view. Nevertheless, over the years I became a legend, a myth, which became my greatest advantage because no one believed in myths. That is, until one night.

"It was in Istanbul, Turkey, years later where I had dispatched a particularly evil man, a rug salesman. Now, Istanbul was not the backwards fishing village Mykonos was. There were men in this city who believed in my kind, and determined to hunt me down. I will not tell you how they overcame and restrained me, but for the first time in my second life I was helpless. I was subdued and locked in a special coffin, inscribed with all manner of talismans to prevent me from escaping. Then they packed me onto a steamer headed for an island, a place where they took their superstitions equally serious. Upon arrival I was to be slain, and my body parts severed. They would be buried so that there was no chance of another resurrection. During my incarceration I came to accept this, partially because there was no joy in what I did anymore. Revenge was no longer a sweet dessert, nor did it hold any personal satisfaction. The love of my life had died years ago, and there was no way of getting her back. I tell you, without love… it was a four-day sail from Istanbul to the destination of my execution place, Santorini. Lying inside that coffin in the cargo hold with nothing to do or see, I made peace with myself and even forgave those who betrayed me over those past two centuries. That done, I became restless and attuned my mind to the goings-on of the people above, for my faculties had grown immeasurably keener now than ever before.

"A wedding was to take place between two crew members. My hearing, as acute as it was, allowed me to listen in on the happy couple and share in their merriment as the day grew close. I knew their names, where they came from, and the dreams they'd pursue upon becoming a married couple. The years fell away as I recalled the loving moments with my own Helena, and I began to look forward to their upcoming nuptials as if they were my own.

"Finally the big day came. The celebratory noises on the top deck filtered all the way down to the hold. I listened intently to the captain as he conducted the marriage ceremony and heard the young bride make her vows to her new husband. The service ended with a kiss and the joyous celebration of all those in attendance—music to my ears! Then the happy couple retreated to their cabin and made preparations to disembark onto the same island that I was to be executed. The box in which I was imprisoned was put onto a skiff along with other supplies, and lowered into the water. The newlyweds boarded shortly after. I don't think they had any idea I was next to them, hidden among so many other containers. But I was aware of them, especially of her. In fact I was so close that I could smell her perfume—a cheap blend unworthy of her. I thought, if she were mine…and at that moment I found my reason to live! By the time we reached land fifteen minutes later I had made my plan. Upon docking, the passengers disembarked first, the supplies next, and I at the end. Listening very closely to what was going on, I felt my coffin being handed off to three island locals who placed it onto a donkey cart. For the next two hours we traveled along sequestered paths to the far side of the island. Though still, I was far from idle. I was busy learning about these men as they talked; their names, and what they did for a living. It was mid afternoon when we finally stopped. I felt my coffin being lifted from the cart and lain on the ground. They would not to wait until nightfall to execute me; they would do it now, because they knew that the Vrykolakas would be at its weakest during the daylight hours. The talismans were removed, the lock was unlatched, and the lid was opened. Staring up, I saw the three men standing over me armed with all manner of weapons.

But they saw nothing! They looked into an empty box and I simply rose and walked away. How, you ask? Living hundreds of years affords one the time to enhance certain aspects of the mind, one of them being thought manipulation, glammouring, they call it these days. I am doing that with each of you as we speak. As for the sun's effects, yes, they are lethal, but the longer the Vrykolakas exists, the more tolerance he builds up against it. Suffice it to say, I was free once again.

"Later that evening I followed the bride and groom from a distance. I no longer needed to have either of them in sight, for I had attuned myself to Mira with a kind of extra sense that I'd developed over time. Ah, the mind is capable of such remarkable things, is it not? I followed them easily, and when I learned that they would be dining at a nearby restaurant that evening, I decided to join them. Hurrying ahead I introduced myself to the owner of the establishment first who graciously allowed me to take over the duties of his dining room, after he'd suddenly grown ill. The bride and groom arrived moments later, as expected, and upon seeing Mira for the first time, my mind was made up, exquisite! Laszlo may have been a good enough man, but he could never give her what I had to offer. And, I would have gladly taken the time to make him understand that, but he never gave me the chance. As soon as he laid eyes on me he was overcome with an irrational fury. After an awkward altercation I could see that there was no use in trying to reason with the madman, so Mira and I were forced to take our leave.

"Later, when I bestowed my eternal gift on Mira, she begged me to teach her the ways of the Vrykolakas. That night, we consummated our love. And, like an honorable man, I sent her to bid her husband goodbye. Alas, my generosity was my undoing. Two old Greeks convinced the misguided bridegroom that he still had rights over my woman, and the cowards then used her to track me down. When they arrived at my lair, I challenged all three of them to settle the matter like gentlemen. Standing here as we are now, I believe the outcome of that confrontation speaks for itself."

With this pause in Stelio's story, the great table became still. Emylene withdrew her hands and turned accusingly to Laszlo. Up until now both he and Stelio's versions of the story were pretty much in sync. But at this juncture they differed drastically, especially where Laszlo claimed that Stelio had been slain.

"Laszlo, you told me that you, Anatoly and Kostas killed the Vrykolakas," accused Emylene, "And that you helped."

"I thought, I hoped," came the reply with equal dollops of doubt, regret and guilt.

"What do you mean, you weren't sure? You told me you were there on your knees by the Necromanteion. You chopped off his hands and then your friends tied ropes around his neck and severed his head with an axe. That's what you told me."

Stelio emitted a hoarse laugh at which point Laszlo bowed his head, a silent confession to an ugly truth he had long held secret.

"I mean, I don't know what happened exactly," replied Laszlo, his face awash in shame.

"Because he ran!" roared Stelio. "It is true that the two Greeks managed to tie ropes about my neck, but where was the third man? Where was the bride groom?"

"I thought it was over," he mewed. "I cut Mira from her bindings and we fled."

"You deserted your friends?" Emylene sputtered.

Using his hands in grand gestures, Stelio filled in the missing scene.

"As I said the Greeks had me by two ropes, but my hands were free. Your Laszlo had already stolen away with my bride. Before the other two could secure their ropes around the nearby trees and finish me off, I pulled them to me, one wrist-turn at a time, until I dragged them both down into the underground cavern from where I attacked. They were brave men, those two, and to celebrate their heroism, I ate their hearts."

Emylene stared daggers at Laszlo as she recalled the lie he told her that day in the restaurant. She also remembered his sudden rage when she doubted that his wife had become the victim of a vampyre. Now she realized that what he was really angry about was the guilt over having run out on his two comrades. With no more explanation or apology from Laszlo, Stelio resumed his story.

"Please," he gestured to Emylene who complied by placing her hands back on the table.

"After that, I pursued the fleeing couple across Santorini but they had already boarded the skiff and returned to the steamer. I, of course, had no choice but to follow. Over the course of the next few days on the ship, I taught my bride how to nourish herself back to health. How she took to my instruction! Laszlo had no idea I was even there. The dullard thought that he was her savior. I could have laid waste the entire ship, but I had no quarrel with the crew, so we took just enough sustenance to keep us alive. Truth be told, Mira was in no shape to fend off undesirables if we were discovered, even with my help. Besides, I was curious to see what Laszlo planned next. He was proving to be quite the entertainment.

"Once the ship landed at Dubrovnik, Laszlo lit out and, to his credit, travelled by day, making it difficult for me to track them. But I knew where they were headed, having learned their history in the preceding days. Besides, Mira's scent was a part of me now, impossible to lose. I found them in the backwater village of Laszlo's youth and, I confess, I almost felt sympathy for the boy as he stood in front of his town elders pleading for a remedy to his wife's ailment. I was not surprised when these bumpkins decreed that she should be put to death. Indeed, their sentence seemed like the answer to my prayers. Their attempted execution would afford me my opportunity to effect her escape. I would wait for just the right moment and then my bride and I would leave together as easily as two wisps of fog melting into the night air.

"But, again, I underestimated my rival when his family spirited Mira off to that desolate farm of theirs in the country. What could he be planning this time, I wondered?

"Unfortunately, my hesitation was my undoing, for I waited too long to prevent a kind of deviltry that even I hadn't come across in all my years.

"There I stood, several yards back in the forest, bemused as I watched one of Laszlo's family draw a charcoal sketch and his aunt invoke the aid of her ancient ancestors. Magically, these strange men dressed in cowls marched out from the woods. Before I could react they encircled Mira in a protective formation from which she could not escape, and I could not penetrate. Then, the aunt spoke words that were foreign to me, and, in a flash, the entourage disappeared from one astral plane and re-appeared in another—the drawing! My poor Mira stared out at me, terrified while the ancient ones forced her back along the crooked fence and beyond my sight. Imagine my astonishment! Joy within my grasp one moment, calamity the next. I punished myself severely for that miss-step, I can assure you.

"After the awful deed was done and the gathering broke up, I followed the aunt home, in order to wring a remedy out of her. Stubborn woman she was, stubborn to the death! Believe me, before I left that village, as much as I punished myself, I punished the aunt even more.

"After that, I had no choice but to follow Laszlo to America in hopes that one day I would learn how to free Mira from her diabolical incarceration. When he opened his shop, I opened my own down the street. Years passed, but I never gave up hope. I suspected Laszlo was aware of my presence. I assumed he must have decided to keep Mira imprisoned until he was sure I had either gone or given up. I thought about torturing him for the key to Mira's freedom, but he was so witless that he would have died before giving it up. I confess I was stymied until I hit upon the idea of employing an accomplice. Yes, Emylene, a lonely, disaffected youth with more enthusiasm than intelligence. While she thought she was seducing the local haberdasher, I was filling her head with necromantic suggestion. Then, when the little princess was primed and ready, I sent her on her mission. Which brings us to the moment at hand."

Stelio ended his tale and the oak table returned to its rigid form. Emylene, Laszlo, Vandy and Mira stood in silence as they digested all that had been revealed. Stelio smiled with the satisfaction that his story had finally been told and everyone in the room now had a much better appreciation of him.

"Laszlo, I must say that you have been an unexpectedly formidable adversary, and you may think I brought you here tonight to exact my revenge. But instead I invite you, all of you, to join Mira and myself to be part of the future I have...."

Before Stelio could get into the specifics of his grand scheme Emylene interrupted him.

"The first night I brought Mira here, you said something."

Stelio smiled and recited his speech word for word.

"I look at you and I see the seed of something that could become a rare and magnificent flower. But to realize this you will need to have full control over your emotions, you will need to know what to do and when to do it without letting pride, remorse or misguided zeal get in your way."

Emylene felt sick to her stomach at the realization of what those words meant.

"You weren't saying that to me, were you? You were saying it to *her*."

Stelio replied in an almost apologetic manner.

"Emylene, don't be hard on yourself. I have had over 200 years to plumb the depths of the human psyche and learn how to bend it to my will. I can offer you the same…"

Laszlo began to laugh so hard that he had to back away from the table.

"You thought you made Emylene do what you wanted her to? You thought *you* gave her the power to release Mira through your 'necromantic suggestion'? You stupid vampyre! Emylene's father was born in Slovakia. His cousin and my aunt were one in the same—Daphna Stropnicki, the witch who banished Mira into the charcoal sketch! Emylene gets her powers from our family, not from you. There are things at work here, revenant, that are beyond your powers."

But Stelio's confidence was unflappable.

"My friend…"

"I am not your friend, nor your ally. I am your executioner!" shouted Laszlo.

"Shut up!" commanded Emylene.

It was another classic mistake by the old man, running off at the mouth, and Emylene had to bark at him good and proper to shut him up. Her mind began flashing from Laszlo to Stelio, to the tattoos, to the beads Laszlo used to protect her in the hotel room. And then something suddenly twigged in Emylene's mind.

"It was you the other night, wasn't it?"

"Confess, Emylene. It was your secret desire—to be with me, to be taken by me. I heard and came to you. That night was but a taste of what I can offer you."

Emylene did not answer. She was lost in the moment that overcame her that night in the hotel room, that exquisite torture. Stelio had her now and he knew it.

"You think I'm evil, Emylene, but tell me, what is the nature of evil? The people who judged you by what you wore as a child, are they evil? I was robbed of my love, Helena, and then of my life by her father who believed he was only trying to protect his daughter. Am I evil? Was he? Who is worse? Who should be vanquished and who should be rewarded? If what I did was born out of good intentions, and those good intentions led me to Mira, then how am I to blame? Perhaps fate itself is the culprit and I am simply its vessel. The truth is a perverse mistress, is it not? Once long ago, I conceived of a plan to save my city from pirates and corrupt politicians. I am trying to do the same thing now. I am not a villain. I am an architect, a builder of cities creating the paradise I conceived of centuries ago with all of you as its city fathers. So you see, Laszlo, you are wrong. Not only are we allies, but through Mira, we are family, bound by blood."

"Not my blood!" argued Emylene.

"Especially yours. Isn't that true, Theo?"

Up until now, Emylene's father had been a forgotten footnote in the melodrama that was currently unfolding. So when Emylene, Vandy and Laszlo heard his name spoken, they were justifiably surprised. But, that didn't compare to their bewilderment when he actually entered the room from a hidden door behind the curtains. Taking his place next to Stelio, Theo looked different than he did back in the street. His skin was still the pallor of the undead, but his eyes shone with an animated intensity that made him look like a hybrid of the two species.

"There, Theo. Did I not return your daughter and wife to you as promised?" asked Stelio with a look of self-satisfaction.

And that's when it came to Emylene that all the pieces of the puzzle assembled in this room were part of Stelio's grand design. He intended to establish Other-Town as his kingdom, and would rule from behind the scenes. To do that he would need others to act as figureheads, people to whom the masses could relate to on a daily basis. Who better than the Stipe family who were already considered royalty in this part of town? Looking around the room Emylene realized that Stelio's manipulations among those assembled was absolutely Machiavellian. Theo and Laszlo were emotionally tethered to Mira; Emylene had grown sympathetic to Laszlo, and even though Vandy left her husband long ago, their relationship still had currency. He didn't need to turn them to get their cooperation. These inter-dependent relationships would allow Stelio to exert his influence on any one of them by threatening the other whenever it suited him.

Laszlo was thinking something else entirely: that his original plan to offer Emylene for Mira was now off the table. It would be all he could do to escape with his life. If he was going to do something, it had to be now.

"Emylene, this is what you wanted. Go to your father," Stelio commanded.

"Emylene, do as you are told. Come to me," ordered Theo in the same flat tone he'd used earlier.

But Emylene detected something in the timber of his voice, a sense of urgency. And when she looked at him, she noticed a strain building around his eyes.

"No!" shouted Vandy, who put herself between the two.

"Your daughter came all this way, she sacrificed everything. Let her make her own decision," interjected Laszlo.

"Are you crazy?" shouted Vandy defiantly.

Vandy pulled out her hatchet, ready to defend Emylene against anyone who would touch her daughter. Tensions were about to boil over. The question was, would Emylene defy her mother and go to her father, or would she try to kill him to save her mother? Then, to everyone's surprise, Theo grabbed his crotch, doubled over and emitted a painful yelp.

"What the hell?" blurted Emylene as she watched her father drop to his knees in agony.

"Omigod! Do vampyres get kidney stones?" shouted Vandy.

Then it dawned on Vandy and the others in the room that Theo had not been turned, and she rushed to her husband's side.

While all eyes were on Vandy and Theo, Laszlo discreetly pulled a lighter from his pocket and lit the heavy drapes that hung on the wall behind him. Vrykolakas are impervious to most mortal traumas, but fire is as lethal to them as the sun. The flames ignited, surprising everyone. Emylene knew Laszlo had given her this moment and she wasn't going to fail him. While everyone tried to shield themselves from the fire, Emylene unsheathed a garlic-laden stake and attacked Stelio. A vampyre's response is much quicker than a human's, but with the distraction of fire and smoke in such close quarters, Stelio's evasive tactic was off by a hair. He crouched to avoid the fatal blow. In doing so, Emylene's stake found its mark just above his heart. Though wounded, he still had the strength and agility to grab Emylene by the throat. It wouldn't take long for the master vampyre to choke the life out of the twenty-year-old mortal. Emylene remembered the tattoos that were so painfully inscribed on her arms. She ripped off the bandages and pressed her arms into his flesh. Their power was not strong enough to do serious damage, but it was enough to cause Stelio to loosen his grip for a second, just long enough to enable Emylene to reach into her pocket.

From inside she pulled a string of beads and wrapped it around his neck twice, producing an excruciating pain. Mira screamed like a banshee upon seeing her master in distress. She bared her fangs and razor-like fingernails and lunged at Emylene, but Laszlo was ready for her.

"Forgive me," he cried.

Stepping in her path, he staked his wife with one swift thrust. Mira stared down at the weapon that protruded from her abdomen. Stelio was still clawing at the evil-eye beads when Vandy rushed to her daughter's aid and plunged the wooden stake deep into his chest. Still the Vrykolakas fought.

"Protect your master!" cried Stelio to Theo.

Grimacing with pain, Theo got to his feet and reached for one of the ancient decorative axes that hung on the wall. He raised the weapon over his head and swung—but not at either his wife or daughter. Stelio's head flew off his shoulders with one clean swipe, and his body dropped backward into the flaming drapes. Vandy looked at her husband with question marks in her eyes, but there was no time to respond to a single one of them. The room was quickly filling with smoke and the flames were already eating through the walls. Screams of panic from humans and vampyres alike were heard in the adjacent club, as both species tried to escape through the bottleneck by the front entrance. Theo led his wife and daughter out the secret door from which he had entered, and brought them all into a small passageway. When they had a moment to think, Vandy realized she was holding onto her husband's hand, his warm hand. She grabbed it at the wrist with her other and felt a pulse running through it. Laszlo shrugged and offered his wife the explanation.

"They needed someone to make deals with the outside world, someone who could manage in the daytime. They figured it was smarter not to turn me," he explained. "Sorry I couldn't tell you before."

With sweat and soot streaming down her face, Emylene hugged her father who was still suffering from his kidney stone attack.

"We need to get you to a hospital," said Vandy.

Any breathable air was quickly being smothered by the acrid smoke filling up the small hallway and making visibility near impossible. Holding his middle section, Theo led his family along a passageway to a set of stairs that led up to ground level and out to another alley—an entrance he and Vandy had built years ago to add a little mystery to their comings and goings. The trio emerged into the night air coughing and sputtering from the smoke, but glad to be alive. It was only when they turned back to see how narrowly they'd escaped, that Emylene exclaimed, "Laszlo? Where is Laszlo?"

Her mother answered: "I saw him put a stake in Mira. After that..."

"We can't leave him," Emylene implored.

"We can't go back in there," argued Vandy. "This place will be crawling with demons any second, and your father needs a doctor. We have to get back to the city now!"

Vandy was right. Stelio's execution was being felt on a psychic level by every revenant in the district, sending them all into a hellish rage. Instead of neutralizing and dispersing the ranks, his death only incited them. Ungodly shrieks and howls were heard from every basement and rooftop within a twelve block radius. Other-Town spit and fumed like a volcano erupting.

"Killing Stelio won't be enough!" cried Emylene. "We need to burn this place to the ground!"

Vandy shook her head, no. You could only tease death for so long in a place like this before it turned on you.

"There's no time. We have to save ourselves!"

But Theo stood by his daughter's decision.

"Emy', give me one of those stakes," he demanded.

Emylene pulled a stake from her tool belt while Theo yanked off his coat and wrapped it around the stick of wood. Vandy withdrew a lighter from her pocket and handed it to her husband. Theo ripped his coat into shreds with a knife and shouted, "Torch it!"

Daughter and the wife did as they were told, and then all three took off at a gallop, setting fire to as many storefronts as they could. Black-cloaked demons came charging out of the burning edifices like a plague of locusts, attacking every living thing in their path. Fire, smoke and chaos filled the streets, yet, through all of this, Emylene had other concerns.

"So, that secret room of yours, you spying on me?" she demanded as the family dodged attackers.

"We weren't spying," replied Vandy.

"Yes we were," confessed Theo. "We wanted you to have your freedom, Emylene, but we also wanted to be there in case you needed us."

"They have a name for that in the suburbs, you know; helicopter parents!"

"That's a horrible thing to say," replied Vandy, "as if we'd ever be caught dead in the suburbs!"

Before Emylene could reply, a vampyre sprang from behind a burning car and wrestled Theo to the ground. As the demon prepared to sink its teeth into Theo's throat, both Emylene and Vandy jumped on its back and pressed their tattooed arms into the demon's flesh. The revenant emitted a shriek as the tats seared its putrefied skin and then ignited its body, sending a plume of fire a dozen feet into the air. Emylene fell back choking on the sooty remnants. Vandy cradled Theo who lay there with his arm broken and twisted from the attack.

"Theo, are you okay?" asked Vandy.

"The bad news is I peed my pants, the good news is I think I passed the stone."

"You've also got a broken arm," she replied.

Emylene knew the flames would act like a beacon and bring more demons down on her family. They had to get out of there. She peered through the fog to get her bearings, but the smoke and screaming had turned the streets into a war zone. Which way to safety?

With chaos at every turn, there was no way to be sure which direction to go. They pulled themselves together and followed their instincts. Emylene and Vandy shouldered the injured Theo over the burning tendrils that snapped, crackled and popped under their feet. Their lungs burned from the poisoning air, making every step a struggle, until the trio could go no further and collapsed on the pavement, exhausted. Emylene listened for tell-tale signs. Angry, urgent voices all around them confirmed they'd been overtaken by the orgy of death. Footsteps approached and stopped inches from where her head lay on the concrete. Finally, she would meet him, the one she imagined since she was a child. Whether he be the handsome stranger who would dance her into her grave or the thief who would carry her soul off into the night, she was ready to face him. But when she lifted her eyes, she was not prepared for what stood before her.

"Girly, get off my hose!"

Staring upward, Emylene and her parents found themselves surrounded by a team of firefighters. The heavy footsteps and booming voice belonged to a burly fire chief who towered over her, dressed in heavy khaki overalls and a helmet. The three had made it past the demarcation line to safety.

But Emylene wouldn't release the hose she had fallen onto, and shouted back, "Let it burn! Let it all burn!"

The chief looked down at the little waif. He could have thwacked her aside like a horse swatting a fly, but something in her voice convinced him that she spoke from a higher authority, and he turned to his men.

"Drench the perimeter, confine the fire. Let everything inside burn."

The chief's men deployed their hoses and began dousing the street as ordered.

"Emylene, I still need to get your father some help," whispered her mother.

"Go ahead. I'm good," she answered.

Vandy helped Theo to a nearby ambulance to get his arm attended to while Emylene staggered a few feet away to watch Other-Town burn. She was actually thankful for the moment alone for she needed to say goodbye to someone who perished in the fire. When Emylene saw that no one was looking, she withdrew something from inside her great coat: Stelio's severed head. She had picked it up in the club's secret room and kept it tucked away until now. The eyes looked at her and blinked. Somehow, defying all the natural laws of the universe, his soul stubbornly clung to life.

"I am talking to Stelio who once loved a woman named Helena. I'm talking to Stelio who made me feel like a woman even if he didn't know it. I am doing this for the good Stelio. I hope you find peace."

The lips parted in an effort to speak, but no words came. Emylene prayed those words would have been, "Thank you," and then she took the head by the scalp and tossed it across the demarcation line into a heaving pit of fire, and watched it burn. Moments later, more survivors emerged from the inferno and scrambled past the Stipe family to safety. Other figures were not as lucky: the black-cloaked devils that could not cross over. Death had come to reclaim its own. She could see them some twenty feet away, their faces a mix of terror and rapture as they lit up like Roman candles and were released from their un-lives. It was a harrowing sight, and Emylene almost felt sorry for them. But her deepest sympathy lay with Laszlo, whom she believed had perished in the club. The only thing that gave her comfort was the hope that he, too, was finally at peace.

EPILOGUE

City officials let Other-Town burn itself out until there was nothing left in the quadrant but ash, bent husks of steel and burnt cinderblocks. With Stelio's demise, the spell over the larger city eased and, although there were scattered reports of sightings and bitings, nobody took those stories seriously, and eventually, they became the stuff of urban legend. The populace returned to their mundane lives, working their forty-hour weeks and getting hammered, juiced or high on the weekends. Crime and poverty crept back onto the main streets and settled in as though they had never left.

For Emylene Stipe, life returned to normal, if normal was a Sunday afternoon picnicking at your own gravesite. When the weather was favorable, she would come to the cemetery and spread her blanket out in front of two headstones. One was engraved, Emylene Stipe, May 2, 1992—December 26, 2011, Our Little Princess. The one next to it was engraved. "Laszlo Birij 1944—2012, beloved friend." On the first occasion, Emylene planted a little slip of paper in his grave, the I.O.U. Laszlo handed her that night in Other-Town. On successive occasions she would talk and joke and laugh to herself and offer up silent prayers. Sometimes, she spent all afternoon telling stories about the past and making wishes for the future. It was her way of dealing.

After the purge, Emylene needed to get as far away from the Goth scene as possible. She missed Laszlo, and as often happens when a loved one dies, would see his image in the faces of elderly men she passed on the street. It made her sympathetic to the needs of people of that generation. With the financial help and support of her parents she opened Stipe Funeral Insurance Brokers, offering low cost funeral insurance to the elderly. For a time, it would give her peace. She would need it. She had no idea how complicated life was about to get.

Steam rollers and shovels worked day and night to clear the rubble throughout the city blocks that Other-Town had once subverted, so that life could sprout up again. Until then, no one living or dead would take up residence in the quadrant. Almost no one. One of the last remaining structures, a house that stood at the edge of the old demarcation line, was said to be haunted. Another urban legend. Some said lights could be seen at night emanating from inside the hollowed husk. In truth, they came from beneath the frame, in the safe room that Laszlo had built months in advance, and for this very purpose.

"Shhh. You're safe, *babika*. Drink. Soon you'll be strong again."

Laszlo cut his arm in the one spot that was tattoo-free. His bride bowed her head and drank.

"She's Venus in blue jeans
Mona Lisa with a ponytail
She's a-walkin' talkin' work of art
She's the girl who stole my heart"

THE END

TODAY I AM A MAN

LARRY RODNESS

About the Author

Larry Rodness began his entertainment career as a professional singer at the age of 19 and has been performing in and around Toronto Canada for over 35 years with his wife and singing partner, Jodi. They have three children, Adam, Jonathan, and Erin.

In the 80's Larry studied musical theatre writing with P.R.O. under Broadway conductor Layman Engel, which led him to write for dinner theater. He then moved into the screenplay arena where he has written over a dozen screenplays and has had 3 scripts optioned to date. "Perverse" is his second novel.

If you enjoyed Perverse,
consider Larry Rodness' *Today I Am a Man*:

Fifty-year-old Steven Goldman waits for Todd Holloway, a fifteen year old student, to leave school, and beats him up in front of the boy's friends. Afterwards Goldman calmly goes home to have dinner with his family while he waits for the police to arrest him. The key to his seemingly reprehensible behavior becomes apparent through a series of flashbacks to his childhood, when his family moved from the harsh Canadian winter to the raw heat of Los Angeles in the early sixties.

ISBN: 978-0984117529